Once Upon A Secret

A MODERN UN-FAIRY TALE

ZION

This novel is a work of fiction. Any resemblances to real people, living or dead, actual events, establishments, organizations, or locales are intended to give the fiction a sense of reality. Other names, characters, places, and incidents are either products of the author's imagination or are used fictitiously.

Copyright © 2013 by Zion

Published by 21st Street Backroom Publishing

All Rights Reserved. No part of this book may be reproduced or transmitted in any form or by any means, graphic, electronic, or mechanical, including photocopying, recording, taping or by any information storage retrieval system, without the written permission of the publisher.

Second Edition

ISBN: 978-1-940097-49-7 (Kindle)
ISBN: 978-1-940097-48-0 (paperback)
Library of Congress Control Number: 2014952412

Printed in the United States of America

Cover Design by Firstborn Designs
www.firstborndesigns.com

A Very Special Thank You To:

Grayson Kellum
Tamara Anderson
Tori Glaze
Personal Impressions
The Pink Banana
Miss Sassy Boutique
Adult Video LAX
Chateau Exxxperience
Nancy's Nook
X-Spot
Zion

Prologue
The Parable of the Lost Son
Luke 15:11-32 King James Version

[11] And he said, A certain man had two sons:

[12] And the younger of them said to *his* father, Father, give me the portion of goods that falleth *to me*. And he divided unto them *his* living.

[13] And not many days after the younger son gathered all together, and took his journey into a far country, and there wasted his substance with riotous living.

[14] And when he had spent all, there arose a mighty famine in that land; and he began to be in want.

[15] And he went and joined himself to a citizen of that country; and he sent him into his fields to feed swine.

[16] And he would fain have filled his belly with the husks that the swine did eat: and no man gave unto him.

[17] And when he came to himself, he said, How many hired servants of my father's have bread enough and to spare, and I perish with hunger!

[18] I will arise and go to my father, and will say unto him, Father, I have sinned against heaven, and before thee,

[19] And am no more worthy to be called thy son: make me as one of thy hired servants.

[20] And he arose, and came to his father. But when he was yet a great way off, his father saw him, and had

compassion, and ran, and fell on his neck, and kissed him.

21 And the son said unto him, Father, I have sinned against heaven, and in thy sight, and am no more worthy to be called thy son.

22 But the father said to his servants, Bring forth the best robe, and put *it* on him; and put a ring on his hand, and shoes on *his* feet:

23 And bring hither the fatted calf, and kill *it*; and let us eat, and be merry:

24 For this my son was dead, and is alive again; he was lost, and is found. And they began to be merry.

25 Now his elder son was in the field: and as he came and drew nigh to the house, he heard musick and dancing.

26 And he called one of the servants, and asked what these things meant.

27 And he said unto him, Thy brother is come; and thy father hath killed the fatted calf, because he hath received him safe and sound.

28 And he was angry, and would not go in: therefore came his father out, and intreated him.

29 And he answering said to *his* father, Lo, these many years do I serve thee, neither transgressed I at any time thy commandment: and yet thou never gavest me a kid, that I might make merry with my friends:

30 But as soon as this thy son was come, which hath devoured thy living with harlots, thou hast killed for him the fatted calf.

[31] And he said unto him, Son, thou art ever with me, and all that I have is thine.

[32] It was meet that we should make merry, and be glad: for this thy brother was dead, and is alive again; and was lost, and is found.

Once Upon A Secret

Nikole

"Oh, I'm sorry," I said as the cute professor and I reached for the tongs at the same time.

"Oh, no, Ms. Turner! You go right ahead," he replied.

"Professor Lions, I told you to call me Nikki. I'm twenty, not forty," I said, smiling as I placed some salad on my plate.

"Well, Ms. Turner, no matter how old you are, a man should always speak to you with respect."

I smiled. "I'll remember that." I walked toward my table in the Hampton University café.

He was watching me. I didn't have to turn around to know that. *I'm gorgeous and I know it*, I thought. Everyone knew it. With my long golden hair, light gold complexion, gray eyes, pink lips, and small frame, I got approached by guys on an hourly basis, and girls complimented me all the time.

Last year I was a sophomore, and I didn't know how to make good grades. Yeah, I'm smart, but college is a little overwhelming. I had brought home one A, two B's, a C, and two D's. I had only one male teacher, and I flirted with him whenever I saw him; that was how I got one of my B's.

So, this year, I bought nothing but tight ass clothes, and I made sure all of my teachers were men. Professor

ZION

Lions taught my Psychology 203 class, where I sat in the first row, with my skirt high and my cleavage out.

I think I started fucking them after midterms; I had one B, two C's, and three D's, and I knew I couldn't take that home. So, one day, I approached Mr. Phillips, my Strategies for Start Up teacher, in his Buckman Hall office.

"Mr. Phillips?" I knocked on his door and saw he was on the phone. "Oh, I'll come back later."

As I turned to leave, I "accidentally" dropped my keys. I knew my skirt was way too tight as I seductively bent over to pick them up.

"Oh, I've got to call you back," he rushed before hanging up the phone. "Nikki! What can I do for you?"

I stood up and turned around with a bright smile. "Hey, Mr. Phillips!"

"Hello."

"Umm... I got my midterm grades back."

"Uh huh... ?"

"And I have a D in your class."

"That's right."

"Well, I was wondering if there was any extra credit I could do to help my grade."

"I'm sorry, but no."

"No?"

"It's in your syllabus. I do not give out extra credit. My class is easy. Just do the work and pretend like you're trying to learn and you pass."

I threw myself down on the chair in front of his desk and pouted. Tears came to my eyes as I said, "But I am trying. It's just... I can't keep up."

Once Upon A Secret

Mr. Phillips stared at my thighs, and I pretended not to notice that my skirt had slid up so far that my panties were showing.

"Mr. Phillips?"

"Oh! I'm sorry, Nikki. I lost my train of thought."

Of course, he did. "Mr. Phillips, I'll do anything. I need an A in this class."

Usually when a person says she'll do anything, I thought, *it's pretty much understood that that is not true*. So, I really was not expecting what happened next.

My teacher shut and locked his office door and sat in the chair next to me. "I don't give out extra credit, but I do give out bonus points."

"Oh, my God!" I jumped up excitedly. "How can I get those?"

He looked me up and down and licked his lips.

"Well," he started.

"Well?"

"What are you willing to do?"

"I mean… whatever," I answered nervously. *Where is this going?*

"Hmm… you tell me what you want to do." He stared at my legs as he rubbed his right thigh.

I looked at the door to make sure it was shut. "I don't want anyone to… find out about this."

"About what?" He smiled.

I knew what I had to do. I was actually shocked that I was prepared to do it. But, nobody goes to college to fail. *This is for the grades*. I took a deep breath and slowly got down on my knees in front of him and looked up in his face. Then, I unbuckled his belt, undid

ZION

his pants, and pulled out the fattest penis I had ever seen. This old man had to have been in his late fifties and there he was with this fat ass, thick ass slug in my face. He wasn't even hard. It felt like a whole pound of slick flesh just resting in my palm and laying over my hand. I looked back up at Mr. Phillips and asked, "How much will my grade go up if I do this?"

"I'll let you know when you're done."

Dear, God! And with that, I took a deep breath and shoved the whole thing into my mouth. I had never sucked a dick before, but I had seen a lot of women do it in the pornos I'd watched. As I gripped the shaft with my right hand and sucked really hard on the head, he moaned. I could feel his penis grow in my mouth and I had to keep adjusting my jaw to fit him. I went from using one hand to two really quick. I moved my hand up and down and bobbed rhythmically. Then, I removed my hand and put my head down as far as I could until I gagged; that really wasn't that far on that fat thing.

"Oh, yeah," he moaned.

I spat on it and continued to jerk it off. Then, I slowed down and sucked his balls. Those hairy, hairy balls. There was no way Mrs. Phillips had been putting her mouth down there. I beat his dick with my tongue. As I put the head in the back of my throat, I hummed *Moonlight Serenade* by Glenn Miller. He really liked that. I kept going until I could feel his penis throbbing in my hand and mouth. I sucked his head and beat his dick as hard as I could. Then, at an almost perfect moment, I pulled back to remove some hair out of my eye and he shot his cum all over my face. *Oh shit!*

Once Upon A Secret

Uuh... I kept jerking him off until his entire load had been released. After giving my professor one last suck, I looked up at him. His head was tilted all the way back, and his eyes were closed. I had heard that guys got turned on when they saw their cum on girls' faces, so I sat at his feet and waited. *Hurry up, Old Man.*

"Was that your first time?" he asked.

"Yeah," I said.

He exhaled deeply. "I could tell."

"What?!"

He lifted his head and looked down at me. "Umm, you don't want to keep that on too long; it's going to get hard." He pointed at my face. Then, he sat up straight and said, "Uh, excuse me." I stood up and got out of his way. He handed me some tissue. After fixing himself back up, he asked, "What's your grade now?"

"A D," I answered.

"Right. You have a C now."

"A C?!"

"I'm actually being generous."

"But I need an A!"

"Then you're going to have to earn it, either in the classroom or," he stared at my breasts as he tucked his shirt in, "in my office."

"Wait! I have to do that again?" The thought of putting that slick thing in my mouth again was repulsive. The thought of another pube in my mouth almost made me gag!

"If you want the bonus points," he said without even looking at me.

I felt like a slut, a whore, a prostitute... worth-less.

ZION

"Is there anything else I can do for you?" he asked when he finally looked at me.

"No," I grabbed my purse and left.

The walk back to McGrew Towers was longer than usual as I thought about what I had just done... for a C! I had definitely thought my performance was A material or, at the very least, B! Hell, B- is fine with me.

In the lobby, I waved to the RA, got on the elevator, and went to my room, 501. After I let myself in, the first thing I saw was my half-naked roommate.

"Yasmine, where are your clothes?"

She was wearing what looked like a tube top. It had just enough fabric to cover her breasts; and that's it.

"Don't be mad at me! I didn't know you were going to be here! I thought you were staying at Lonnie's house."

Lonnie was my Mexican boyfriend. He was nothing special. He was doing the same thing everybody else's boyfriend was doing. Lying, cheating, apologizing, repeating the steps and giving a girl just enough hope to think he will change for the better. But, she was right. I had told her that I would be staying at his house for the weekend.

"Yeah, I might go over there later." I sat my things on my bed and then sat at my desk. "But I've got to handle some things first. I got my midterm grades back."

"Oh, Lord. What did you get?" she asked. After I handed her my grades, she yelled, "Nikole! What is wrong with you? See, I know what it is. It's 'cause you don't get yo' butt up and go to class!"

Once Upon A Secret

Even though she was fussing, I laughed. I could not take her seriously without pants on, and, when she got excited, her thick Macon, Georgia accent came out extra heavy.

"So, I went to Mr. Phillips and tried to get an A."

"Nikki, you can't ask for one, you have to earn one."

"Well, I did more than ask."

"Oh, Lord! What did you do?"

After I told her about everything that had just happened, her mouth dropped as she yelled some more. "Nikole! I can't believe you did that!"

"Yeah, and he only gave me a C!"

"What did you think you were going to get? You got to give up the cupcake for an A!"

I checked my e-mail while she continued to rant.

"Oh, my God!" I yelled; shocked.

"What?"

"All of my professors want to see me."

"Hmm… I wonder why," she said sarcastically.

"You don't think Mr. Phillips told, do you?"

"Nikole! Yes!" Yasmine was still yelling.

I exhaled deeply and set up times to meet with them all. I was getting my things together when my roommate asked, "You're not going like that, are you?"

I looked at myself in the mirror. I still had on the too tight clothes.

Before I could answer, she said, "No, you're not! Go and put some sweatpants on!"

I laughed. I loved how she was so concerned and protective. Yasmine was and will always be a real friend.

ZION

"For real, for real! You don't need to go. But you ain't gon' listen to me, are you? Nope. Do you need to go in the 'treasure chest'? Yes, you need to go in the treasure chest." She hopped off the bed and opened the drawer that was underneath it. She pulled out a small, decorated box and opened it. It was full of Lifestyle condoms.

"Yasmine, who can fit in these lil-ass condoms?"

"Girl, all condoms are the same size, except Magnums. Nobody can fit a Magnum. Nobody's penis is that big."

"What? Who told you that? Lonnie wears Magnums. At least, that's what he told me he wore. I don't actually know for sure." Lonnie and I only never had sex. I was a virgin saving myself for marriage. That's another reason why I didn't leave him. Yea, he was cheating on me. But, I wasn't having sex with him so, I kind of understood.

"Mmm hmm." She shook her head. "He lyin'. Take these." She handed me a handful of Lifestyles.

I laughed, put them in my purse, and said, "Okay."

The first teacher I went to was Doctor Anderson, my Theatre History teacher, in Armstrong Hall. I knew she wouldn't want any favors. One, because I had a B in her class and, two, because she was a middle-aged, White woman. I'm pretty sure she couldn't even fathom the idea of lesbian sex.

"Hey, Doctor Anderson," I said as I walked in the office she shared with Professor Jones, another theatre professor. I looked around and saw that we were alone.

"Hello, Nikole! You weren't in my class today." She looked over her glasses at me and locked her fingers.

"Oh, yea! I'm sorry. See. What had happened was—"

"Uh huh," she said, knowing a bad excuse was coming.

I laughed. "Ay! I'm sorry. I'm just a little overwhelmed."

"Okay... and you have good grades, but you're always either severely late or not present at all." She continued to look over her glasses as she bit at her peeling lips.

"I know..."

"And you know, after you miss three classes, you start to drop one letter grade per absence?"

"Yes, ma'am."

"Okay," she said, picking up her attendance book. "So, according to this... you should have failed my class."

I just stared at her.

"But I didn't put that in, and you have a B."

"I appreciate that."

"Well," After a long and drawn out pause she said, "Shut the door."

I immediately became nervous as I closed the door. *Oh no, Doc A! Please don't make me lick ya dry ass pussy! Please!*

"I have a cousin who just graduated from college with a bachelor's degree in film and directing. Now, for some reason, he wants to direct pornography. Unfortunately, he doesn't have enough people to get his business off the ground."

"Umm, okay..." I started to scratch my palms as I stood as close to the door as possible.

ZION

"Well, I will give you extra credit if you work for him as a PA."

"A Production Assistant?"

"Yes," she said, and I laughed.

"Oh, my goodness… I thought you were going to say something else."

"Oh, no! I would never suggest something that horrid." She assumed I thought she was going to ask me to star in a movie. *No ma'am. I thought you was gone ask me to lick that hairy twat!* "Well, here's his number." She handed me a business card. "Call him ASAP!"

"Yes, ma'am."

"Okay. That's it."

"Okay. I'll talk to you later, Doc A."

"Alright," she said.

I left her office, walked down the steps, turned the corner, pushed open the door, and headed to Elmo's office. Elmo was my professor for two classes—Financing New Ventures and Creativity, Innovation, and Product Development. I walked in, and, before I could say hello, he said, "Shut the door, Nikki."

I did.

"Phillips told me what you did."

My heart dropped. *God… damnit!*

"I have no intention of telling anybody about it, but you have a D in my class," he said as he unbuckled his pants and pulled out his penis. "Now, you can either suck your way to an A, or I can fuck the shit out of you, and you won't ever have to attend another class."

"I don't know what you're talking about." *What in the hell was going on?!*

10

Once Upon A Secret

"Oh, really?"

"Yeah."

"Well, since you don't know what I'm referring to, I must be mistaken."

I swallowed hard.

"But maybe a failing grade will refresh your memory."

"What?"

Elmo leaned back in his chair and stared at his penis as he made it jump around in his lap. *What in the hell? Boy!*

"I could run right now."

"But you won't. You'll be known as the HU slut, and you'll have to tell your parents how you thought this was a good idea. I'm sure they'd love to hear that."

I froze while looking at him. All it took was for someone to whisper something about someone else and you immediately became a hashtag; on twitter, that fucking yak app, the school newspaper! Even people at other schools will be talking about you and they don't even know yo ass!

In his horny moment of need, he grabbed my hair and pulled me into him. "Get on your knees!"

I did.

Then, he pulled my head back. "If you bite it, I swear to God… " And he shoved himself inside my mouth.

I cried and gagged as he face-fucked me. He kept a fast rhythm and didn't slow down at all. Ugh, that long black thing was playing peek- a- boo with my innards. I swear his tip dipped down in my stomach juices and came back up. Just as I thought I was going to throw up, he pulled out, grabbed my shoulders, and picked

ZION

me up. I thought we were done, but he grabbed my arms and dragged me to the back of his desk. After he bent me over, he lifted my ass with his left hand, while he used his right hand to hold my head down. Then, he pulled my sweatpants down, revealing my red lace thong.

"Oh, yeah," he said, sucking his teeth as he slapped my ass and squeezed my cheeks. As I felt his hard cock push against my virgin slit, tears filled my eyes. When he pushed inside me, it hurt. It hurt worse than I ever imagined it would. He was so big, and he thrust forward forcefully, ripping through my hymen.

My teacher grunted. "I didn't know you were a virgin." As he kept thrusting, he said, "Oh, you're getting an A for sure."

Y'all, I was a virgin in my twenties. Do you know what that means? For twenty years, I had been fighting off the advances of boys and men. I was a strong black woman and I was not defined by what I could offer between my legs, but what my mind had to offer. I was saving myself for marriage and I gave my sweetness away to an old horny man for an A. So, my intelligent ass can have the right to sleep in and not go to his class again. As my face was getting rub burn from the desk, I just let the tears slide down and took the time to stare at my reflection in his name plate.

Hello, Nikole Turner, you whore. Are you enjoying that fat ass dick being rammed in your pussy right now? Feels good, doesn't it? Way better than waking up at nine am to make a TEN AM CLASS!

When he finally removed his hand from my head, my back arched up, and, for a moment, my face had some relief. Elmo's thrusting now hurt less, but I was so ashamed of myself that I hurt all over. He wrapped his hands around my waist and bent over, kissing and licking my ear. He then lifted my shirt and ran his tongue up and down my back. Uugh, I never knew a tongue could feel so disgusting. Then the unthinkable happened. I could feel his orgasm burst inside my once tight hole.

Immediately, I panicked. *What if I get pregnant by this man?*

My professor pulled out of my vagina, and I could feel his cum running down my thighs as he sat down in his chair. I couldn't move. I didn't know whether to cry or throw up, so I just stayed bent over his desk. And what if my movement made the sperm swim faster?

Elmo slapped my ass. "Good job, Nikki." He let out a sigh. "That's an A for Financing New Ventures."

I turned around and looked at him, confused. "What? What about my A in Creativity, Innovation, and Product Development?"

"What? You didn't think that covered two classes, did you?"

My mouth dropped, and he laughed.

"No, no, no... you're going to have to do that again. And, next time, you'll need to convince me that you want to do it." As tears ran down my face, he said, "Aw! Don't cry. You wanted this, remember?"

I nodded.

"Yeah... I hate to kick you out, but I do have to get ready to teach a class."

I didn't move.

ZION

"Here. I'll help you with your clothes." He pulled up my thong and pants all at once, leaving me uncomfortable. "Okay?"

I nodded and left. Once outside of Buckman Hall, I ran all the way back to McGrew Towers. I threw open the door to my room and ran inside.

"Nikki?" Yasmine looked at me as I threw things all over the room. "Nikki, what's wrong?"

I found a bottle of douche and ran to the bathroom. When I finished, I went in my room and threw myself on my bed and cried hard for half an hour. The whole time, Yasmine sat with me and passed me tissues.

"Nikki, you know I'm not used to you crying. What's wrong?"

I sat up. "You're going to hate me."

"Oh, Lord! What did you do?"

I looked at the huge painting of Jesus she kept next to her bed and told her everything that had just happened, and again, she was upset.

"Nikole, what did I just tell you? Did you at least use the condoms?"

I put my head down. "No."

"What? What do you think I gave them to you for? Decorations? Toys? Pocket Pals?"

I started crying again. "He came inside of me."

"What did you say? I know you ain't say what I think you said!"

"He came inside me," I repeated. "That's why I douched before I came in here."

"Oh, my God! Are you on birth control?"

"No, I was a virgin." It got quiet for a few seconds.

"Oh, Nikki." My roommate hugged me, and I cried some more.

When I wiped my eyes, I looked down and noticed Yasmine was wearing pants. "Thanks for not being naked."

"You're welcome," she said, and we shared a laugh.

I didn't go see any more of my professors that day. Instead, I went to dinner with my roommate at five. Afterward, I stayed outside while Yasmine went upstairs. I called Doc A's cousin.

"Hello."

"Hi! May I speak to Jermaine?"

"Speaking."

"Oh!" I was a little shocked because he sounded gay. Well, I mean, like, he clearly sounded like an unbothered feminine man... if that makes sense. And I was immediately unsure of how I felt about gay porn.

"Can I help you?" he asked.

"Oh, um, I got your number from Professor Anderson. And she said you could use me as a PA."

"Oh, yeah! She did call me and tell me to expect a ring from you. What's your name again?"

"Nikole Turner."

"Okay. Tomorrow's Saturday. What are you doing?" he asked.

I actually had planned to spend the day with Lonnie, but he didn't know that. So, I said, "Nothing."

"Okay, cool. Can you meet me at my house in Virginia Beach?"

"Uh... "

"You don't have a car, do you?"

"No, sir."

ZION

"Okay, well, I guess I could come get you."

"Okay, are you sure? I know it's kind of a long drive."

"Oh, it's not that far. Thirty minutes, if I go the speed limit. Ten, if the HOV lane is open, and I can practice my NASCAR," he said.

I laughed. "Okay. Well, I can get my parents to bring me back if you can take me home. I stay on the corner of Kempsville and Indian River."

"Oh, where?"

"In those townhomes across from Applebee's and Golden Corral, on Carriage Mill Road."

"Oh, yeah. I know where that is. I actually used to talk to somebody out there."

"Oh, really? Do you mind if I ask who?"

"His name was Michael… I think. He stayed across from the BB&T."

"Was his father a pastor?"

"Oh, I don't know. I know his dad was Latino and his mom was white. I think he had a sister, too."

"Yeah, I know who you're talking about. I'm actually kind of close to the family. I go to their church."

"Oh! And I'm all on the phone tellin' other people business. Let me shut up. Okay. I'll come get you tomorrow. Is ten o'clock okay?"

"Yes, sir."

"Ugh! Please stop calling me sir."

"Oh, I'm sorry."

"Don't be sorry. This is my cell phone number, so text me your address."

"Okay."

"Alright, Nikole. I'll see you tomorrow, hun."

"Okay. See you tomorrow." I hung up and went back up to my room.

"So, are you still going to Lonnie's house?" Yasmine asked, walking around in her too short nightgown.

"I don't know. Today has been one of them days."

"Pff! Girl, today was crazy. You just need to take you a shower and go to bed."

I looked at the clock. It was 6:45. "I guess you're right,"

"I know I'm right!"

I laughed, gathered my towel, washcloth, and body wash and headed to the bathroom I shared with seven other females, which was one of the many things I disliked about Hampton University. I got into the only shower stall and washed and scrubbed until the water ran cold. Then, I dried off and went back to my room.

"Girl, your phone been ringing ever since you went to the bathroom!"

I looked at the phone. Six calls from Lonnie. "Wow!" I called him back.

"Hello."

"Yes, Lonnie… "

"Hey, baby."

"Hey."

"Are you still coming?"

"Didn't I say I was coming?" I know I had agreed to stay home, but I guess not.

"Yeah, but I haven't heard from you all day."

"I'm in college, Lonnie. I'm busy."

"Yeah, I know."

"I'll be there in an hour or less."

"Okay. Love you."

ZION

"Love you, too." I hung up.

"Why are you still messing with that boy?" Yasmine asked.

"I don't know." I shrugged my shoulders. "I'm bored." I didn't know why I was still messing with a cheater, but I was still going to his house on a regular basis. After getting dressed in a pair of sweatpants and a sweatshirt, I called a cab and went downstairs to meet the driver.

The ride wasn't long. Lonnie didn't stay more than a few miles away from the school, but the trip cost me $6.75. I paid and thanked the man before walking through the gate to the side door. Lonnie always left the side door open for me because the front door made too much noise and might wake his mother. I walked through the kitchen, into the living room, and found Lonnie lying on the couch, watching TV.

He looked back at me. "Hey, baby."

"Hey," I sat on the love seat.

"You're not going to give me a kiss?"

I just looked at him. Ever since his mom called me in August and told me that she had found Lonnie in his bed with some nappy-headed chick named Monique, I hadn't been able to look at him the same or be the same around him. All the more reason I should have left his ass alone, right?

"Come here."

I picked up my phone and started pretending to text.

He sat up really fast. "Nikole!"

I looked at him. "What?"

"Come here."

Once Upon A Secret

I went back to my phone. The big, muscular Mexican got up and stood in front of me, and I pretended to ignore him. He took my phone.

"Oh, my God!"

"Uh huh," He put my phone on the floor, and then he bent down and got in my face. "Give me a kiss."

"No."

He leaned forward and kissed me. He pulled back and looked at me, and I smiled. I knew what to do to get him up, and he knew I liked when he was aggressive with me. He leaned in again, and we started making out. He slipped his hand inside my sweatpants, between my thighs, and started to rub my clit. I moaned and spread my legs a little. We kept kissing, and, with his left arm, he lifted me out of the love seat and stood me up. He pulled my pants down, and that was when I snapped back into reality.

"No. Stop." I sat down and pulled my pants back up as fast as I could while remaining seated. "I'm not ready yet."

He let out a loud, disappointed moan and laid back on the couch. As far as Lonnie was concerned, I was still a virgin; he would have been pissed to find that my vagina wasn't as tight as it should have been.

"You know I love you, right?" he asked.

"Nope."

He looked back at me. "What do you mean no?"

"Mo… nique."

"She was just some ho," he said as he looked back at the TV.

"If you loved me, you wouldn't have fucked her."

ZION

"If you fucked me, I wouldn't have had to fuck her," he said.

I got quiet, and he looked at me and saw the hurt on my face. He laughed. "I'm just playing, baby."

I jumped up, finished pulling up my pants, grabbed my phone, and left out the side door. He ran out after me and grabbed me from behind, holding my waist.

"Baby," he whined, "I was just playing."

"Let go of me, Lonnie."

"No."

"Yes."

"No."

"Yes, I have to go back to my room. I've got a busy day tomorrow."

"Doing what?"

"I've got a lot of homework to do." I wouldn't dare let him know I had a job working in the porn industry.

He let out a deep sigh. "Okay." He turned me around and kissed me. "I love you."

"Mmm hmm."

"Say you love me, too."

"Bye, Lonnie."

He gave me a huge bear hug. "Say it!"

"Okay! I love you!"

He smiled, kissed me on my forehead, and started to run in the house. "Bye, baby."

I started walking back to campus. It was normal for me to only spend an hour or less at my boyfriend's house. Everything about him annoyed me some days. When I'm away from him, he's all I want. When I'm with him, I can't stand his ass. I didn't want to spend any more money on a cab. Even though it was after nine and I knew that the Hampton city streets were no place for a girl like me to be walking alone, I had to clear my head. So, I made a left on Kecoughtan, a right on Settlers Landing, and that was when I really got into deep thought.

That day, a lot of stuff had happened. I had gone from being a virgin to being a slut in only a few hours. And what would happen now? Would my professors give me bad grades if I didn't fuck them? I didn't want to be that person. I didn't want to lose my virginity to a sixty-year-old man. I didn't know what I had gotten myself into, but I prayed and prayed that it would never happen again. I wanted the A, but, as a Christian, I couldn't believe what I was doing. I wasn't even having sex with the guy I was in love with. Sure, he'd cheated, but, wasn't I the reason why? Yup. And as soon as everything downstairs snaps back, I'm gone give it to him.

By the time I reached my dorm, I had asked myself so many questions, but I didn't have an answer to many. I walked into my room, and Yasmine was in the dark Skyping her boyfriend at her desk.

"Mmm," she grunted as she looked at my face. "Well, babe, I'm going to talk to you later. Me and Nikole are about to have a movie night."

"Okay, I love you," he said.

"Love you, too," she hung up and looked at me. "He pissed you off, didn't he?"

"Yeah," I said as I stripped myself of my clothes.

"I knew it! Why do you keep going over there? Why? You can do so much better."

ZION

"I know I can, but... I just can't stop talking to him. I love him."

She shook her head. "Well, let's watch a scary movie."

"Okay." I set up Netflix, and we had a good night, screaming in the dark.

The next morning, I was in the lobby at nine fifty, waiting on Jermaine. Almost at ten on the dot, he called.

"Hello," I said.

"I'm outside. McGrew Towers, right?"

"Yeah." I walked out of the front door. "I see you."

"Oh, hey."

I got in the passenger side of his GMC Denali. I looked at him and gave him a "hello" smile.

"Oh, my gosh! You're gorgeous!" he said.

I laughed. "Thank you."

"You're welcome," he said while putting the car in drive. "Thank you so much for helping me today."

"Oh, no problem."

"When we get back to my house, I'm going to briefly explain what I need you to do to help me out. And I'm actually going to shoot a few scenes today, so, if you're ready, then you can stay and help."

"Oh, okay."

"Yeah, so today should be fun."

For the rest of the ride, we were quiet while the radio played. We got off on the second Indian River Road exit, made a left on Kempsville, and a left on Whitehurst Landing. We drove down a little and pulled up to his house. It didn't look big from the outside, but he was young, so it was cool that he owned his own home.

"Do you have roommates?"

"Oh, no, baby. I live by myself. I can't be worried about niggas not paying their part on time."

He unlocked the door, and we went inside. The first thing I noticed was how the house was decorated.

"Oh, your house is so nice."

"Thank you. I hired my mom to decorate for me. I don't know how to do that stuff. I'm not one of those gays. Come on. Let's go to the office."

I followed him down a hallway to an office. He sat behind the desk and pointed to an empty chair. "You can sit right there."

I sat.

"Okay, so basically you're going to be my production assistant, meaning you're going to assist me on and off the set. A lot of times, you'll be my voice, so the actors and everybody else need to respect you as if you are me."

"Everybody else?"

"Yes, the light man, cameraman, makeup, costumes, all of them people."

"Oh, okay."

"Yeah, like," he checked his computer, "it's almost eleven o'clock now. People are going to start coming in and setting up. Today, I'll introduce you to the crew. But the next time you're here, you'll come see me first. We'll meet, and then you will go upstairs and relay the messages. You'll be in charge until I come upstairs. The only thing you do not do is direct a film. If I am

ZION

not upstairs, there should not be a damn camera rolling!"

"Okay."

"Got it?"

"Yes."

"Good. Okay, what days do you think you can get on this side?"

"Umm, it will be hard because I don't have a car."

"Right, but, if you did, when could you come?"

"Well, Mondays and Fridays. I'm out of class by one. Tuesdays and Thursdays, I get out at 3:15, and, Wednesdays, I get out at 7."

"PM?"

"Yes."

"Wow. Okay, well, I like to shoot every day. So, do you do anything after class?"

"Not really."

He gave me a look. "What's 'not really'?"

"I do my homework... sometimes," I said.

"Cool. I'm going to need you every day. And we'll talk about transportation later."

"Ok."

"Let me explain what we're doing today. We are going to try to finish shooting a video we started yesterday."

"Does it have a storyline?"

"Uh, yeah. Girl walks in on her boyfriend masturbating, starts sucking his dick, and then they start fucking."

I was shocked. I assumed he was doing gay porn.

"What's wrong?"

"Well, that storyline is so... overdone. No offense."

Once Upon A Secret

"Oh, no, you're fine. That's what you're here for. Tell me your opinion."

"Umm, well, first, if you're gay, why not do gay porn?"

"I thought about it, but, I want to make a name for myself in the industry; I feel hetero porn is easier for me to do."

"Well, if you're gay, then all the freaky, kinky, nasty stuff that you like, you can put on the screen."

"You're right. I'll think about it some more. But do you have any ideas for girl-boy porn?"

"Well, I have one that I think may be good."

"What is it?"

"Well, you know how men get gang raped in prison?"

"Yeah."

"Well, the scene is in the showers of a female prison, and all the women are either trannies, or they're wearing strapons, except one. And that one drops the soap."

He burst out laughing. "I see where you're going with that. Ok! Ok! That's pretty good." He paused and looked at me. "Have you ever thought about getting in this industry before?"

"I thought about it. But it was just a thought."

"You thought about acting or directing?"

"Uh, just writing scripts."

"Oh, okay, maybe you could do that for me. I'll pay you more."

"I'm getting paid for this?" I said, a little too excitedly.

ZION

"Uh, yeah. You thought I was just going to make you work for free?"

"Well, yeah. Doc A said I had to do this to help my grade, so I just assumed—"

"Oh, no, baby. I pays my people."

"Oh, okay."

"Do you want to know how much?"

"Yes." I smiled.

"If you come every day, it's a hundred fifty dollars a week to be my PA. Miss a day, and I take away thirty bucks. Now, if you write scripts for me, I've got something else in mind."

"What?"

"Follow me." He got up, and, as we were about to leave his office, we heard the front door open. "Who that?" he yelled.

"Steve!"

"Oh, come here, Steve." In a matter of seconds, a fat Asian man was in the hallway in front of us. "This is Nikole. She's my new PA."

"Hi," I said.

"Hey," he said out of breath. He stunk and was covered in sweat.

"Steve!" Jermaine shouted. "Why are you dripping sweat?"

"Man, it's hot outside."

"Steve!" Jermaine shouted again. "It's October. It's cool out."

"Whatever, man." Steve waved him off and walked away. "I'm going upstairs to set up."

When he was gone and we could hear him running up the stairs, Jermaine said, "Steve is the set manager.

Once Upon A Secret

He's in charge of how the rooms look and props and whatever. Okay, come on."

I followed him down the hall, and he opened the door leading into the garage. It was a single car garage, and inside was an older Mercury Sable.

"Now, I wouldn't normally do this, but you seem decent, and I need you, and I ain't driving back and forth from Virginia Beach to Hampton." He took a set of keys off the hook. "This was my first car in college. Now it's your employee car."

"Oh, my God. Are you serious?"

"Yeah, but only if you write scripts for me. You write and PA, and you get one fifty a week, and I'll keep gas in the car."

"Oh, my God!" I jumped on him and hugged him. "Thank you, thank you, thank you!"

"No problem. But you better be good at what you do."

"Oh, yes! I promise!"

"Alright, baby. Let's go back inside, and I'll show you around."

We went in, and he showed me around downstairs: the kitchen, office, living room, and backyard. And then, we went upstairs, and he showed me his room.

"This room is off limits! I don't want no bitch's hair or Steve's sweat nowhere near my private area."

He showed me the other two rooms where he filmed the videos, and Steve, two other ladies, and one guy were in one of the rooms. "Nikole, this is Erin, our makeup girl; Ashley, our costume girl; and Diontae, the cameraman. Y'all, this is Nikole, my PA."

ZION

They all looked at each other and smiled as if they were in on a secret I hadn't heard about.

"Hey," they said simultaneously.

I smiled and waved. Erin was a red-haired white girl with big, square eye glasses and green eyes. She was a little over five feet and had an average build. Ashley had big brown hair and long fingernails. I got a vibe from her that made me feel like we weren't going to get along. But Diontae had pretty caramel skin and curly hair that was tapered on the sides. He was over six feet tall and had big, muscular arms. He was the sexiest thing I had seen in a long time.

"Are any of the girls here yet?" Jermaine asked.

"Brittany's in the bathroom changing," Ashley answered.

"She the only one that's here?"

Nobody answered.

"Oh, my God." He looked at me. "That's another thing I need you to do. Call these motherfuckers and see where they at!" He walked out, scrolling through his phone.

I was debating on whether I was going to follow him or not when Ashley popped her gum twice and then asked, "So... Rachel, how do you know Jermaine?"

I looked at her. "Are you talking to me?"

"Uh, yeah," Ashley said, and Erin laughed.

"You know that's not her name," Diontae spoke up.
Oh, so she was trying to be funny?

"Well, what's your name again?" Ashley asked.

"Nikole," I said.

"Well, Nikole, how do you know Jermaine?"

"He's my professor's cousin. I'm doing this for extra credit."

"Oh, what school do you go to?"

"Hampton."

"Hampton? You think you're hot shit, huh?"

"No, I just go to the school. Where did you go?"

"Salem High," she said as she stood up. "Brittany!" she yelled into the hallway. "You need some help?"

A muffled, "No," came from the bathroom.

"Mmm hmm... open up. I'm coming in," Ashley announced as she went in the bathroom to help the girl.

I just stood in the room with the other two.

"She's not that hard to get along with," Erin said. "She likes to act harder than she really is."

"Ok," I said under my breath.

"Now, who you really have to look out for is Charlotte," Diontae said.

"Mmm hmm," Erin co- signed.

"Who is Charlotte?" I asked.

"Who's asking?"

I looked, and there was this tall, slim black woman with long, beautiful black hair that stopped at her breasts.

"Hey, Charlotte," Erin said.

"Are we doing my scene today?" Charlotte asked.

"I think so," Diontae answered. "We just have to shoot a few more sex positions and the—"

"Right. Where's the costume girl?"

"In the bathroom helping Brittany," Erin said.

"Are my girls here?"

"No, ma'am," Diontae said.

"Where's Jermaine?"

ZION

"In his office," Diontae answered, and Charlotte looked at me as she walked past and through the door.

When I heard her footsteps going down the stairs, I asked, "Who is she?"

"She's Jermaine's assistant director. She directs the lesbian porn," Erin said.

Just then, Ashley and Brittany walked in.

"Did we hear Charlotte?" Ashley asked.

"Yep," Diontae and Erin said.

"Oh, I'm glad I'm here on time," Brittany said.

I couldn't help but stare at her. She was gorgeous with the most beautiful hazel eyes and long blonde hair. She was wearing a threadbare gray T-shirt that I could see her breasts through. She wasn't wearing a bra, and she had on the shortest pair of shorts. So short that her butt cheeks were hanging out. And, to complete the look, she had on knee high tube socks.

"Umm, hi. I'm Brittany." She stuck her hand out. Lord, y'all, I had been staring a little too long.

I shook her hand. "I'm sorry for staring. You're just really beautiful."

"Oh, thank you! What scene are you in?" The fuck?!

"Oh, I'm not going to be in any of the movies."

"Nikole is the new PA," Ashley said, "from Hampton University."

"PA?" Brittany asked.

"Production Assistant," everyone said in unison.

"Ooooooooh!" Brittany said.

"Come on. Let me do your makeup," Erin adjusted her stool.

Once Upon A Secret

The two went into a corner and proceeded to beat faces. That was when we all heard the front door shut, and everyone got quiet.

In a matter of seconds, we could distinctly hear Charlotte yelling, "What time do we start shooting every day? Then, why are you late? When you're late, we can't get started on time, and that means the movie won't be done on time and can't be uploaded on schedule. Whose fault is that? Yours! Goddamn it! Now, get your asses upstairs and get into makeup!"

The sound of many feet running up the stairs was heard. I looked down the hall and watched as two guys and four girls ran into the other bedroom. Ashley ran behind them. I looked around, confused.

"I think you should go downstairs," Diontae said. "Jermaine might need you."

When I got downstairs, I could hear Charlotte yelling, "Dumb-ass porn stars think they are stars for real."

I started to walk in the office. When Charlotte saw me, she slammed the door. "Why didn't you call anybody?" I could hear her through the door. "And who is this lil' girl?"

Jermaine opened the door. "Charlotte, this is Nikole. My new Production Assistant."

She sized me up. "I got to go check on my actors," she walked out.

"You got to excuse her," Jermaine said. "We actually met during an incident last year. She's good peoples. She's just been hurt before, so now she goes around being mean to everyone. But you'll learn to ignore it.

ZION

Look, my movie is pretty simple today, so I want you to help Charlotte."

"Umm, is she going to be okay with that?"

"Yeah. Whether she'll admit it or not, she needs help. Come on," he said, and we went upstairs. "Charlotte!"

"What?" she turned to look at us.

"Nikole is going to help you out today."

"Oh, no, she's not!"

"Oh, yes, she is!" Jermaine said and walked away.

"Oh, my God," she groaned. "Look. My cameraman is almost here. Go downstairs and help him with his equipment. One thing you'll notice is I move a lot faster than Jermaine. This movie will be done today." She started texting on her phone, and then she looked up at me. "Okay. Why are you still here?"

"Oh," I said and turned to leave.

"This ain't gonna work," I heard her say as I left the room.

The cameraman showed up and introduced himself as Jesse. He was Italian with a greasy ponytail. He set his things up downstairs.

"What's the storyline to this movie?" I asked him.

"She ain't tell you?"

"No."

He laughed. "Yeah, that's Charlotte. This girl comes over to this guy's house to study and surprises him with an orgy."

"Oh, wow!"

"Yeah, Charlotte does some pretty elaborate stuff."

"Okay, let's get started!" Charlotte shouted as she and a group of "high school" kids came down the stairs. "Right now, I need Davon sitting on the couch,

Once Upon A Secret

Idriss outside on the other side of the door, and you other girls sit in the kitchen quietly until I call you. You." She pointed to me. "Stay next to me."

I moved over to her.

"Jesse, you ready?"

"Yep."

"Alright... rolling... action!"

As Davon flipped through his textbooks, there was a knock on the door.

"Idriss!" Davon said as he got up to answer it. When he opened the door, he said, "Hey!"

And Idriss said, "Hey. I'm sorry, but Erika can't come. She just found out she has to work."

"Oh, well. I guess we can study."

"Yeah."

They sat on the couch, and Davon asked a few questions.

Idriss laughed because she didn't know any answers.

"I don't know any of this stuff. But," she said as she bit her lip, "I know a little about anatomy."

"Yeah?" Davon said, not looking at her.

"Well, this is your temple," she said, kissing his temple.

"Get on your knees," Charlotte said.

Idriss did. "This is your neck," she said, kissing his neck.

Davon let out a moan and leaned back on the couch. Charlotte signaled for Jesse to move around the room. Idriss undid Davon's pants and pulled his penis out. She stroked him while she kissed on his neck, and then, in one swift motion, she threw her head down and began to suck his dick.

ZION

I followed Charlotte around the room to get a better view.

"Davon, move Idriss' hair out of the way," Charlotte instructed.

He did, and I was impressed to see how much of his penis Idriss was engulfing. She sucked and kissed and spat, and it sounded like she was slurping some soup that was too hot. By watching that, I knew why Professor Phillips wasn't impressed by the blow job I had given him. After about ten long minutes, Davon came in the back of Idriss' throat, and she spat it on his balls and then sucked it off. My mouth dropped; I was overly impressed.

"Okay, Jesse. Keep rolling," Charlotte said. "Hey! Y'all in the kitchen!" The three girls came running into the living room. "I need you to wait for your cue outside."

The girls left the house. "Okay, Idriss. Check your phone."

Idriss picked up her phone and pretended to check for text messages.

"Oh, my God!" she said.

"What?" Davon asked as he zipped his pants back up and redid his belt.

"Okay, so, Erika said the power went out at her job, so she's on her way over."

"Okay."

"And she's bringing two of her co-workers."

"Why?" Davon asked, confused. "Do they need help in school, too?"

Idriss laughed. "No, you get four pussies tonight."

"What?"

Once Upon A Secret

There was a knock at the door. Idriss answered, and the three girls walked in wearing the worst fast food costumes ever: short shorts, super tight shirts, and baseball caps with a toy chicken glued on top.

"Keep rolling. Nikole, what do you see wrong with this picture?" Charlotte asked me.

"Umm."

"I'll tell you. Erika has only one hard nipple, and Becca's nipples aren't hard at all. Fran, you're fine." Fran smiled brightly. "Do you know how to get them hard?" Charlotte asked as she turned to me.

"Ice?" I asked.

"Yes! Now go to the kitchen and get some ice."

I went to the kitchen, got a glass, and filled it with ice. When I got back to the living room, both Erika and Becca had their shirts up over their breasts.

"Okay. Now rub their nipples until they get hard. And make sure you lick the ice first, so it doesn't stick and the poor girls get ice burn."

I licked the ice cube and slowly rubbed Becca's nipple. She giggled.

"Nikole," Charlotte called me.

"Yes," I answered.

"Are you going to make love to Becca?"

"No."

"Then, can you stop being so gentle with her and hurry up? Time is money."

"Okay," I said and moved faster.

"It's okay," Becca whispered. "She makes everyone nervous."

I just smiled and hurriedly rubbed both girls' nipples.

ZION

"Okay. Now the nipples are wet, so you have to fan them," Charlotte said, and I did. "Okay. Girls, pull your shirts down, and Nikole come back over here. And... action!"

Becca held up a case of beer. "I brought drinks," she said.

"Cool," Idriss said. "Come in."

Everyone walked over to the couch, and Erika was the first to notice the shape of Davon's hard penis through his pants.

"So, what have you guys been studying?" she asked.

"Everything," Idriss said as she sat next to Davon on the couch.

"Oh, really?" Erika asked. "Well, maybe you can tutor me on something," she said to Davon, and she pulled down her shorts while the other girls began to drink their beers.

She kept her legs straight while she bent all the way over to help herself step out of the shorts. While she was bent over, Jesse moved in for a closer look at her pink thong. Erika turned around, so her back was to Davon as she pulled her thong down. Jesse got a close-up of her pussy. She kicked off her tennis shoes, pulled her shirt up over her head, and threw it, and the cheesy hat, onto the floor. I mean, clearly, she had done this before, because she was more than comfortable. If it were me, I would have at least kept my shirt on.

Davon pulled his dick back out, and Erika climbed on top of him. As she proceeded to bounce up and down on his thang, she moaned loudly. *My, God*! Now, Idriss, who was still sitting next to Davon on the couch, slapped Erika's ass, and she let out a playful

Once Upon A Secret

moan. Davon grabbed at Erika's breasts and sucked her nipples. She grabbed the back of his head and bounced harder. Davon leaned his head back, so he could watch her, and she looked back at her ass bouncing up and down.

"Erika, I need you in backward cowgirl," Charlotte said, "and get ready, he's coming in the back door."

It didn't hit me right away what that meant. But I soon found out when Erika climbed back on, and he inserted his penis into her asshole. My mouth dropped. I could only imagine the pain she was in. It wasn't like his dick was small or anything! He was a pretty decent size. And he just eased it right on into her ass. Let me tell you something... no. Not my ass. That's just not Christian. God didn't ordain that nonsense! Davon wrapped his hands across her midsection and pulled her back to him, and then he let his fingers do their exploring on her womanhood. He used one hand on her clit and burrowed the other hand deep inside her, caressing and teasing the flesh that parted like curtains. She began to breathe harder, faster, and deeper, and she looked into the camera as she hollered out for Davon to keep touching her. Then she came all over his fingers.

I didn't know if I was impressed or disgusted. It was just... way too much going on. Charlotte pointed to Idriss, and immediately, Idriss began to help Erika off of Davon and onto the couch. Erika got in the doggy style position and started sucking Davon's dick, and Idriss began to eat Erika out from the back. Wait, let me back up right quick. Erika began to suck Davon's dick after he had just fucked her in her ass hole! If that

ZION

isn't the most disgusting- she's eating shit! She has to be. Who does that? Charlotte waved to Fran and Becca, and they put their drinks down and started making out. That was when I understood what Jesse meant when he said Charlotte did some elaborate movies.

"Fran, help Becca with her shirt."

Fran took off Becca's shirt and hat, and Becca took off Fran's hat. Then Fran bent down and started sucking Becca's titties while playing with her pussy. Becca moaned. Then she motioned for Fran to sit up, so she could help her out of her shorts. Once they were both naked, Fran got on top of Becca, and they started doing a sixty-nine. Let me tell you something, y'all... it was too much.

Davon was grunting and had grabbed Erika's head. He was guiding her mouth down his shaft, but, with a mouthful of dick, she was moaning loudly because Idriss was violently eating that twat.

My eyes were darting all over the room. I didn't know what to focus on. But Charlotte did. She barked directions and told Jesse where to move until, finally, the two girls had humped each other's faces until they came. They climbed off of one another and slowly started making out. Erika screamed and came in Idriss' mouth, all while sucking Davon's dick. But once she was done, she sat up, and Idriss sucked Davon until he came in her mouth again. And the scene ended with Erika touching her dripping pussy and Idriss licking cum off her fingers.

"Alright. Hit the showers," Charlotte yelled. And immediately, everyone got out of character and ran

Once Upon A Secret

upstairs to clean up. "So, how'd you like that?" Charlotte asked me. "Did I go too fast for you?"

"No," I said, "but I was shocked at how much you can control at once. That's going to be a great movie."

"Yeah. Jesse's going to edit it ASAP and upload it as soon as he's done. Come on. Let's go to the office."

"Oh, should I pick up the costumes?"

"No, that's what the costume girl is for. Come on."

I followed her into the office, and she shut the door behind me. "So, I realized that there is a lot that I could use your help with. All of the yelling I did today is your job as a PA. So, I'm going to need for you to get really comfortable as soon as possible."

"Okay, but… " I hesitated.

"But what?"

"I'm supposed to be Jermaine's PA. If I'm helping you, then who's helping him?"

"See, Jermaine doesn't need help. He needs focus. And can't nobody give him that but him. If you work for Jermaine, I guarantee that you'll be doing almost all of his work, and you might as well direct your own movies, instead of just being someone's assistant."

"Yeah. I see what you're saying, but my teacher told me to help her cousin out for extra credit in her class. Plus, Jermaine wants me to write scripts for him."

"Hmm," she thought for a second. "I'll talk to Jermaine about what you're going to be doing around here. But, you did a good job today. When are you coming back?"

"Hopefully, tomorrow. I have to talk to Jermaine."

"Oh, we don't film on Sundays, so he might not need you." There was a knock on the door. "Come in."

ZION

Jesse stuck his head in. "I'm leaving. I'll e-mail you the video before I upload it."

"I trust you. Just upload it as soon as you finish editing it."

"Okay. Cool."

"Alright. Good job today. I'll see you on Monday."

"Tuesday."

"Excuse me?" Charlotte questioned him.

Jesse stepped inside of the office. "Charlotte, remember I asked for Monday off? That's the day I'm proposing to Jordin."

"Oh, yeah. That's right. Okay. I'll see you Tuesday."

"Alright," he said and walked out.

"Well, I guess you should go see if Jermaine needs you."

I left the office and went upstairs to a completely different environment. Everybody was laughing and joking, and nothing was being filmed.

"Hey!" Jermaine shouted when he saw me. "How did everything go downstairs?"

"We're done. Do you need me up here?"

"You're done?" Jermaine nearly shouted.

"I told you that you needed to get on it," Diontae said, "and stop laughing and joking all day."

Jermaine smacked his lips. "Whatever." He looked at me. "No, I don't need you."

"Okay. Well, when do you want me to come back?"

"I'll call you. But let's go down to the garage."

I followed him down to the garage.

When we got to the garage, Jermaine said, "I made sure it's full of gas, but I haven't driven it in a while, so, all that oil and shit, I don't know if that's good. But

Once Upon A Secret

let me know if anything acts up, and I'll take it to the shop." He pushed the garage door opener and handed me the keys. "Here you go. Go ahead and start it up."

I smiled and hopped in the driver's seat. As soon as I started the car, I squealed with excitement.

Jermaine waved to me. "I'll call you!"

I waved back. "Okay!"

I was so happy to be driving with a full tank of gas that I didn't know what to do. I backed out of the garage and pulled onto the next street, so I could make a phone call. I dialed my friend Byron's number. He used to be a football player at Hampton. That year, he couldn't get financial aid, so he wasn't enrolled, but he stayed less than a minute from my house, and we stayed in touch.

"Hello," he answered.

"Hey! Where are you?"

"My parents' crib."

"I'm two seconds away. Come outside."

"Okay."

I hung up and drove around to Thompson Way. I pulled up in front of Byron's house. He was standing outside, waiting on me.

"Yo! Where you get this?"

"I got a job, and they gave me a car."

"What?" He got in on the passenger side. "Where you working at? I need a job."

"I'm a PA."

"What's a PA?"

"Production assistant. I help direct movies."

"Word? You doing it big! What kind of movies?"

ZION

"Umm… " I was nervous about telling him because, when I first told him I wanted to direct porn, he was highly upset, "Uh—"

"Aww, man. You doing that nasty shit?"

"Yeah."

He shook his head and looked so disappointed. "Well, I guess you got to do what you got to do."

"Yeah," I said, and he shook his head again.

"So, what you about to do?"

"I don't know. I got a full tank of gas, so I can go anywhere."

"True. Well, I got to get back inside and apply for some jobs."

"Okay."

He got out, and I drove off. I knew he wasn't applying for jobs. That was a lie to cover up how pissed he was. I decided to go see my friend Jen. She stayed around the corner from me in Carriage Mill, which was right up the street. I made a right on Canterford Lane and pulled up in front of her three-story townhouse. I knocked on the door, and her mom answered.

"Hey, Nikole!"

"Hey, Mrs. Matos. How you doing?" I gave her a hug.

"Fine. How's school?"

"Good."

"You like it?"

"Yes."

"That's nice."

"Is Jen home?"

Once Upon A Secret

"Yes. Come on in." She held the door open for me, and I stepped into the foyer. She went up to the third floor, and, in a minute, Jen came downstairs.

"Hey, Nikole," she said as she walked down the stairs toward me. Even though she was four years older than me, we had become fast friends a year or so earlier.

"Hey," I said as I held the door open, so we could talk on the front porch. "You sound really good now."

"Thank you."

The year before, Jen had torn her esophagus. But, since she had healed up, she had been sounding better and better.

"Whose car are you pushing?"

"Uh, mine. I guess. Temporarily."

"What? How did that happen?"

"I got a job as a production assistant for an adult film director."

I was comfortable telling Jen the truth because she was one of the nastiest and kinkiest people I knew.

"Oh, really? I didn't know you were a freak jank!"

"No," I laughed. "I'm helping direct porn, not starring in it."

"Mmm hmm. Where at?"

"Up the street, behind Anytime Fitness."

"Really? I didn't know anyone was doing it that close."

"Yeah."

"I could be a porn star."

"Uh, yeah, I believe it." I laughed.

"Put me on."

"Maybe."

"I'm serious."

ZION

"I know, but I just got the job, and I don't want to work with anybody I know yet."

"I feel ya. So how much you getting paid?"

"I'm getting a hundred fifty a week, plus the car, plus a full tank of gas."

"Oh, that's cool. But you know you could be making that plus more if you worked with me at Consequences in Richmond."

"Richmond?"

"Never strip where you live."

"You're a stripper?"

"Yeah. I get paid over five hundred a night in tips and a thousand or more on the weekends."

"Wow! How many hours do you usually work?"

"I usually do the eight pm to three am shift."

"Oh, I don't know." I instantly replayed the day before, thought about where I had come from, and decided that adding stripping to that would just make me the newest freak of the week.

"Well, think about it. It's not really that bad, especially when you're bringing home that money every night. In fact, I'm moving out this weekend."

"Oh, really? Where to?"

"Apartments of Merrimac in Hampton."

"Oh, that's not too far from the school."

"Nope, and you already know you can come over and cook anytime."

"Oh, that's what's up."

Jen knew I loved to cook. I used to cook all of the time for her and her family. After I started at Hampton, I cooked for Yasmine and a few other friends at Lonnie's house.

Once Upon A Secret

"So, you going to tell ya peoples about the job?"

"I'm going to try my best not to."

"Yeah, well, the Johanson's Halloween party is coming up and so is Thanksgiving break. How you plan on coming home?"

"The car... oh."

"Yeah. Exactly."

I understood where she was going. If I drove home, my parents would definitely want to know who the car belonged to and why I had it.

"Well," I started, "Thanksgiving break is only Wednesday through Sunday. I'm sure Jermaine wouldn't need me or the car for those days."

"Jermaine? What kind of Rock the Boat name is that?"

I laughed. "He actually said he used to mess with Michael."

"Oh, who knows when that was? You know Michael's married now."

"To who?" I said overly excited about this newly spilled tea. Do y'all know what tea is? Tea is gossip, but juicy gossip. Gossip that makes your mouth drop.

"His best friend Scarlet."

I frowned up my face. "Wait! Scarlet is a girl's name."

"Yup."

"He married a girl?"

"Yup."

"But I thought he was gay."

"Yeah, so did everybody else. But he said that was just a confused phase he was going through, and now he is completely in love with Scarlet."

ZION

Ain't no way in hell! "Well, how does she feel about his confused phase?"

"She's cool with it."

"Whaaaaat? Ain't no way."

"Mmm hmm."

We sat there quietly for a while, and I tried to imagine being cool with Lonnie having a gay past. And it didn't take me long to come to the conclusion that I didn't like butt-fucked niggas. After Jen and I said our goodbyes, I got in the car and headed to Hampton to surprise Yasmine with a night out.

Scarlet

I was taking a shower when I heard Michael holler for me.

"Scarlet! Baby, I'm home."

I ignored him and continued to wash myself. My husband was a light walker, but I heard him walk in the kitchen to check for food. Then he walked down the hall and checked each room until he got to ours.

"Scarlet?"

I turned the water off and pulled back the shower curtain. I was about to get my towel when Michael walked in and saw my naked brown body.

"Oh, my God!" I shouted as I tried to cover my private parts.

"Oh, I'm so sorry," he said and ran out.

Once Upon A Secret

I laughed. This was my favorite part of the day. I dried off and put on my silk robe and went to look for my husband. I found him in his office.

"Look, Scarlet, I'm sorry about that—"

"Yeah. Uh huh," I said, crossing my arms and leaning against the door frame. "Why didn't you call for me? I would have answered."

"I did. Maybe you didn't hear me."

"Right... well, you know you've got to make this even, right?"

"What?"

"You've seen me... now, I want to see you."

"Me?"

"Yeah."

"But what if someone comes?"

"Nobody's coming. Stop being such a little bitch."

He hesitated before saying, "Okay." He stood up and undressed, starting with his straight legged denim jeans, dress shirt, tie, cardigan, and leather loafers.

"Umm... remove the underwear please."

"But—"

"Ah ah ah... you saw me."

"Okay." He pulled down his fresh white Hanes, revealing a very erect penis.

"Hmm, so you must have liked what you saw earlier," I said, and he smiled.

"Yeah." He bit his bottom lip. "So are we even now?"

I stood up straight and walked toward him, and I backed him into his office chair. Then I straddled him and sat in his lap. I put my face close to his and whispered in his ear.

ZION

"We're even," I said as I ran my fingers through his straight, brown hair, "but I want more."

I kissed him. It was a long, sensual kiss. He held me as I wiggled in his grip, his powerful hands gently caressing my back. Then I reached down, took his hard dick in my hands and gently started to stroke. I began to kiss and suck at his neck, and he closed his eyes in pleasure as he held me close and smelled the mango body wash I had just used in my shower.

He pulled my face to him and kissed me again, this time with more tongue. I moaned softly as we kissed. I unrobed myself, exposing my perky breasts. Without hesitation, he took each of my soft, brown nipples into his mouth and made them hard with his lapping tongue. I sat up a little and inserted him into my wet vagina. I bounced, slowly at first and then faster, and Michael kept licking my nipples. I was soon trembling through the wave of my first orgasm. I grabbed a fistful of Michael's hair as I shook and squealed with pleasure. He pulled me close until I finished.

Once I finished, shivering from the ecstasy I had just felt, I stood up, and Michael and I watched the cum drip from my pussy, down my leg, and onto the floor. He leaned in and licked my navel, while one of his hands made its way down to my warm, slippery pussy lips. He softly caressed my tender womanhood while his tongue danced in and out of my firm navel and played with my small belly button ring. I moaned softly and again ran my fingers through his hair while he did so.

Then Michael turned me around, so my ass was in his face. He took a soft cheek in each hand and lightly

Once Upon A Secret

massaged the skin while kissing each one and the dimples on my back. And, every so often, he would put one of his hands between my legs to massage my warm, wet pussy. Then he coaxed me into bending over in front of him while I, again, straddled his lap, so my ass was in his face. He pulled my cheeks apart and licked small circles around my orifice. He guided one of my hands to play with my pussy while he attended to my ass and started alternating between sucking on the back of my soft pussy lips and exerting pressure with his tongue against my tight hole. Eventually, his slimy tongue was able to push a little into the opening.

I moaned louder then as my experienced fingers skillfully massaged my tiny, throbbing clit. Michael spread my cheeks as far as they would go and worked his tongue further into my tight, scalding hot orifice so that when he withdrew it, my tight ring muscle winked at him as his saliva oozed out. He continued French kissing my warm butthole for a long time as my hand kept massaging my clit until, finally, I climaxed again. He held my hips tightly as I bucked and squealed. He pushed his tongue deep into my contracting asshole where it clenched down on him in a rhythmic succession until my orgasm was done. I collapsed onto the floor and just laid there.

"So, what made you decide to be shy today?" Michael asked in reference to the role-play we had just done.

"I don't know. It just came to me."

"Oh... Ok!," he said, while lying on the floor next to me, brushing the hair out of my face. "Baby... "

"Yeah," I said with my eyes closed.

ZION

"I think you're pregnant."

"What?" My eyes shot open, and I lifted my body up. Michael sat up, too. "Your breasts are *huge*."

"Okay! And? I'm black. My breasts get huge!" I grabbed my robe and stormed out.

But that didn't stop him from following me. "Okay, Scarlet. You're twenty-three. Puberty is over for you, Hun. Now, why are you so upset?"

"Michael, we just got married. I don't want to be a mom right now. I'm still trying to be a wife."

He walked over to me, guided me down on the bed, and sat next to me. "Look, I'm going to be a great daddy and you going to be a great mom or whatever."

I kept staring at the wall. He turned my head, so I was looking into his eyes.

"We can do this. I'm going to graduate in May, and I'm going to sell the last dresses. My little girl will want for nothing, you hear me?"

I looked down at my lap.

"Jack and Brittany will be happy."

I smiled when he mentioned my foster parents. "Yeah."

"You want me to go get a pregnancy test?"

"Get about six." I stood and started walking to the bathroom. "I want to make sure this shit is legit."

Once Upon A Secret

CHARLOTTE

After that long day on the set, I stopped by the ABC store to purchase some liquor for my liquor cabinet. In the past year I had been drinking a lot more than usual. Sometimes, I would pass out and wouldn't wake up until the next night. I used to live alone in my Riverwalk home, but I had started dating a younger girl a few months earlier, and she had moved in with me. I'm not going to lie. I wasn't completely happy with my life. I had hired somebody else to run my online store, so I was bringing in plenty of money and not working to do it. And then there were the adult movies; they had quickly become my passion.

I remember how I had met Jermaine last Christmas. That was a crazy night. I was having a threesome with my ex-girlfriend and my fuck buddy in her house, and, at the same damn time, Jermaine was upstairs fucking her brother. The parents came home and caught all of us; it was wild. A few weeks later, I ran into Jermaine at a bar, and he told me about his idea to direct adult movies. He sounded so passionate about the idea that I decided to go into the business with him.

Before I could even attempt to open the front door, it was opened for me.

"Hey," my girlfriend, Paris, said.

"Hey." One thing I loved about Paris was she was always happy to see me, and she didn't want to be bothered with anyone else but me.

ZION

"What's in the bags? You buy me something?" she asked. I pulled the bottles out and sat them on the counter. "Oh."

"What's wrong?" I asked, and she took a deep breath.

"Babe, you've just been drinking so much lately, and it's like… you're not even here anymore."

I started to put the bottles away.

"You go to work, and then you come home and drink until you pass out. And then, when you wake up, you leave. It's like I'm not even a part of your life." She hesitated before asking. "Why do you even want me here?"

I didn't know what to say, so I took a minute to think, a long minute.

"Yeah. That's what I thought," she said and walked up the stairs, leaving me in the kitchen speechless.

By the time I had made it halfway up the stairs, she was on the phone, talking low to someone. I stopped to listen.

"Yeah. It's what I've been saying all along. She doesn't love me. She's still in love with her, and I could never be her… no, I'm not staying here. I'm going to pack my shit tonight… I don't know. Can I stay with you for a while?… Okay, thanks." She took a deep breath. "I'll be there in an hour." She hung the phone up, and I still didn't know what to say.

Was I still in love with my ex? Yes, but she and I would never be. I blew that chance when I proposed to her with the same ring my ex-boyfriend had given me when he proposed to me. Plus, out of anger, I told her that the only reason I was with her was because she

Once Upon A Secret

looked like her mother, the woman I had been in love with for over fifteen years.

The previous October, I was introduced to Paris at the Johanson's Halloween Party. One thing led to another, and my ex and I had a threesome with Paris. So, naturally, when I became single again, I gave Paris a call. And now, she was ready to leave me.

I walked in the bedroom as Paris was putting on her jacket. She picked up her suitcase and started to walk past me. "I'll come back tomorrow for my stuff."

I grabbed her arm.

"Charlotte, please." She looked me in my eyes. "I'm not what you want. Let me go."

I pulled her in front of me.

"Charlotte, don't."

I took the suitcase out of her hand and started kissing her neck.

"No, stop."

I kept kissing her and held her tight.

"Charlotte, no, you can't keep doing this every time I—"

Then, I kissed her on the lips to shut her up. I pulled back and looked her in the eyes. "I love you." It was the first time I had ever said that to her.

Her eyes got wide. "I love you, too."

Then she threw her arms around my neck and gave me the deepest, longest kiss. I took off her jacket, and she pulled off her pants. That night, I ate her out until she came three times and fell fast asleep.

Afterward, I went downstairs and poured myself some Hennessy on ice. Then, I went to my office and logged on to the porn site to see if Jesse had uploaded the new video. He'd titled it "Davon Studies These Sluts." I smiled and clicked play. Just like at the shoot that day, the video started off with Idriss sucking Davon's dick. I kept watching and saw Erika climb on top of the male porn star. I opened my desk drawer and pulled out my vibrating bullet. Then, I pulled off my pants and underwear and sat down with my left leg on the desk and my right leg dangling over the chair arm. I watched Erika bounce on top of Davon, and I rubbed my breasts through my shirt. I turned the bullet on, put it in my hole, and then sucked my juices off the toy. I placed it on my clit and rubbed it around in circles. The faster Erika bounced, the faster I moved the bullet. When she got up to turn around, I pulled out a six-inch vibrator, turned it on high, and inserted it in my wet pussy. I made sure my movements matched Erika's as I lifted my shirt up to expose my breasts. I licked my fingers and rubbed my nipples. I was moaning loudly and moving my hand faster and faster until I came all over the vibrator. I removed it, and the cum flowed out of my pussy and down my crack.

That night, when I got back to the dorm, I showed Yasmine the car.

"Nikooole! Look at you!" she shouted as she walked around that old Mercury Sable. "How did you get *this*?"

Once Upon A Secret

"I got a job."

"You got a job? Doing what?"

"I'm the production assistant for an adult film director."

She just looked at me for a while and then burst out laughing. "Oh, my gosh, Nikole. No, you're not."

I laughed, too. "Yes, I am."

"Mmm mmm mmm... well, at least, you got a car."

"I *know*! So, let's do something tonight."

"Like what?"

"I don't know. Anything! We can go anywhere."

"Well, let's go to IHOP. I want a coffee."

"Okay." We went back inside the dorm so we could change. But after we took those nice, hot showers, we just laid in our beds, wearing our robes.

"Nikole... "

"Yeah... "

"I don't feel like moving."

"Me either."

"Can we just watch Netflix and go out tomorrow?"

"Yeah."

"Or next weekend?"

"Uh huh," I said.

But neither one of us moved. And we just fell right to sleep. The next day was Sunday. Yasmine was up, bright and early, getting ready to go to chapel, or, as my friend Michael liked to say, she was going to see Educated Jesus.

"Nikole, are you going to church today?" Yasmine asked.

"Nope, but I'll meet you in the café afterward for brunch."

ZION

I didn't like going to chapel. I had been in church all of my life and was used to something different. The chaplain read her whole sermon and prayed for things like financial aid, cool roommates, nice teachers. My pastor, Bishop Matos, prayed for wisdom and patience and things like that. And he referenced real life situations like bills, diseases, relationships, and homelessness. I knew the chaplain was trying to preach on a level everyone could understand, but her messages were for what Bishop Matos called "Babies in Christ." I didn't need a "baby" word. I needed something much deeper.

"Well, you need to go!" Yasmine said. "I know you ain't forgot about these past two days."

"No, but you know how I feel about chapel."

"Yeah, and I feel the same way. But you need to make time for God. He makes time for you."

"I know," I said as I rolled over. "I'll go next Sunday and see Jesus."

"Mmm hmm, you better, Nikole Turner," Yasmine said, and then she walked out of the room.

That was one thing I loved about my roommate. She was always looking out for me and making sure I was doing right.

I turned on some cartoons and laid in the bed. Memories of me and my professors kept popping up in my head, and the thought of Professor Elmo cumming inside of me made me feel dirty all over again. But then I remembered the movie. It was so… erotic and filthy. I had considered writing adult film scripts, but I guess it didn't really hit me that I'd actually be watching that stuff. I decided to write some scripts for Jermaine and e-mail him.

An hour later, I took a shower and got dressed. It wouldn't be long before I would have to meet Yasmine in the café. Suddenly, my phone rang. It was Jermaine.

"Hello."

"Girl, I just read one of your scripts!"

"Oh, did you like it?"

"What? I loved it! You're earning that car, girl!"

I laughed, "Thank you."

"I'm going to make a few phone calls, and we're going to shoot that tomorrow. Can you be here as soon as you get out of class?"

"Yes, sir."

"Cool. I'll see you tomorrow."

"Alright."

"And stop calling me sir!"

I smiled to myself, thinking life was finally turning around. I printed the script and went to the café.

"What is this?" Yasmine asked as I slapped the script down in front of her.

"A script I wrote. Read it."

"A nasty script?"

"Of course."

"Eew! No!" She pushed it away as if it had the cooties.

"Yasmine, stop being such a... I don't know. Read it!"

"Okay, okay," she said, pretending to cry. She picked up the script and, ten seconds later, slammed it down. "Nikki!"

"What?"

ZION

"Two girls and a guy?"

"Keep reading."

She read for about a minute before she said, "I can't read this and eat at the same time."

I laughed.

But her face was seriously disgusted. "Something is wrong with you. Let's talk about something else."

I laughed again, and we ate and talked about our relationships.

"You talk to Lonnie today?"

"Nope," I said.

She shook her head. "There's *no way* I can go all day without talking to my man."

"Well, I don't want to be bothered all day. Just call me when you're getting ready for bed and tell me how your day was, and that's it."

"Whaaaaat? I would lose my mind if I didn't hear from my baby all day."

"Well, I'm not the clingy type."

"I don't think it's clingy. I think it shows you care when you call to say, 'Hey, how you doing? What you been up to?' But, if he just didn't call… we'd have to fight."

"Mmm, well, I know I'm different."

"Does he know about your new job?"

"Nope."

"You going to tell him?"

"Nope."

"Nikole!"

"You know how Lonnie is; he is a psycho. If he finds out I'm connected to porn in any way, he will whoop my ass."

Once Upon A Secret

"Mmm, just promise me you won't star in any one of those movies."

"I won't," I said.

She leaned forward and slapped the table. "Nikole!"

"Yasmine!"

"I don't want to see your naked butt late one night."

I laughed. "You won't."

"'Cause you'll hear me scream," and then she screamed. People all over the café looked up, and we both burst into laughter. Crazy girl!

"Let's go."

The next day, I made sure I was in Dr. Anderson's class at eleven o'clock.

"Oh! You decided to show up today," she said.

"Word!" my friend Isaac shouted.

"Hey!" I waved to the class and sat next to Jen Ramsey from Pittsburgh.

"Yo! Where you been, dude?" she asked.

"Everywhere!" I said and looked at Doc A.

My professor smiled and then continued to give notes. I wrote what she said down, and, when class was over, she asked to speak with me. My friends said their goodbyes, and I waited for my professor to speak.

"So," she said, "how's everything going with Jermaine?"

"Good," I said. She nodded.

"I imagine it's very interesting."

"Oh, it is! It's one thing to watch it on your computer at home. It's another to watch it in front of you!"

She gave one of those silent laughs. "I can only imagine. Okay. I just wanted to make sure he was treating you right."

ZION

"Oh, yes, he is."

She gathered her things. "Have you cooked for him yet?"

I laughed. I was always cooking and bringing in food for her and Professor Jones. "No, ma'am. I haven't had time."

"Oh, okay. 'Cause those ribs you cooked for me and Mrs. Jones were amazing!"

"Oh, thank you!"

"No problem. Well, I'll see you later."

"Okay."

I left Armstrong Hall and made my way to Martin Luther King Hall. I was thinking about what Doc A had said about cooking for Jermaine. Now, one thing Nikole Turner can do is throw down in the kitchen, hunny! Believe that! Maybe, one day, I would cook for the cast and crew. I was pretty sure they only ate fast food before and after the shoots.

I walked into my Psychology 201 class in Room 117 and smiled at Dr. Lions.

"Good morning," he nervously shouted.

The class stopped talking and looked at him.

"Good morning," I said as I sat in my seat in the first row.

I crossed my legs and leaned forward a little. It was cold outside, so I didn't have any skin showing. But I had sat in that same position every day for the whole semester, and I knew my professor was imagining the legs and cleavage he had seen every Monday, Wednesday, and Friday before.

Lions started teaching, and I listened intently. I answered every question he asked correctly. And every time I did, his smile got wider and brighter. I liked Professor Lions because he actually cared about his students. Most professors taught and graded, and that was it. Lions taught, asked questions, made sure we understood, and basically motivated us.

At the beginning of the semester, he stood before us and said, "I don't care how smart you are... I don't care... at all. Sometimes, when I see a student solve a problem really quickly or in an innovative way, I'm impressed. That's great, but it wasn't necessarily because they were more intelligent; they may have just worked on the problem harder or longer. In fact, that is what we've found: students who work harder and longer on something do better in the long run, and those students will recover more quickly from failure."

When class was over, I got my things, stood up, and smiled at my professor, and then walked out with the other students. I practically ran to my car, which was parked in the shopping center in front of campus. I couldn't wait to get to Jermaine's house and see my script actually turned into a movie.

When I walked into the house, Ashley was walking upstairs. She looked at me and smiled. "Hey."

"Hey," I replied. I went into Jermaine's office, and he jumped up immediately and gave me a hug.

"Yesss, bitch! Yesss!" he yelled.

I laughed, and saw Charlotte standing in the corner. She was smiling.

"I think this script is going to help blow our website up! And I ain't tryna fuck it up, so you're going to help Charlotte direct it today."

I looked over for her approval.

ZION

"Hey! I'm cool with it! It's your masterpiece."

"Okay. Thank you," I said.

"Come on," Jermaine said excitedly. "Let me introduce you to the cast."

He opened the door and practically pushed me into the hallway and up the stairs. We went into one of the bedrooms that everyone was in, and Jermaine stood in the middle of the floor and did a quick two claps.

"I need quiet please! Okay. First, let's give it up for Nikole, who just got her job and is already showing out!"

Everyone clapped, and Erin let out a whoop.

"Okay." Jermaine reached for a handsome, muscular caramel man with a short haircut. "This is Marcus. He'll be playing Todd."

"Hi." I shook his hand. "Nice to meet you."

"Okay." Jermaine pointed to a tall, brown-haired white girl. "You already know Fran. She's playing Tammy."

"Wait," I said.

"What?"

"Todd and Tammy are a black couple." Everyone just looked at each other. "I mean, I'm looking at the fact that Yohe is so different. I wanted two black people to help her stand out."

"Ooooooh," everyone said, as if now they were seeing the light. *Come on, y'all. Keep up!*

"I can call in somebody," Charlotte stepped out into the hall.

"Okay. Well, last but not least," Jermaine said, reaching his arm out, "this is Louisa. She will be playing Yohe." Louisa was gorgeous. She was six feet

Once Upon A Secret

tall with bronze hair, green eyes, olive skin, slim, perky breasts, and a tight ass. She was perfect.

Charlotte came back. "My girl will be here in five minutes. She was actually on her way home from Lynnhaven Mall."

I gave a wide smile. It was actually going to happen!

"Okay, Ashley!" Jermaine yelled. "Let's help Mr. Marcus and Ms. Louisa into costume, so Erin can go ahead and beat these faces to the gods. Then, we can get started ASAP."

"Yes, sir," Ashley said, and she took the two actors into the other room.

"Umm, Jermaine," I started nervously.

"Yes, baby."

"Uh, I was wondering, what do you guys do for lunch?"

"Meaning what? What do we eat? You hungry?"

"No, no, no... I mean, no, I'm not hungry. But, yeah, what do you eat?"

"Oh, well, basically we order pizza or we go out. Why?"

"Well, because I'm a pretty good cook, and I was thinking, maybe, one day, I could cook for the cast and crew."

Jermaine laughed. "Honey, you are going to be too busy to even think about cooking." Then, he walked out the room and downstairs.

Just then, I heard the front door open, and Jermaine say, "My God, you a ratchet-looking bitch!"

Charlotte and I ran downstairs and saw an average-sized black woman standing in the foyer. She had an old sew-in in her hair. It was nappy up top, and the

ZION

weave was tangled and matted and shooting out in the back. She was dark with grey contacts, and it appeared she was wearing only one fake eyelash. She was wearing a pair of baggy gray sweatpants and a green Norfolk State hoodie with some purple and pink Crocs. And, she had long, acrylic, stiletto nails.

"Bitch!" Charlotte yelled. "You look like every fucking black porn star stereotype. Why didn't you tell me you was going to show up looking this... this... goddamn ugly?"

"Oooh," Jermaine said as he grabbed my hand and pulled me into his office. "We don't want to be a witness to anything."

"I can do hair," I said.

"What?"

"I know how to do hair. If you can find me a brush, a flat iron, and some oil sheen, I can make her look presentable enough for the shoot."

Jermaine just stared at me. "You're assisting directing and writing scripts. You wanted to cook for us, and now you want to be my hair girl? Is there anything you can't or won't do?"

I laughed. "You won't catch me in one of your movies."

"Hmm... you say that now. Come on before Charlotte kills that girl."

We went back into the foyer. The girl was crying, and Charlotte was yelling, "I can't believe you would embarrass me like this!"

"Charlotte!" Jermaine called.

"What?"

"Nikole said she'd do her hair."

Once Upon A Secret

"Thank you, Nikole," Charlotte said a little sarcastically. "You wrote a wonderful script. I promised you a decent-looking actress, and now you have to do her hair because she looks like a fucking park girl!" For those of you that don't know, a park girl is a girl from the park. The park is like the hood or ghetto. Hoods around here have park in the name. Diggs *Park*, Foundation *Park*, etc.

"Get your nappy headed-ass upstairs!" Charlotte yelled as the chick ran her ass upstairs to get in costume and makeup.

I didn't know why the actresses put up with how she talked to them, but they did. Cause if she yelled at my ass, it would be another fucking story.

"Sorry about that," Charlotte said to me.

"Oh, it's okay."

"No, it's not okay!" Charlotte barked. Lord, why does this lady keep yelling. "When I say I'm going to do something, I do it. I said I was going to get you a porn star, and, instead, I got you a hot mess that *you* have to fix." She shook her head and headed to the office. "I'm so embarrassed."

No, you so dramatic. When she shut the door, Jermaine said, "Let's hurry up and do this bitch's hair."

We went upstairs and into the main room.

"Ashley!" Jermaine called.

"Yes," Ashley said from the doorway.

"Nikole needs some oil sheen, a brush, and a flat iron. Do you have any of those?"

Ashley stepped close to him so that their bodies were touching, and she whispered, "For that mess in the other room?"

ZION

"Yeah."

"Hell no. You're not gonna mess up my shit!"

"Ashley, if her hair is not done, we don't shoot, and, if we don't shoot, then we don't upload the video, and *we* don't get paid."

Ashley looked at me. "Fine," she said through her teeth.

And, in forty-five minutes, my actress was bad. I had her hair cut with bangs, feathered, and spiral curled down her back. She looked more like she was going to walk down the runway than do a porno.

Jermaine ran and got Charlotte and, when the two of them came back, the whole mood had changed.

Charlotte's face lit up like a proud mamma. "She's gorgeous."

"You ready?" Jermaine asked.

"Yeah."

"Okay, Nikole, call Marcus in here for places for the top of the scene."

"Okay." I started to walk out the room when Jermaine stopped me.

"No. Call from here."

"Oh, okay." I cleared my throat. "Marcus, can I get you for places for the top of the scene please?"

Marcus entered in pajama pants, and the new actress, Shayla, entered, wearing lingerie. Let me tell y'all something. That boy Marcus is fine as wine, you hear me?! Good, God! Muscles just percolating every god damn where, whoo! The two actors both climbed in bed and under the covers. Marcus pretended to read a newspaper, and Shayla pretended to read a magazine.

"Camera's rolling," Diontae whispered to me.

Once Upon A Secret

"Rolling," I said aloud.

Diontae double-checked to make sure everything lined up, and then he whispered, "Ready."

"Action!" I said.

Tammy read her magazine as Todd put his newspaper down.

"Babe," he said.

"What?" Tammy replied, obviously annoyed.

"I've been thinking."

"Uh huh…"

"I want to have a threesome."

"What?" Tammy put down the magazine.

"Please?"

"No!"

"I'll let you pick the girl," Todd said.

Tammy thought about that for a moment. "Hmm."

"*Yeah*?" Todd put his face close to hers and stuck his bottom lip out.

Tammy laughed. "Okay."

"Really?"

"Yeah."

Then, Todd jumped on his wife and started kissing her.

"Diontae," I said, "go around the right side of the bed and get a close up of them kissing."

Diontae moved quickly to the other side of the room, and I followed. And, after about thirty seconds, I said, "Scene!"

Marcus and Shayla kept kissing.

Jermaine cleared his throat. "Umm, Nikole, in film, we say cut."

ZION

"Oh, okay. Cut!" The two stopped. I looked at Ashley. "Can you get them into their next costumes please?"

"Sure thing," Ashley said and led the actors into the other room.

"So how does it feel to be the director?" Charlotte asked.

"Good," I nodded. Jermaine smiled and put a piece of gum in his mouth. Soon, Marcus and Shayla came back in the room. "Oh, we're going downstairs," I told them.

"Okay," the two turned on their heels and walked downstairs.

Once in the living room, I had the couple sit on the couch.

"Umm, can I get some popcorn please?" I asked the crew.

Steve wasn't there that day, so everyone looked at each other before Ashley ran to the kitchen to pop some. I examined Shayla in her night shirt and slouch socks. I tossed her hair a little bit. Then, I looked at Marcus, who was still in pajama pants, still fine, muscles still winking at me.

"Perfect," I said. "Louisa," I called, and she came to me. "I need you on the other side of the door please."

"Okay," she went out the front door. Ashley came back with the popcorn in a bowl.

"Give it to Shayla please." She did.

"Okay, Diontae. Are you ready?"

"Rolling!" he said.

I looked at the couple. "Action!" I said.

Todd cut the TV on, and Tammy began eating popcorn. The doorbell rang. "Oh, thank God! The

Once Upon A Secret

pizza's here!" Tammy jumped up to answer the door with Diontae following her. She swung the door open, and her mouth dropped as soon as she saw Yohe.

Yohe wasn't wearing a bra, and she had size D breasts bouncing on her chest. Her Chico's Pizza T-shirt was too small and showed her midriff. She wore a forest green denim skirt and a pair of white Chuck Taylor's.

"Hi," she said. "That'll be $25.23."

Tammy looked her up and down, and then looked back at Todd. "Umm, come in."

Yohe stepped inside.

"Uhh, Todd. Pizza's here."

Todd turned around, and, once he saw Yohe, he sat up. "Oh," he said.

"Is everything okay?" Yohe asked.

"Yeah," Tammy said, and then she kissed her.

"Wait! What are you doing?" Yohe yelled, and Tammy kissed her again. This time, Yohe didn't resist.

Todd took the pizza from Yohe and sat it on the coffee table. The two women kissed each other deeply and ran their hands up and down each other's bodies as they walked blindly toward the couch.

Tammy softly pushed Yohe onto it. Then, she looked at Todd and said, "Todd, keep the girl entertained for a minute. I need to go upstairs for something."

Once Tammy was gone, Todd turned and faced the delivery girl. She grabbed the back of Todd's head and pulled him toward her. Their lips pressed against each other's and parted, letting their tongues meet. Her tongue filled his mouth, and he pushed his tongue into hers. They kissed for a few minutes, and Todd played

ZION

with Yohe's nipples through her shirt. When he pinched them, Yohe broke the kiss and took in a deep breath. Then, she moaned softly as she exhaled. She had her legs crossed, and Todd looked down at them.

"Oh, God! You got me turned on," Todd said and kissed on her neck.

"Oh... God," she said between gasps of breath.

"God won't be helping you tonight," Tammy said as she came back into the living room. She had changed into a purple corset with matching leather boots and no panties. "I think we should go upstairs," she said.

The three of them started up the steps.

"Cut!" I yelled.

Diontae ran up the stairs, and everyone followed. Once in the room, I stood next to the cameraman, and he pointed to the doorway.

"Rolling," he said.

"Action!"

The couple and their guest walked through the doorway and to the bed. Tammy and Yohe pushed Todd onto it. Then, the two started to undress him. Yohe grabbed the elastic on his right side, Tammy grabbed his left, and they both pulled his pants down, revealing Todd's large penis.

Yohe's mouth dropped. My mouth dropped. "My God! You're... huge," she said, shocked. And yes. He. Was. And I experienced something I had never experienced before. Ladies, have you ever looked at a penis and it looked *good*? Like, immediately, your pussy, which has been silent *all of your life*, just starts smacking her lips like, mmm, *I want him*. And all you can think about is climbing on top and riding him till

Once Upon A Secret

you can't stop cumming? Ever experienced that? Well, bitch, that's what I was going through! I had just lost my virginity and now my pussy lusting after the dick. But, I digress.

So, Tammy sat next to Todd and said, "Wait till you feel him inside of you."

She took the tip of his penis into her mouth. She sucked on it a little bit, and then she shoved the whole thing in her mouth and sucked long and hard. Yohe watched enviously.

"Can I suck some?" she asked.

Tammy pulled the penis out of her mouth, grabbed the back of Yohe's head and shoved her down on it. "You like that?" Tammy asked Yohe.

That poor girl bucked and squirmed, but Tammy didn't let the back of her head go. And, eventually, the delivery girl calmed down and enjoyed swallowing Todd's penis. Tammy laid on her back and began to play with herself as she watched her husband enjoying his fellatio treatment. Soon, Tammy started moaning louder and breathing heavily.

Yohe stopped sucking Todd and started licking Tammy's wetness. Todd looked over at the two and pulled at his dick a few times before leaning over and kissing Tammy's leg. He kept kissing and licking her leg and thigh all the way up to her vagina. Then, he and Yohe attacked Tammy's vagina.

We all watched as Tammy gripped the comforter with her hands and feet. Her legs shook, and we could tell that she was fighting to keep from squeezing the two heads between her thighs. It was obvious she wasn't acting because her whole body began to jerk

ZION

forcefully, and she screamed so loud that I thought the police were going to be called. Damn, woman!

When her screams and shaking subsided, she said, "I haven't cum that hard in a long time."

Yohe smiled and looked at her. "Wait until we fill you up," she said and winked at Todd. The couple looked at each other confused. That was when Yohe stood up and pulled her skirt down, revealing a hard, seven-inch dick.

The couple's mouths dropped, shocked. Jermaine, Charlotte, and I did the same. Everyone was on script, but the shock factor had everyone's minds blown. Yes, I asked for a trans. But, I had never seen one in real life!

"Is something wrong?" Yohe asked.

"Is that a penis?" Todd asked. Nobody said anything. Todd looked at his wife and then ran out of the room.

Yohe pulled up her skirt. "I should leave."

"Wait!" Tammy said. "Come back."

Yohe walked to the edge of the bed, and Tammy crawled toward her. When they met, Tammy held Yohe's penis in her hands. She stroked it for a little bit, and then she put it all in her mouth. The Chico's delivery girl grabbed the back of Tammy's head and leaned her own head back.

Diontae got a close up of the girl on tranny action. The two separated and laid on the bed, holding each other and kissing. Diontae went into the hall and recorded Todd peeping into the room, watching and rubbing himself.

Yohe laid on her back, and Tammy guided her new friend's penis into her wet pussy. She ground her hips

Once Upon A Secret

slowly as she and Yohe kissed each other and caressed each other's bodies. Todd stepped into the room and jerked himself as he watched the two fucking on the bed. In a matter of seconds, he climbed onto the bed and got up close to Tammy's ass. He spit on his dick, rubbed it all over, and then he put it in her ass *slowly*. I think moving slow is the key concept in anal sex.

"Goddamn! This ass is tight!" Todd groaned as he buried himself deep inside of her.

Tammy just bit at her bottom lip and breathed heavily through her nose. Todd and Yohe found a synchronized rhythm, and both began to rock their hips slowly. Tammy went back to kissing Yohe and moaned into her mouth. Todd grabbed onto Tammy's hips and sped up his pace. Yohe, also, began to thrust her hips faster until they both were slamming so hard into Tammy that I feared they were going to cripple her. Scared me!

All three of them fucked and screamed, filling the room with cries of passion and the wet slapping sounds of their sweaty, naked bodies.

"Oh... God!" Tammy screamed as she came for the second time that night. Tammy's cum drenched Yohe's cock and hips.

"Yeah! Cum all over my dick!" Yohe yelled as she looked into Tammy's face.

Again, we could see Tammy's body shake wildly as she came, and she yelled out loudly. When she came this time, I heard her pussy making noises. Todd slid his cock out of her ass, so she could roll off of Yohe and catch her breath. Then, he moved between Yohe and Tammy. Once he was on his back, he pulled the two close to him and took turns kissing them softly.

"And cut!" I yelled.

All of the crew clapped, and the actors laid in bed, exhausted.

"That was intense," Jermaine said.

"*Yes*," Erin said.

"It was awkward because you get horny, but, then you ask yourself, 'Am I gay for liking this?'" Diontae said, and we all laughed.

While everyone was laughing, I got a phone call from a 757 number I didn't have saved in my phone. "Hello," I took the call in the hallway.

"Hi. May I speak to Ms. Nikole Turner?"

"Speaking."

"Hi, Ms. Turner, this is Adam Baker with Dominion Law Associates. We are a debt collection agency. Any information obtained will be used for that purpose. Ms. Turner, Capital One has hired us to collect a debt that you owe to them. Are you aware that you owe Capital One $532?"

"Umm, yes, sir. I haven't been able to pay anything because I'm in school right now and without a job." I didn't tell him about being a PA because, that's my business.

"Okay. Well, Ms. Turner, is there any way you can set up a payment plan and possibly pay $25 a month?"

"No, sir. I really don't have any money. But income tax time will be here in January. I can probably do something then."

Once Upon A Secret

"Okay. Please hold while I make a note on your account." There was a long silence, "Okay, Ms. Turner?"

"Yes, sir."

"I have noted here that you will try to make a payment when you get your tax return."

"Yes, sir."

"Again, I have to tell you that Dominion Law Associates is a debt collection agency, and any information obtained will be used for that purpose. Good-bye," and, immediately, he hung up.

I had been avoiding Capital One since I got the credit card seven years ago, but I didn't know how much longer they were going to put up with my excuses. Almost immediately, Jen called.

"Hello."

"Wassup? What are you doing? And what's all the noise in the background?"

"I'm at work. I just directed my first scene, and everybody's kind of excited."

"Oh, okay. Well, look, I moved into my apartment this weekend."

"Oh, that's what's up."

"Yeah, so don't you want to come over and cook for me before I go to work?"

"Umm." I checked my cell phone for the time. "It's going on six. What time do you have to leave?"

"I'm going in late. I'll leave here at ten."

"Okay. I'm on my way."

ZION

Jen

I hung up the phone and continued to unpack. The day before, I had unpacked the cookware, plates and silverware. Nikole was only twenty, but she cooked like an old black woman. I remember when I had my accident last year, she cooked a homemade soup for me, and I nearly ate the whole pot on the first day. After that, I got Nikole to cook for me whenever possible.

As I was unpacking, I found a picture of my ex-girlfriend and me in our Halloween costumes from the previous year. I remembered being so happy to be with her, but she was my ex for a reason. I had never been brought down to a low like I had when I was with Fish. I continued to stare at the picture; I was smiling so hard, and I remember thinking that night I was the happiest woman on earth. I ripped it up and threw the picture in the trash. I continued to unpack and break down boxes, and, in thirty minutes, there was a knock at the door.

"Hey!" Nikole said after I had opened the door for her.

"Hey! Come on in." I shut the door.

"So, what do you want me to cook?" she asked.

"Anything," I said. "I've been waiting for this all day. I just didn't get a chance to call you."

She laughed. "Okay." She went in the kitchen, washed her hands, and began to pull out pots and pans and food.

Once Upon A Secret

I looked over when she was bent over looking in the refrigerator. I had never noticed how sexy Nikole was. Her figure was perfect, and I couldn't stop staring at her. When I finally realized what I was doing, I hurriedly looked away. I didn't know how long I had been staring, and I hoped she didn't see me.

"Mmm, that smells good," I said as I inhaled deeply.

"Mmm hmm, I know it does," Nikole said.

"What is it?"

"Chicken Marsala, white rice, fried corn, and salad."

"Oh, my God." I almost started to drool immediately. "Do you need any help?"

"Nope," she said as she gathered all of the trash and went to the trashcan. "Who is this?"

"Who?" I asked as I unwrapped a picture frame.

Nikole set the trash on the counter, reached in the trashcan, and pulled out a few pieces of the torn picture.

"Is this you in the Catwoman suit?"

"Yeah."

"But why is it torn up?" She looked a little longer. "Is that your ex?"

"Yeah."

"Wow! I wish I could see her face, but her mask is covering most of it." She looked on for a few moments more before putting the pieces back in the trash and then covering them with the contents from the counter. "So, it's a Monday night. How much money do you plan on making?"

"Five hundred," I said.

Her mouth dropped. "Are you serious?"

"Yeah."

ZION

"Wow!"

"I told you to get on it."

"Yeah, but I don't think I'd be comfortable with men seeing my naked body."

"You don't get completely naked."

"Oh, what do you strip down to?"

"Pasties and a thong,"

"That's naked!" Nikole shouted.

I laughed. "Well, what did you expect? You don't come out in your winter clothes and strip to your bra and underwear."

She came in the living room with me and plopped herself onto the couch.

"Do you wear a costume?"

"Yep."

"Do you have a stripper name?"

I smiled. "Baby."

"Baby?"

"Yeah."

She laughed hysterically.

"Why Baby?"

"I don't know."

"Wow… " She hesitated. "So you like it?"

I looked at her. "I love it!"

"Hmm… "

"Mmm hmm… "

She sat on the couch while I continued to work, and, in about forty-five minutes, the food was done. We ate, we laughed, and, after we washed our plates, Nikole went back on campus, and I began my hour and twenty-five minute drive to Consequences.

Once Upon A Secret

MICHAEL

"Do you need any help?"

I nearly jumped out of my skin! Who told that woman to sneak up behind me?!

"Oh, I'm so sorry! I didn't mean to scare you."

"Oh, no, you're fine. But no, I don't need any help."

The young lady smiled and walked away. Trick. Anyway, I looked down at my hands. In my left hand, I was holding a plush blue elephant, and, in my right, I was holding a Minnie Mouse in a pink dress.

"Michael, really?" Scarlet ol' pregnant ass was walking toward me from the women's department.

"What's wrong, hun?"

"I'm only three months. We don't even know what it is yet."

"First off, don't call my child an *it*. He or she is a baby. A little prince or princess."

"Well, can you wait two more months before you start buying baby toys and clothes?" Oh! She had a lil' attitude!

"Scarlet, why are you so upset?"

"I'm not upset," she crossed her arms.

"Well, you seem pretty upset to me. We just left the doctor and saw the baby. This is real."

A little tear fell down her face.

"Aaw," I hugged her.

"Michael, I'm not ready. I don't want to be a mother. I just want to be your wife for a few more years. I don't know how to take care of a child."

ZION

"Well, I'm going to help you. That's what I'm here for. I'm not going to just sit around and stare at you." My wife hardly ever cried so, if I didn't know before, I knew then. That heifa was pregnant. I wiped the tears from her eyes and kissed her. "I love you. I won't let anything happen to you *or* our baby."

She smiled. "I love you, too."

I kissed her on the forehead. "Okay, let's get out of this cheap ass store. You ready to go see my mom?" She nodded.

We left K-Mart and went across the street to my parents' house in Carriage Mill. I knocked on the door.

"Hey, y'all."

"Hey," we said together and walked into the foyer and up the stairs into the living room on the second floor.

"So, what's up? You called and said you have something to tell me, so… "

"Well… " I was smiling so damn hard. "We're having a baby."

My mamma's eyes grew to the size of golf balls, and she looked at Scarlet's stomach.

"What?" she started smiling.

"I'm not showing yet," Scarlet said.

"Aww! I'm going to be a grandmamma." Then, she frowned. "I'm going to be a grandmamma."

"Well, you knew this day was coming, Ma." She betta had got herself together! Ain't nobody frowning about my baby!

"Yeah, but… you know… I still wasn't prepared. Have you told your dad?"

"No, we're going there next."

Once Upon A Secret

"Uhh… "

"What?"

"I think you should tell him by yourself."

"Why?"

"Because you know how he is. He's going to want to have a man to man talk with you. So, *you* should go to the barber shop and leave Scarlet here." Uugh, I don't know *why* my parents are so dramatic. Sigh, that must be where I get it from.

I looked at Scarlet. "I'll be fine. It's not like she's going to kill me or anything," Scarlet smiled at my mamma. Them heifas do not get along, and I had never left them alone before.

"Umm, okay," I said and walked to the door. I looked back at Scarlet, and she smiled and waved. Crazy bitch.

In ten minutes, I pulled up to the barber shop. It was a Tuesday, so there was only one client in the shop getting a cut by Romeo.

I walked in, and Pops jumped up. "Hey, look! It's my son!"

It still shocked me when my dad was excited to see me. Just earlier that year, he wouldn't say two words to me. But he apologized when my sister Jen went into the hospital. Guess he was scared he was gone lose his kids. But when I got married, *oh*! It was like he couldn't get enough of me! "Hey, Pops."

"¿*Que pasa*?" he asked.

"I need to talk to you."

His face frowned up. "Okay."

"Scarlet's pregnant," I said as I smiled.

ZION

Pops smiled so hard, I thought his whole face was gone split in half. "What?"

"Yeah."

"My son! Ay, Romeo!"

"Yeah," Romeo hollered back.

"My son's having a baby! Go get us some drinks!"

Romeo waved my father, Rev. Jose Matos, off. Everybody know the bishop ain't drinking shit.

"Jose, you ain't ready to drink what I'm drinking," Romeo said.

"Aww, whatever, you ugly red nigga!"

"Yeah," I had no intentions on being involved in whatever back and forth they were about to start up. "Well, I left Scarlet at the house with Mom, so—"

"Yeah, you better get over there 'cause ain't no telling what might happen if you leave them two alone. But *mira*."

"What?"

He looked around at the barbers before saying, "Let's go *fuera*."

I followed him outside.

"You know... well, let me ask you this. How does Scarlet feel about the baby?"

"She's not excited."

"Uh huh... why not?"

"'Cause we just got married and she wants to be a wife for a little while longer before being a mother."

"Mmmhmm... well... I got to say this *porque* I'm your father and your pastor. What culture are you going to raise *el bebé* in?"

"Umm... " Here we go with the million and one questions.

Once Upon A Secret

"Right!" He laughed. "Um!" He laughed again. "The reason why I asked is because you don't want to raise a child in confusion. You are Mexican and white, but thank God your mamma and I were able to find a common ground. You never been to Mexico. There's a lot you don't know. And there's a lot you're going to forget to tell your child. Okay? Scarlet is black. I'm sure she has her own views on how to raise a child, right?"

"Yeah."

"Okay. Also, both of y'all have a past." He stared at me. "*¿Entende?*"

"Yes." Oh my God!

"You *sabe* that she lost her mother, and you know... what happened with those men?"

"Yeah."

"*Tu habla* she's not excited about being a mother; she would rather be a wife. Why do you think that is?"

"Uhh... " Can we get to the point please?

"Could it be that she's scared that she'll turn out like her mother? Or she's scared that she won't be able to protect her child from the same things that happened to her?" He looked me in my face, "*Hijo*, you have to take into consideration all of these things when you get married and when you have a child," he paused, "and just last year, you had a... up in your... okay. I ain't got to say it, do I?"

"No." But, I should have known he was going to bring it up!

"Okay. Well, that's all I'm saying. I'm happy for you, *hijo*. I really am; don't think that I'm not. But I want you to raise this child right, and, as long as I'm alive, I'll help you."

"Okay."

"A'ight. Now go get your wife before she kills mine."

Nikole

"Hello?"

"Hello. May I speak to a Ms. Nikole Turner?"

"Speaking."

"Oh, my name is Ms. Rebecca Ives, and I'm with the debt collections department at Chesapeake General Hospital. Any information obtained during this call will be used for debt collection purposes. Ms. Turner, you have an outstanding balance with Chesapeake General for six hundred ninety-six dollars. Are you aware of that?"

Lord, Jesus. "Yes, ma'am."

"Okay. Will you be able to make a payment today?"

"No, ma'am. I'm in school right now. I attend Hampton University, and I'm not currently working."

"Okay, I understand. I have kids in college. I'll make a note on your account. Do you know when you'll be able to make a payment?"

"Um, I'll get my tax return next year, and I should be able to make a payment then."

"Let me make a note… Okay, Ms. Turner, I hope you do well in school. What are you majoring in?"

Once Upon A Secret

"Theatre Arts and minoring in entrepreneurship."

"Oh, that is wonderful."

"Thank you!" Finally, some recognition for my hard work!

"Okay, Ms. Turner, you have a nice day."

"Thanks. You, too." I hung up the phone and threw myself down on the bed.

"Girl!" Yasmine said as she painted her toenails. "Why do you have so many bills? How old are you again?"

"Twenty."

"Mmm! I wish I could help you, but you need God to help you with all of that."

My phone rang again. "Who is that?" she asked.

I looked at the phone. "Another 877 number."

"Oh, God! Nikki, please don't answer."

I silenced the phone. "I definitely need another job."

"Oh, Lord. The last time *you* looked for a job, you went out and started directing porn. I'm going to help you find a job before you start prostituting."

My phone rang again, "Lordy!" I looked at the screen, "It's just Lonnie." I answered, "Hello."

"Hey, baby."

"Don't 'hey baby' me."

"What?"

"What? Lonnie, I haven't heard from you since Friday. It's Wednesday; where have you been?"

"Oh, I haven't been home."

"Well… where have you been?"

"James's house."

"James?"

"Yeah."

ZION

"Who is James?"
"My friend."
"I don't know a James."
"Oh."
"*Oh*?... Okay, Lonnie."
"Yeah... how was your day?"
"Good. How was yours?" I said dryly.
"Good."
"Good. I got to go."
"*Baby*!" he whined.
"What?"
"I want to talk to you."
"I have homework."
"*Baby*!"
"Sorry, Lonnie."
"Okay. Love you."
"Love you, too." I hung up.

Yasmine looked at me as she was putting her polish away. "Girl, I don't know why you put up with that."

"Me either. Watch this." I called Lonnie's house phone back and got the busy signal. "See, Lonnie was on house arrest when he was eleven and couldn't have call waiting. But, his mamma never put it back on the phone. So, basically, Lonnie is on the phone with another bitch right now." I hung up.

"Well, it could be a guy."

"One, I know it's not a guy because Lonnie is a motherfucker. And two, I'll call back in twenty minutes. Lonnie talks to guys for a maximum of ten minutes. If I get the busy signal, it's a bitch."

Yasmine shook her head. "Why don't you just break up with him?"

Once Upon A Secret

"I don't know. I'm bored."

"That's just too much… too much drama."

"Yeah, I know."

She exhaled deeply. "Well, if that's what you want to do. But I think any real man will be lucky to be with you. You cook… good. You can do hair; you're funny, and you're beautiful." She got under the covers, "But you got to see that for yourself."

We both went to sleep, but I woke up to use the bathroom around midnight. I called Lonnie's house phone just to see… busy signal. The next day was a Thursday. I had Professor Phillips' Strategies for Start Up class at nine thirty; Professor E said I didn't have to go to his eleven o'clock Financing New Business Ventures class, but I did have to go to his two o'clock Creativity, Innovation, and Product Development class. I woke up that morning and put on the loosest pair of dress pants I had, and my shape was still showing. I put on a pair of matching heels and a shirt and made that walk to Buckman Hall. I walked up the stairs to the second floor and sat in one of the office chairs that surrounded the conference room table in the center. At 9:37, Professor Phillips walked in, late as usual.

"Good Morning. Good Morning."

"Good Morning," one or two of us said. He hooked up his projector to his Apple laptop and began to teach. I didn't even look at him. I just took notes and stared at either the slides or my notebook.

"What do you think, Ms. Turner?"

I jumped when I heard him say my name, "Uh, uh…"

ZION

"Would you want to open up a salon in a bad neighborhood if the building was good and affordable, but you couldn't guarantee your customers would make it to their car safely?"

"Umm, I don't know because I think women would risk it if the hairstyle is good."

"So, you think a woman would risk getting robbed to get her hair done?" The class laughed.

"Some women might. There are women who live in those areas… they're not scared."

Professor Phillips thought about it, and then said, "See me after class."

"What?"

"Yeah, I want to pick your brain."

Oh, my God, no! For the rest of class, I didn't hear what he said. I was so scared of what might happen next. At ten forty-five, he looked at his watch. "Okay, you all can go to Elmo's class. Ms. Turner, come with me to my office." The rest of the class went downstairs and across to the MLK building.

Mr. Phillips' secretary was sitting at her desk, outside of his door.

"Good Morning," she said.

"Morning," we said as he turned his key to let us inside.

"Shut the door," Phillips said. I did, and, before I could turn around, he was unbuckling his belt.

"Wait."

"Uh uh," he said as he dropped his pants. "Let me pick your brain." He ran toward me, grabbed the back of my head, forced me on my knees, and shoved his penis in my mouth. He thrust in and out until I gagged.

Once Upon A Secret

He liked that and went harder and faster. He was literally in my throat, and, even though I was gagging, he was not stopping. I couldn't breathe, so I did the only thing I knew to do. He pulled back and, as he was pushing in, I bit down hard enough to scrape the skin off of his head and part of his shaft. He yelled out and stumbled back. I stood up and grabbed the door knob, but, before I could open it, Phillips grabbed my hair and pulled me back. He whispered in my ear, "You don't go anywhere until I tell you to!"

Then, he threw me up against the cinder block wall. I hit my head and tumbled to the floor. Phillips pulled his pants all the way off and picked me up.

"Please, let me go," I whined.

He didn't even respond. He laid me on my back on his desk, undid my pants, and pulled them all the way off, along with my panties. Just then, there was a knock on the door.

"Yeah?" Mr. Phillips yelled.

"Mr. Phillips, are you okay?" the secretary said through the door.

"I'm fine," Mr. Phillips said. He looked down at me and then picked me up off of the desk, "If you say anything," he whispered, "I'll ruin your life." I just stared at him. "Put your clothes back on and get out."

I frantically pulled up my underwear and pants, "And now you have an F in my class for that little stunt that you pulled."

He sat in his chair and stared at his penis. I just grabbed my things and calmly walked past his secretary.

ZION

In the hallway, my phone rang. I didn't look at the number before answering.

"Hello," I said as I power walked to the exit.

"Hello, may I speak to Nikole Turner?"

"Speaking."

"Hi, Ms. Turner. I'm with Chartway's Debt Collection Department, and I first have to say that any information obtained during this call will be used for the purpose of collecting a debt."

"Okay," I said as I hurried back to McGrew Towers.

"Ms. Turner, did you know that you owe Chartway seven hundred sixty dollars for a credit card ending in four, six, seven, three?"

"Umm, yes."

"Okay. Are you prepared to make a payment on this debt?"

"No, ma'am; I am in school, and I don't have a job."

"Okay. Well, how do you pay for school?"

"Excuse me?"

"You pay your tuition, but you can't make a payment on the credit card?"

Hold the hell up! "Ma'am! I don't have a job, and I get financial aid!"

"Well, how do you take care of yourself?"

What the fuck is up with these questions?! "My family takes care of me."

"And they can't loan you $25 a month to help pay off this debt?"

"What?" I hung up. The debt collectors were getting worse and worse. I needed to do something about it.

Once Upon A Secret

Casey

I slapped my alarm clock and slid out of the bed. Six p.m. Time to get ready for work. I walked to my bathroom and cut on the shower. The pipes clanged on the inside of the walls as the water flowed. I left the room and went into the kitchen, started the coffee, and turned on the news. Just then, I got a knock on the door. I looked through the peep hole and saw Mrs. Twine, my elderly black neighbor who stayed down the hall. I opened the door.

"Hello, Mrs. Twine."

"Hey, Casey. I just wanted to pray for you before you go to work."

"Okay, Mrs. Twine," I exhaled impatiently.

"Oh, Lord." She grabbed my hands. "Please protect Casey as she goes to that dreadful strip club. Don't let any hurt, harm, or danger come to her. Please keep all drugs and alcohol from her lips, and keep your arms around her. In the name of Jesus I pray, Amen."

"Amen," I said. "Okay, I'll see you."

"Wait. I cooked you a lasagna. It's in my apartment."

"Okay, Mrs. Twine, but I got to take a shower. I'll leave the door unlocked, and you can leave it in the kitchen."

"Okay, baby." She walked down the hall to her apartment, and I shut the door and headed back to my bedroom. Mrs. Twine was genuinely concerned about me, and I loved that someone in the world was. She was kind of annoying, but one thing my daddy taught

ZION

me was, old ladies are somebody's mother, and I should treat them as if they were my own.

The pipes had stopped rattling, and as I washed myself, I began to think the same thing I thought every night before I went to work. What would my daddy think of me now? My mom died when I was born, and I never really had a woman's influence in my life. But my daddy never neglected me, and he instilled morals in me. I know for a fact, he wouldn't even be able to look at me if he knew his little girl was showing her body off to random men. I didn't even like looking at myself anymore. I only had one full body mirror on the front of my bedroom door and that was it.

I got out of the shower, dried off, and as soon as I stepped out of the bathroom and into my bedroom, I could smell lasagna.

"Oh, God," I said aloud.

One thing about Mrs. Twine—she could cook her ass off. I stayed on my treadmill, trying to stay at a decent size. I threw on matching bra and underwear set, a pair of black skinny jeans and a sheer orange button up. I opened my bedroom door, looked in the mirror and tossed my red hair from side to side. My hair was the one thing I got from my mother. It was really long, down to my butt because I never cut it. Other than life, it was one of the only things she gave me. After I brushed it back into a neat, high ponytail, I went to the kitchen.

"I'm just warming some up for you. You do have time to eat, don't you?" Mrs. Twine asked.

"Yes, ma'am," I said as I sat on one of the bar stools and patiently waited for her to serve me. She placed the plate on the placemat in front of me. "Thank you." I took a bite, "Oh, Mrs. Twine! Why is your food so good?"

She laughed and set a glass of milk next to my plate.

"I never told you?"

"Told me what?"

"I used to live in Chesapeake, Virginia in a neighborhood called Fernwood Farms. I used to babysit lots of kids from the neighborhood and from church."

"Uh huh," I said with a mouth full of food.

"Don't talk with food in your mouth, dear," she said as she walked around the counter and sat on the bar stool next to me. "Well, I got tired of taking care of kids at my age. I mean, there was a reason I only had one daughter, and she was grown. So, I stopped babysitting, and I decided to open up a restaurant in the shopping center in the front of the neighborhood. Drink your milk." I guzzled down half the glass. "Now, I never went to culinary school, never went to college. And my husband, God rest his soul, was *so* nervous. He didn't see how it was going to work. But I hired all culinary school graduates, and it didn't take long for business to start booming. And these kids taught me, too." I dropped my fork on the plate, and Mrs. Twine looked over, saw I was done, and picked up my plate to put it in the sink.

"So, what happened to the restaurant?"

She put the plate in the sink and headed to the door.

"Have a good night at work. God is with you, baby,"

"Wait!" I turned in my seat. "What was the name of the restaurant?"

ZION

"Good night, Casey," she said and left the apartment. I looked at the clock. 7:15 pm. Time to go to work.

Tori

It was nine o'clock, and I already had a full bar of men begging for drinks. I worked at Consequences Gentleman's Club in downtown Richmond, and the craziness was just about to begin. One of our dancers, Jen, brought a friend in to join our team. Jerry, the manager, exchanged glances with the DJ, "Get on stage for Amateur Hour," he told her. Between you and me, I'd worked at the club for a little over a year, and we'd never had an Amateur Hour at the club. Casey, Emily, Jordin, and Jen watched from the bar.

"Who is she?" I heard Jordin ask Casey.

"She's with me," Jen said. Casey and Emily looked at each other behind Jen's back.

"Well, let's see what she's got," Casey said.

"Okay! Listen up!" The DJ said. "It's Amateur Night here at Consequences!" Everyone clapped. "Introducing Nikki, Nikki, Nikki!" The DJ played "I Luv Dem Strippers" by 2 Chainz ft. Nicki Minaj. The girl came out in a clown costume, and everybody, except Jen, laughed.

"Who the fuck gave her that costume?" Jen asked. The other girls shook their heads and laughed.

"Don't look at me," Emily said. The girl on stage just stared out into the audience,

Once Upon A Secret

"Go, Nikki!" Jen yelled and clapped. All of a sudden, the girl ripped open the clown costume and revealed a purple lace bra. She dropped the top half of her costume and danced to the pole. She put her finger in her mouth, wet it with her tongue, and slid it down from her chin to her chest, down her stomach till she got to the top of the clown pants. Then, she turned her back to the audience and slowly pulled the pants all the way down to her ankles. The men went crazy when they saw her butt cheeks surrounding a purple lace thong. She pulled her right foot out of the clown shoe and the right pants leg. Then the left foot out of the clown shoe and the left pants leg. Then she walked to the back of the stage a little, did a back flip, and, before her legs could hit the floor, she wrapped them around the pole, bent her body up, grabbed the pole with her hands, stretched her legs straight out to the sides, and let her body drop to the floor in a split. Then, she did a crabwalk toward the back of the stage, stood up, and ran and jumped to one of the other stages. The crowd went wild, and the girls' mouths dropped. Then the girl took off her clown wig and whipped her long golden hair. All the men stood up, threw money onto the stage, and Nikki posed with the pole as the song went off.

Jen jumped up, screamed, and clapped. Then, she grabbed her friend and took her into the New Girls' dressing room.

"Hmm," Casey said,

"She was good," Emily said.

"Not great," Jordin said as she flipped her straight brown hair. She looked at me. "I need a shot."

"And?"

ZION

"And give it to her, bitch!" Emily yelled in her friend's defense.

"Who you calling a bitch?" I yelled back.

"You, obviously."

"Excuse the fuck out of you." I pulled my blonde hair back into a ponytail.

"Don't forget. I'm how you get paid, whore."

"Look at the pot calling the kettle black."

"Oh, yeah?"

"Yeah, bitch."

"Kiss my ass, Tori!"

"Fuck you!"

"Fuck *you*!"

Jordin and Casey pulled Emily away from the bar and to the dressing room. That was when Emily lifted her skirt, revealing the lip tattoo on her right ass cheek.

"Kiss... my ass... *Tori*," she sang, all the way to the dressing room.

"You okay?" Clarence, the other bartender, asked me.

"Yeah," I said and walked to the kitchen.

Nikole

"Oh, my God! You were so good," Jen said after I got off stage and into the dressing room.

"Really?" I asked. "I was so nervous." Nervous my ass! I killed that shit. Clown suit and all.

Once Upon A Secret

"Well, we couldn't tell," a man said. "Hi!" He stuck his hand out. "I'm Jerry. I'm in charge of all of the VIP rooms, treatment, and, essentially, all of the girls."

"Oh, okay… but why are you repeating this? You already introduced yourself before I went on stage."

"Oh, did I? I'm sorry. I can be a bit forgetful. But I would love to add you to our team."

"Really?"

"Yes! When can you start?"

"Tonight!" Damn, right! Let's get to the money!

Jerry laughed. "Well, you are an amateur, so I need you to watch the girls. So, stay tonight, mingle with the guys, introduce yourself, and get a feel of the place. I'm sure Baby will show you around. And, if you want to come back tomorrow, then we'll handle the paperwork."

"Okay! Thank you so much!"

Jerry laughed again. "You're a cute kid. Baby, I need you to get ready," he left the dressing room.

As soon as he walked out, three women—a redhead, brunette and a blonde—walked in. The blonde had her skirt lifted, singing what sounded like a made up song,

"Hey," the redhead said. "I'm Casey."

"Hi," I said.

"I'm Jordin," the brunette said. "And this is—"

The blonde stepped forward. "I'm Emily, but you can call me Luna."

"Oh, nice to meet you." I stood up and stretched out my hand. The girls just looked at it, and Emily laughed.

"We don't shake hands here."

"Oh," I said.

ZION

"Emily," Jen started.

"We hug," Emily said and hugged me.

"Oh," I was a little startled by being toched by this half naked white girl.

As she let go, Jerry stuck his head back in. "Baby, I need you to get ready,"

"You already told me that, Jerry!" Jen said. Jerry just laughed and went back to what he was doing,

"That crack is going to get the best of him someday," Casey said.

"Mm hmm," everyone else moaned.

"I'll be in the other dressing room if you need me," Jen said to me, and then she eyed all of the girls before leaving.

"So, you were pretty good out there," Casey said.

"Yeah, how long have you been dancing?" Jordin asked.

"Oh, I've never danced before," I said, "except in the club or at a party, of course."

"Oh, you can't even tell!"

"But why start dancing now?" Casey asked. "I don't think anybody wakes up and says, '*I want to be a stripper.*'"

"Well, to be honest, I don't want to be a stripper." The three girls' eyes got wide. "I need this job. I have no other choice."

"That's not true."

"So, what were you doing before this?" Emily asked.

"Umm... I help direct adult films."

"Porn?"

"Yeah," I said.

"Oh, can you get me in a movie?"

Once Upon A Secret

"Umm, I can try, but I work in Virginia Beach. That's eighty miles away."

"Aww," she groaned and sat on the vanity next to mine.

"Oh, so you stay in Virginia Beach?" Casey asked.

"Actually, I stay on campus in Hampton."

"Oh, what school do you go to?" Jordin asked.

"Hampton University."

"Wow," Casey said. "That's good."

"Thank you."

"Well," Emily said as she stood up, "you'll find that this place is full of sharks. You'll have no friends… except me." She placed her hand on my shoulder. "I'll be in the other dressing room if you ever need to talk, okay?"

"Okay," I said. The girls all waved goodbye and left the dressing room. The other new girls all eyeballed me and continued to do their makeup. I began to put my clothes back on and started thinking about what Jen had told me: "You are not going to have any friends here. And that's okay. You're here to make money, not friends. And the number one bitch to watch out for is Emily. She is a sociopath and a crazy motherfucking bitch. Do not try to be friends with her." I looked in the mirror and began to touch up my makeup. I was going to keep my eye on Emily, but, so far, she hadn't given me a reason to be on edge.

ZION

Paris

It was two a.m., and I was downstairs in my pajama shirt and matching shorts, smoking a blunt and dialing my friend's number.

"Hello," he said when he picked up.

"What the fuck, Carl?"

"Hello?"

"What?"

"Paris?"

"Yeah, who the fuck were you expecting? Charlotte?"

"*Wow*! Really?"

"Yeah, really. I got her phone right here." I clicked on a text from him to my girlfriend. "I miss you, too. When can I see you again?"

"Oh, my God, Paris."

"*Oh, my God, Paris?* Carl, you're trying to fuck my girlfriend!" He hung up. "Hello... *hello*? I know this nigga did *not* hang up on me." I called him back, and he ignored the call. "Look, nigga! Don't you ever call this phone again!" I pressed END and threw both phones down on the couch.

"What the fuck is going on down here?" I turned around, and Charlotte was standing on the stairs. I picked up her cell phone and threw it at her.

"What the fuck?"

"Carl is *what the fuck, Charlotte*!"

"What are you talking about?"

Once Upon A Secret

"What am I talking about? Carl," I imitated her, "she can't fuck me like you can. I want you to do me like the last time." Then, I imitated Carl, "Ooh, you like that, huh?" She didn't say anything. "How many times have I told you that I wanted to leave?" She walked into the kitchen to get a drink. I followed her. "How many times have I told you that I *know* you don't love me, and you said, 'Paris, I know you're the one'?" She took a long swig from the gin bottle. "So, why keep me here?" She didn't say anything, "When was the last time you fucked him?"

She took another long swig and looked at me, "Are you sure you want to do this right now?"

"Answer the question, Charlotte."

"Last weekend," she said and headed back upstairs.

I don't think my heart ever hurt as bad as it did right then. It was as if she slapped me in the face and didn't give a fuck. I followed her up the stairs to the bedroom, "*Last weekend?*"

She got back in bed with her bottle. "Did you want me to lie to you?"

"No, but I wish you hadn't lied when you said you loved me."

"Oh my God, Paris. I *do* love you."

"Yeah, right. I'm *done* with you, Charlotte." I went into the closet in the bathroom and put on my fur hat and knee high UGG boots.

"What are you doing?" she yelled from the bed.

I walked past her, out of the room, and down the stairs.

"Paris!" she yelled.

ZION

I grabbed my keys, and, when she heard the keys jingle, I heard her jump out of bed. As fast as I could, I ran out of the front door and slammed it behind me. As soon as I made it down the porch steps, Charlotte tackled me in the grass.

"Get off of me!" I yelled.

"No!"

We were wrestling in the grass. I had rolled over, but, she was still on top of me, holding me down while I tried to get her off of me. In about five minutes, I was exhausted, and I just started crying.

"I love you, okay? Is that what you want to hear? Don't leave, Paris. You know I love you."

I just cried in the grass while she held me down. She bent over and kissed me. She got up, helped me up, and wiped my tears.

"Come back in the house," she said as she pulled my arm to lead me into the house.

I pulled away from her and shook my head. "*No.*"

She looked at me.

"What?"

"Let me go, Charlotte."

Then her face balled up, and she threw my arm down.

"Fine, bitch! Leave! I don't need you! You need *me*!" she yelled as she walked into the house.

I got in my car, started it, and put it in reverse. That was when I saw Charlotte throwing all of my clothes out of the guest bedroom window. I put the car in park and ran into the yard to get my clothes. Charlotte started pouring gin out of the window, onto the clothes. As I tried to grab my things, the liquor was sprinkling on my head.

Once Upon A Secret

"No!" she yelled. "Don't touch them! I paid for that shit!" I grabbed an armful of clothes and shoes and walked to the car. Next thing I knew, the gin bottle came flying over my head, hit the top of my car, cracked the sunroof and ricocheted off into the driveway and smashed.

"What the *fuck*?" I yelled as I turned around. Charlotte ran out of the house toward me and snatched some of the clothes out of my hands.

"What are you *doing*?" She ran back to the pile and threw the clothes down. "Charlotte!" She lit her lighter, bent down, and set the clothes on fire. It was burning slowly, and I ran toward the pile.

"What is *wrong* with you?"

She grabbed me and held me back. "No! I paid for all that shit!" Then she pushed me toward my car. "You want to leave? Leave!"

"Fuck you!" I got into the car.

"Yeah. Fuck you, too," she said and walked back to the large blaze. I backed out of the driveway, and, before I pulled off, watched Charlotte light a cigarette and slowly exhale as she watched the fire. I put the car in drive and headed down the road. I didn't know where I was going. Charlotte had been taking care of me ever since we got together. She had burned all of my clothes, and I only had five hundred dollars in my bank account.

Fuck.

ZION

Scarlet

I was staring at my belly in the mirror. I had on nothing but my bra, underwear, and a silk robe. My stomach wasn't big yet, but, I had a noticeable pudge. I hurriedly smeared Vaseline all over my stomach and stared at it. I hated to say it, but, I was *not* excited about being a mother. And I felt bad about that. Didn't every girl want to be a mother at some point? Everybody was excited, except me. My phone rang; I picked it up and saw it was Brittany, my foster mother.

"Hey, Mom."

"'Mom'? What's wrong?"

"What?"

"Scarlet, you only call me Mom when something's bothering you." I didn't say anything. "Okay. Let's do lunch."

"I'm not hungry."

She was quiet for a moment. "Well, are you busy?"

I looked down at my stomach. "No."

"May I come over?"

"Yes."

"Okay, sweetheart. I'm on my way."

"Okay."

I hung up and continued to stare at myself in the mirror. In about fifteen minutes, there was a knock on the door. I opened it, and Brittany's mouth dropped when she saw me standing there with my robe open.

"Oh, sweetie," she said as she hugged me.

"Hey, Mom," I said as she hugged me.

Once Upon A Secret

"Let's talk."

"Okay," I shut the front door and led her to the living room. I plopped down in the recliner, and she sat down slowly and smoothed out her dress. I looked at her, how perfect she looked. Her blonde hair was flipped and each curl was perfect. She and Jack were the few white people I knew that didn't age. She looked the same way she did the day she adopted me. And that was when I burst out crying.

"Scarlet… baby." She waited for me to quiet down a little bit. "You are not your mother… you are not me. You are Scarlet Waters-Matos. You were born in Chesapeake General Hospital, and you're going to be a *great* mother. What happened to you won't happen to your baby. And you have a family who is going to help you." I was still crying, but I could hear her get up and go to the bathroom. In a few moments, she was back, and she held my head up and wiped my eyes. "Don't cry, baby."

"You're so beautiful."

She looked confused. "What?"

"I've been in here all day watching myself grow. I'm getting uglier by the second. My body will never be the same again. But, you… you're flawless and have been flawless forever."

She sat on the couch again, "You ever notice how mostly men get pot bellies and women don't?"

I just looked at her. What the fuck did that have to do with my depression?

"When a woman gets pregnant, her muscles move so the baby can grow. Well, they never come back together completely so fat can spread everywhere. A man never gets pregnant, so his fat doesn't spread."

"So, you're saying I'm going to be a fat ass after this?"

"No, I said all of that to say, you watched your stomach grow for a baby. I never had that chance. You think I'm flawless and beautiful because I'm thin, but I hate my body for the same reason. In about two months, you're going to feel that baby kick. I never got to experience that. You don't even know how hard I tried to get pregnant before we adopted you. I never loved *anything* or *anyone* as much as I love you. I'm not flawless, I have a major flaw. But I am getting over it more and more every time I look at you."

I looked down at my stomach, "It's a girl."

Brittany smiled. "Is that what you want?"

I nodded. "But I know it's a girl because I think about Michael so much more, and when he's not here, I just want to be with him. I feel like I've fallen in love all over again." Brittany smiled, and I looked at her. "Do you want to go out for lunch?"

"Yes."

"Okay," and I went in my room to get dressed.

Nikole

It was 8:00 on Saturday morning, and my phone was ringing. I looked, and it was Jermaine.

"Hey, Jermaine."

Once Upon A Secret

"Hey, Nikole. Are you coming in today?"

"Uhh, yeah."

"Okay. What time were you planning on coming?"

"One."

"Uhh, no, that's not going to work. Can you be here by ten? We need to have a meeting."

"Okay."

"Okay. Thanks."

I hung up and sat up on Jen's couch. The night before, I had danced for the first time and made $625. Jen made a little over a thousand. Jermaine paid me $150 for my first week of work, and he had put the car on full. So, the first thing I did was pay Dominion Law Associates $532 online at five that morning when I got back to Jen's house. I went into the hall closet, grabbed a towel and wash cloth, and went into the bathroom to take a shower. I got out of the shower and headed to my bag of clothes in Jen's room. She was laid out across the bed, asleep. So, I just dropped my towel and got dressed right there. When I was fully dressed, I woke Jen up.

"What?"

"I got to go to work. I'll leave my stuff here and be back when I'm done."

"Okay."

I hopped in my car and drove to Virginia Beach. It was 9:45 when I pulled up to the house. I saw Charlotte's car outside and none of the other crew, so I immediately began to worry what the meeting was about. I knocked on the door, and in a few moments, Jermaine answered.

"Girl, why you knocking? You always just walk in."

ZION

"Well, I thought things might be different today because we're having a meeting and all."

"Oh, girl, you can just walk right on in."

"Oh, okay."

Then he pushed me back, stepped outside, and pulled the door shut.

"Charlotte and her girlfriend got into it," he whispered, "so she is a real emotional roller coaster today."

"Okay."

Then we went in the house and headed for the office.

"Good morning," I said as I walked in.

"*Hey*," Charlotte said with a smile. I had never seen her that happy in the week I'd been there.

"Hey," I said as I sat down in a chair. Jermaine sat behind the desk.

"Okay. Let's get started," he said. "First off, Nikki."

"Yes?"

"Your video got over 1,000 hits already."

"Really?" I asked.

"Wooooo!" Charlotte yelled and clapped in the air.

"Yes, really," Jermaine said. "That brought us a lot of money, really fast. So, we want to use another one of your scripts."

"Yeah, sure. That's what I wrote them for."

"Okay. It's either the college girl who sneaks her boyfriend in her dorm or the girl who has sex with her mom's drunken boyfriend." He looked to Charlotte, and she thought for a moment.

"Well," she started, "Jermaine, I don't know why you keep running from this, but we haven't done gay porn yet."

"Um… " I started.

"In the industry boy on boy is gay. Girl on girl is lesbian."

"Oh, okay."

"So, I'm thinking we do the college dorm idea with two guys."

"That's not hot," Jermaine said.

"We can make it hot! And we can make it work!" I blurted out. "At my school, the rule is 'no sex on campus,' and girls complain because we can't have guys up to our rooms, except from seven to ten p.m. on the weekends. But gay people can have their partners up, no problem. So, they can have sex whenever."

"Yeah, but two guys? I don't know."

"Look, we start out shooting the outside of a male dorm. We go inside and see a sign at the front desk that has the female in room visitation hours. Then, the camera will shoot slowly around the lobby, showing guys talking to girls. We see two guys walk in. One signs in. Then, they laugh a little bit as they walk to the stairs. Once we're in the room, boom, it happens." They both looked intrigued, so I kept going. "The guy's roommate walks in, and, before he can get out of the room, the two grab him, and they have a threesome. Movie goes off with them kissing each other." Jermaine's mouth was wide open, and Charlotte's eyes were wide.

"Dayumm!" Jermaine said. "That *is* hot! I'ma have to call Robin and tell her thank you for sending me Nikole."

I laughed.

ZION

"So, when can you have the script to us?" Charlotte asked.

"Well, do you really need a script? That's pretty easy to do. The words can be improvised."

"Yeah, you're right," Jermaine said.

"No, no, no!" Charlotte yelled. "If we gon' do this, let's do it right. We need a script. Something we can refer to in the future." I started to see the emotional roller coaster Jermaine had warned me about.

"Okay, but it would look even better improvised because it would look more natural," I said.

"How long have you been doing this?" Charlotte asked. "Huh?"

"A week."

"A week. I've been working with Jermaine for nearly eight months. I think I know a little more than you. Write the script."

"I'm sorry. I've been studying theatre, acting, and directing for more than eight years, so I think I may know a little bit more than you. If you need a script for reference, I'll write it after the movie, so what is improvised will be set lines." I don't know who she *thought* she was talking to, but she had the right one that day!

Charlotte hesitated and then burst out laughing, "Yeah, you're right. Okay."

Jermaine gave her a scared look. Her emotions had changed that fast.

"So, when do you want to start shooting?" I asked him.

"When can I get a dorm room?" He gave me the eye, and I knew what that meant.

Once Upon A Secret

"I'll see what I can do."
"Good!"
"Okay, so what are we doing today?"
"Well, let's do the other script. Girl has sex with her mom's drunken boyfriend."
"Okay. Who have you chosen to act in this one?"
"Well," he pulled out a binder from the desk drawer and sat it in front of me. "Here is a book of girls and guys we've worked with in the past." He opened the binder, and it had about ten pages of four 4x6 headshots of different people. "The front is a headshot, and the back is their contact information." He flipped through the pages. "This is Margie." He pointed to a brown haired, older woman. "I like her for the mother." I nodded.
"Okay." He flipped through some pages. "This is Amy." He pointed to another brunette, but she looked about eighteen and had chubby cheeks.
"How old is she?"
He took out her picture and read the back. "Uhh, twenty-five."
"Oh, she looks so young."
"Yeah, that's why I picked her for the daughter."
"Okay."
He put the picture back in its protective sleeve and flipped through more pages. "And here is Roger."
Roger looked as if he were forty-five years old. He had his beard cut low, and his brown hair was tossed all over his head. He also had chubby cheeks, but his cheeks and around his eyes were red.
"Umm."
"No?"

ZION

"Well, he could work. He's just… different."

"Did you want to look for anybody else?"

I yawned. "No, he's fine."

"Long night?"

"Yeah."

"I remember those days. I can't do that no more."

I laughed.

"Okay. Well, you can go for a few hours. I'm going to call up the actors and see when they can come in. Then, I'll call you to let you know when to come back."

"Okay." I got up to leave.

"Bye," Charlotte said through a fake grin.

"Bye," I waved to the two. When I got in the car, I called Byron.

"Yo."

"Where are you?"

"My parents' crib."

"You want to ride to the store with me?"

"Where you goin'?"

"Lynnhaven Mall."

"A'ight," he grunted as if he were sitting up.

"Were you sleeping?"

"Naw, man. Laying on the couch, watching TV."

"Oh, well, I'm like two seconds away, so come outside."

"Aww, man! You at that nasty place?"

"Uhh, yeah."

"A'ight, yo."

"A'ight."

We hung up, and I drove a few streets up to his house. He got in the car, and we went to the mall. Once inside, I took him to Frederick's of Hollywood. When he saw the window displays, he got really nervous.

"Where are you taking me, yo?"

"It's a lingerie store."

"But why did you bring me?"

"Because I need a costume for the Johanson's Halloween party, and I need someone's opinion."

"Oh, God."

"Come on." I grabbed his arm and led him into the store. All of the costumes and their accessories were up front. There was an ice princess, a queen bee, a Mrs. Clause, and many more. "What about Wonder Woman?" Byron didn't answer. I looked up and he was nervously looking around like a child scared to leave his mother's side. "Precious?"

"Huh?" He looked my way.

"What about Wonder Woman?"

He smacked his lips. "Naw, man."

"Okay." I kept looking through the rack. "*Naughty cop*?"

"What? No."

"Sexy Nurse?"

"Man, do Wonder Woman."

"Okay."

I picked up the costume and went into the fitting room. In a few minutes, I stepped out.

"Byron," I called loudly. He had gone back into the mall and was sitting on a bench. He came back in the store and almost immediately tried to cover me up. The Wonder Woman costume was basically a bra and a mini skirt. The skirt was so short that my butt was hanging out of the bottom. "Stop!"

ZION

"Man, cover all that up."

"I'm trying to win the sexiest costume contest."

He shook his head. "*Noooo.*"

It almost amazed me how much Byron cared about me, and we had just met the previous March.

"Why?"

"What do you mean, *why*?"

"Well, I'll just wear this to work then." Once I realized what I'd said, I ran into the dressing room, hoping he didn't hear me.

"What?"

"Nothing."

"Maaan, I told you, you was gon' be in them nasty films."

I stepped back out, still in costume, and said, "I'm not in the movies."

"Yeah, right," he said and walked away.

"Byron... Byron!" He kept walking and sat in the mall. I put my clothes back on and put the costume on the rack. I went and sat next to my friend. "I'm not in the movies, Byron."

"Then, what you need a costume for?"

"For my other job."

"What other job?"

I put my head down. "You're not going to like it."

"Man, what is it?"

"I strip in Richmond."

"What?" he yelled. I covered my face with one of my hands. "Why, man?"

"Because the bill collectors keep calling me, and I didn't know what else to do, so—"

Once Upon A Secret

"Whatchu *mean*? Work at McDonald's, Walmart, anywhere but a strip club."

I didn't know what to say, so I just put my head down.

"A'ight, man," he said real calm. "Do what you got to do."

I looked at him. His head was down, and he looked *so* disappointed. I put my head on his shoulder and wrapped my arms around him. I could feel all of his muscles bulging.

"I'm sorry, precious."

"Man, you good."

"No, I *promise* I'll stop as soon as I pay off all of my bills."

"Whatever."

I looked up at him. "Byron." He looked away.

"Okay," I put my head back on his shoulder, "Let's just sit here then." He started laughing, and I looked back up at him. "I *promise* I'll stop as soon as possible."

He nodded his head. "A'ight."

"Okay. I'm hungry. Let's go get something to eat."

We got up and went upstairs to the food court. I got chicken teriyaki from Sarku Japan, and he got chicken nuggets from Chick-fil-A. We sat down, and as soon as I finished praying over my food, Byron said, "So I'm going in the Navy."

"What?"

"Yeah, man."

"That's good, precious. When?"

"I gotta take the test first."

"Right."

ZION

"You gon' help me study for that jank?"

"Uh, *yeah*!"

"Yeah, I gotta get out my parents' crib, yo."

"Why? What's wrong?"

"Man, my dad don't even talk to me no more, and he just look at me like he's so disappointed in me."

"Oh."

"Yeah, and, when we do talk, it's an argument."

I shook my head. "Take the test, dude. You don't want to be a bum."

"Whatchu mean?"

"You don't want to keep saying, 'Maybe I can do something else,' and you're not in school and something else never comes around, and, next thing you know, it's four years down the road, and you ain't done shit with your life."

"Oh, true."

My phone rang. It was Lonnie. "Hello."

"Hey, baby."

"Where have you been?"

"Whatchu mean?"

"It's Saturday. I haven't talked to you in—"

"Why, every time I call you, you got an attitude?"

"Because you supposed to be my man and you go *days* without calling me."

"Okay. I be busy out here."

"Out *here*? What is out *here*?"

"Out here in these streets."

"What streets? What are you talking about? You know what? I gotta go. I'm out right now."

"Out with who?"

"*Somebody*."

Once Upon A Secret

"A guy?"

"Yeah."

"What the *fuck*?" he yelled it so loud that Byron heard and looked up at me.

"Yes."

"Fuck you, *bitch*," he yelled and hung up. I put the phone down and continued to eat as if nothing had happened.

"Umm," Byron said.

"What?"

"Are you okay?"

"Yeah, we go through this all of the time."

He just looked at me as if to say, "That ain't right."

"Lonnie only sees what *I* do wrong. Not what *he* does wrong,"

"So, you not supposed to be here with me?"

"First of all, I'm grown. I can go *wherever* I want with *whoever* I want. Second, you are my *friend*, not some nigga I'm fuckin', so I can be here."

Byron shook his head. We continued to eat and talk until my phone rang again.

"Oh, God," Byron said.

I looked at the screen. "It's my boss."

As I answered, Byron mumbled, "Which one?"

"Hey, Jermaine."

"Hey, Nikki! Can you get here by 2:30?" I looked at the clock on my screen. It was 1:45.

"Yes, sir."

"Aaauugh! Stop calling me that!"

"I'm sorry," I giggled.

"A'ight. See you in a bit."

I hung up and said, "Okay. We gotta go."

ZION

"Fo' real?"

"Yeah. I gotta go back to work."

"A'ight."

We emptied our trays and started to leave the mall. On the way out, we passed by Frederick's of Hollywood. Byron stopped, "You're not gon' get that costume?"

"Naw."

"But you looked cute in it."

I looked at him. "You're just saying that," I said and kept walking.

"Naw, I'm serious." I turned around, and he was looking at me.

"Get it."

"Okay," I smiled and ran in the store while he waited outside. I got my size and went to the register to pay. The lady looked at Byron.

"Is that your boyfriend?" she asked. I followed her eyes and looked at Byron.

"Oh, no, we're just friends."

"Oh, I was going to say y'all make a cute couple." I laughed. "Well, you never *know*," she said as she handed my bag to me.

"Umm, okay," I said and walked out.

"What?" Byron asked when he saw the funny look on my face.

"That lady said we would make a cute couple."

Byron made a face that said, "She should shut the fuck up". In fact, that's what I call it—the "shut the fuck up" face. "Whatever. Come on, man." We were walking through the department store, when he said,

Once Upon A Secret

"Well, I look good, so I make any couple a cute couple."

"Excuse me! And what am I?"

"You a'ight, but… "

He stopped and looked in a mirror at a makeup counter.

"Boy, please!" I said and slapped him on his back and kept walking. He ran to catch up with me, and I looked up and all of the associates were looking at us, smiling. I looked at Byron. "Why are they staring at us?"

"Who?" He looked up. "Daang, yo." We walked past an older lady at the perfume counter.

"You two are so *cute*!" she said.

"Oh, no, he's the cute one," I said, trying to put all the focus on Byron. But he knew what I was doing.

"Oh, uh huh, you fine," he said. We went back and forth, pushing each other while we were running toward the door. An older white couple opened the door for us.

"Thank you," we said together.

"Aww! You two are so cute," the lady said. I looked back, and she and her husband were smiling at us. Byron and I got in the car and headed toward his house.

"Well, damn," I said.

"What?" he said.

"All that couple shit."

"Oh."

"I told you we shouldn't go out in public together."

One night, Byron had come to my house and said he was trying to meet some girls. So I suggested he go to

ZION

a Norfolk State game because Hampton girls are stuck up and selfish and Norfolk State girls are cool and ride or die. He wanted me to go with him, and I told him that was a bad idea because, if he went looking good, trying to get girls, and I went looking good, trying to get guys, people were going to assume we were together. He said he didn't care.

"Maan, whatever! Let them think what they want." I looked at him. "What?"

"Nothing."

"I'm serious."

"I know, but, how are *you* going to get a girl if people assume we're together?"

"Man, it's not like we be out in public together all the time."

"You right."

"Plus, I don't need a girl right now." I gave him a look, and he started laughing. "I just need to be worried about *me*." He slapped his chest, and I smiled.

"Okay, well, when are you going to take that test?"

"ASAP."

"Okay. You better." We pulled up to his house.

"A'ight, yo."

"A'ight, Precious."

"Don't slip up and be in a movie now."

"I won't! Get out!"

He laughed and got out.

I drove a few streets up to Jermaine's house. Inside, there was a lot going on. I could hear noise upstairs and arguing in the office. I didn't even have to be sneaky; I just stood in the foyer and heard everything.

Once Upon A Secret

"How long has Diontae been filming?" Charlotte shouted.

"Why are you making a big deal about this?" Jermaine shouted back.

"Jesse has been filming for ten years! Diontae just graduated college like you!"

"Charlotte, Diontae is *my* cameraman. He shoots *my* movies. This is *my* movie."

"That you asked *me* to direct."

"No, Nikole is going to direct it."

"What?"

"I changed my mind. It's her script. She should direct it."

I walked up the stairs to the sound of Charlotte going off. Ashley and the actors were in one bedroom getting dressed.

"Hey, guys!"

Everyone said hello.

"I'm Nikole, the PA." They all smiled.

"Can I get a coffee please?" Amy said.

"I'll see what I can find."

"Plenty of sugar, a little cream."

"Just water for me. Thanks," Margie said.

"If you have any honey, that'd be great," Roger said.

"Excuse me?"

"You're the production assistant, aren't you?" Amy asked.

"Yeah, but—"

"Coffee… please!" she barked. Ashley just kept working, looking to see what I would say. I stepped into the room and slammed the door.

ZION

"First of all, I don't know what other PAs you have worked with before, but you will not talk to me like your mind is bad. Second, I'm the production *assistant*. I *assist* the production by way of assisting the directors. There is not *one damn person* on this set who will run around being your errand girl for the next few hours. Now, if you *want* something, I can see if I can find it for you. But I am *not* about to fix your coffee the way you like it or run all over this *damn* house looking for shit that might not be here. Now, as a last attempt to be nice, make a list of stuff you would like before a shoot, and I will keep it on file for the next time we decide to use you. But, if you keep up with the fucking attitude, then I will rip up that motherfucking profile, and we just won't worry about working with you anymore. Is that understood by everybody in this goddamn room?"

"Yeah," everybody said.

"Good." I opened the door and walked to the second room. Everyone was sitting quietly. "What are y'all doing?"

"Shh!" They all hushed me.

"This is the best room to hear them arguing," Diontae whispered. He tapped the spot on the bed next to himself, and I sat down. "Really, I hope Jesse gets to shoot the video because I want to go home." I looked around.

"Where's Jesse?"

"Not here yet."

"What?"

"We keep calling him, but he hasn't answered."

Just then, Jesse ran into the room.

Once Upon A Secret

"Hey, guys! What's—"

"Shh!"

"Oh, who's arguing?" he asked as he sat on the floor.

"Who do you think?" Erin replied. She stared at him for a while. "Remember that scene that Tony and Erika did in here?"

"Naw," he said, and everybody looked at him.

"That was Erika's first time doing anal," Erin said.

Jesse looked nervous. "Okaay?"

"That spot, where you're sitting, was *covered* in shit!"

"Ugh!" he shouted and ran out.

"We cleaned it up, dumbass!" Erin shouted after him.

We all laughed. Then, we heard a door slam and then footsteps in the downstairs hallway. Immediately, we scattered. I went downstairs to check for coffee and the other things the actors had asked for. When Charlotte saw me, she yelled, "Come here!"

I followed her into the office where Jermaine was.

"Charlotte, what are you doing?" he asked.

"Nikole," she said as she looked at me. "Jermaine is trying to get you to direct this whole movie by yourself today. Don't you think that's a little too much for you to handle?" She smiled.

"Um, no. Didn't I just direct a movie a few days ago?" Charlotte frowned. "What's the difference?"

Charlotte just stared at me, and Jermaine stared at her.

"Well, since you're directing the movie, which cameraman would you like to work with—the experienced Jesse or the inexperienced Diontae?"

ZION

I remembered Diontae saying he didn't want to work that day.

"I'll use Jesse," I said.

Charlotte stood straight up and smiled.

"Okay. That's settled," Jermaine said nonchalantly. It was obvious that the whole situation wasn't as big a deal to him as it was to Charlotte. "Nikole, please tell Steve to prepare the living room for a nighttime scene. We need the TV on, and we're gonna need some popcorn. Then, please tell Diontae that he can go home, and if Erin and Ashley are done, they can leave as well."

"Okay. Do you have any coffee, sugar, cream, water, and honey?"

"The *fuck*?"

"Those are the things your actors requested."

"They asked *you* for that?"

"Yes."

"Oh, hell naw!" He stood up.

"Wait!"

"Wait, what?"

"What are you going to do?"

"I'm going to tell them that you aren't their slave. Who the fuck do they think they are?"

"Well, I already told them that, but I was going to get it anyway."

"No," the two directors said simultaneously.

"We're about to start shooting anyway. They can get all of that when they leave," Charlotte said.

"Okay," I replied.

Jermaine shook his head. "I swear porn stars think they above *real* actors and actresses." He looked at me.

Once Upon A Secret

"Next time, remind them that anybody can *fuck* in front of a camera. What they do is not special." He rearranged some things on his desk. "Let's go upstairs."

Jermaine handed me my copy of the script and we went up to the bedroom.

"Hey!" I said to get everyone's attention. "Today, I will be using Jesse as my cameraman, so, Diontae, you're free to go. Also, Erin and Ashley, if you two are done, you may leave as well. Steve, please prepare the living room, and we need the TV on, and we need popcorn."

"In one big bowl or three small bags?"

"One big bowl. And can you place two glasses on the table with a little bit of liquid in them?"

"Yes, ma'am."

"And that is it for right now."

"Okay," everyone said.

Then they all dispersed. I went into the other room to look at my actors. Amy was wearing a red three-quarter sleeve fleece nightgown. Margie was wearing green and blue flannel pajama pants and a blue thermal. And Roger was wearing jeans, a wife beater, and an unbuttoned red and green flannel shirt.

"Did you guys have a chance to go over the script?" I asked.

"Yes," they said.

"Roger, I need you drunk, asleep on the couch, and with a beer in your hand."

"Sitting up or lying down?"

"Sitting up. Amy, you're next to him, and, Margie, you're next to her, asleep. So the movie is going to

ZION

start, and, Amy, you're the only one watching TV. Margie, you're going to wake up, check your watch, kiss your daughter goodnight and tell her not to bother Bill." I pointed at Roger. "Because he's drunk. And once Margie goes upstairs, that's when it's going to start to get sexual. Okay?"

"Okay," they all said.

"Alright. Let me go see how the set is coming along, and we'll get started shortly."

I went into the hall and found Jermaine and Charlotte standing there with big grins on their faces.

"Good job," Charlotte said.

Jermaine hugged me. "I'm so proud! My baby's all grown up."

I laughed, and he let me go. "Steve's done, so you can take them downstairs."

"Okay." I leaned into the room and said, "Let's go, guys."

We all went downstairs, and the actors sat down on the couch while Jesse finished setting up his lights and camera.

"Roger, can you slouch down and lean your head back?" I asked. He did. "Steve," I called, "can I get a half drunken beer in Bill's hand please?" While he was getting the prop, I adjusted the other two actors. "Amy, sit on your knees facing Margie. And, Margie, sit on your knees, but lean on the chair arm and be asleep. Okay? Good." Steve brought in the prop and gave it to Roger. "Perfect. Can I get the lights set please?" Steve cut off the living room lights, and that was when I noticed that the windows were covered in opaque black shades. The set designer cut on a dim blue strobe light in front of the actors, and it looked as if they were watching TV. "Okay?" I looked at Jermaine.

"It's on you," he said.

"Jesse, you ready?" I asked. He nodded. "Okay. Rolling… and… *Action*!"

Margie's head rolled forward and then shot back up. She looked at Bill and then kissed her daughter on the forehead.

"Good night, baby. Don't wake Bill."

"Okay," Amy said.

Margie went upstairs, and Amy continued to watch TV. Immediately, Bill rolled onto his left side and pulled Amy close to him.

"Oh, Sarah."

"Bill, wake up," Amy said. But Bill kept holding her and pulling her closer. "Bill, I'm not Mom. Wake up," and then Bill just stopped moving. "Bill?" She shook him. "Bill!" He didn't budge. She thought for a minute and then slid out from under him. She propped him up, so he was sitting upright and then whispered in his ear, "Bill? Do you want me to be Mom? You want me to be Sarah?"

"Sarah," Bill grunted.

"Okay." Then, Amy took off her nightgown, so she was only wearing a pair of white cotton underwear and white slouch socks. She undid Bill's pants and pulled them down to his ankles. His slightly hard penis lay in his lap. Amy pulled off her underwear, climbed on top of Bill, and slowly slid down on his dick. He didn't move and tried to stay quiet as the young one bounced up and down on his manhood. She rubbed on her nipples and breasts, and I could tell she was actually

ZION

enjoying it and wasn't acting. I looked at Roger, and I knew he was trying his hardest not to moan or make any facial expressions. Amy licked her nipples, and, when she felt herself about to cum, she hopped off and shoved him into her mouth. She sucked only about five times before she stood up and looked at him, analyzing her next move. Then, she laid him on his side, laid down in front of him, facing him, put her left leg on the back of the couch, put him inside of her, and began to slide up and down. She bounced and moaned and made little screams, but Bill kept slipping out. So she turned her back to him, put him back inside, and put his right hand on her breasts. She did some pelvic thrusts, but he still kept slipping out. So she got up, laid him on his back and rode him, bouncing and sliding and grabbing and sweating until she had an orgasm on top of him. She collapsed on his chest and continued to breathe heavily.

Once she was calm, she got off, picked up her nightgown and went upstairs. Jesse did a close-up of Bill, and then I said, "Scene! Good job, guys! You can go get cleaned up."

"Nikole!" Charlotte and Jermaine called in unison.

I turned around. "Yes?"

"It's *cut*, not *scene*," they said, and I laughed.

"I'm sorry. I keep forgetting."

"It's fine," Jermaine said. "Let's go in the office and talk."

I followed the two directors down the hall.

"Have a seat." I sat. "Okay, so I don't know if you heard Charlotte and I whispering, but we think you should direct more of your own work."

Once Upon A Secret

"Really?"

"Yeah, you're good at this."

"Oh, wow!"

"Yeah, but don't forget to see if you can get us a dorm room for that other scene."

"I'll handle that when I get back to campus."

"Okay, so go upstairs and make sure the costumes get put away and tell Jesse and the actors they can go."

"Okay." I stood up.

"But come back when you're done."

"Okay." I left the office and headed for the stairs. Jesse met me at the bottom. "Going up?" He smiled.

"Yeah, I left some things upstairs."

"Cool. Hey. How did your proposal go the other day?"

"Oh, it was awesome. I wanted it to be really intimate and personal, so I got us a room at the Westin."

"Wow!"

"Yeah, I went the cheapest route, though, so I only paid $180 for the room. But, I spent hella… hey, do you hear that?" We stopped at the top of the stairs and listened. "It's coming from Jermaine's room." We walked over, and Jesse turned the knob quietly and peeked in. "Oh… my… God!"

"What?"

He moved out of the way, so I could have a look. My mouth dropped at what I saw. Amy and Roger were having sex in Jermaine's bed, and Margie was watching.

"Damn! You two look hot," Margie said.

ZION

"Oh my God, Jesse. What should we do?" He didn't say anything. I turned around, and he was coming back up the stairs with his camera. "You *wouldn't*!"

"It's *so* much better when it's real. Jermaine will thank me later."

I kept thinking about how serious Jermaine was when he said his room was off limits. And was it or was it not my job to either stop the madness or go tell him?

"Look," Jesse said.

"What?"

"You can watch on this little screen."

"Ew! Gross!"

Jesse just stared at me. "You just directed a whole *fucking* porn scene."

"That's different. That's acting. This is three people fucking *for real*!"

We were whisper yelling. He gave me the stink eye. I looked down at the screen. Amy was holding Roger's head as he was eating her pussy.

"Fuck me!" Amy said. He stood up and put his penis at her hole, and that was when I noticed that Margie was standing next to the bed, rubbing herself. Amy put her legs around him and pulled him into her. Jesse zoomed in, and we saw that her eyes were closed, and she was biting her bottom lip and moaning. Margie rubbed herself faster as she watched Roger stroke in and out. It was only a matter of minutes before Amy was gripping the sheets and moaning out an orgasm. Jesse focused the camera on Margie, who was holding on to the bedpost as she rubbed out an orgasm herself. Then, she crawled on the bed and put her fingers in

Once Upon A Secret

Amy's mouth. Amy stuck her tongue out and licked Margie's cum off her fingers.

Margie looked at Roger's still erect penis and then bent over and ran her tongue over the head. She sucked several inches in and slurped it with her tongue. Then, she shoved the whole thing in her mouth until she gagged. Just then, the door flew open, and Jesse and I looked up. Jermaine was standing over us pissed, looking at what was going on in his bed.

"What *the fuck* are you bitches doing on my *goddamn bed*?"

I wanted to run, but he was blocking the way, so I had nowhere to go. I looked, and Jesse had run in the room and was filming everything.

"I have *one* rule! Nobody is allowed in my room. There are two other rooms! Why the fuck are you fucking in my damn room?" Nobody answered. Jermaine walked in the room and looked around. "Nikole!" He yelled.

I stood up. "Yes, sir?"

He turned around and saw me standing in the doorway.

"Where the fuck were you when all of this was going on?"

"I was right here, sir."

"The whole damn time?"

"Yes."

"So, you thought, as my PA, you weren't obligated to come get me? After I *told* you, I didn't want anybody in my room spreading they *sweat* and *funk* and *diseases* and *shit*! What the fuck is wrong with you?"

I put my head down. "I'm sorry."

ZION

"Ya *damn* right you sorry! Get the fuck out my house! You're fired. And leave my damn keys on the fuckin' kitchen counter." I ran down the stairs, took the car key off my key ring, put it on the kitchen counter, and then ran out the house and down the street to where Byron lived. I banged on the door until his father came and answered it. I had never met him before. He was a tall, handsome man. I tried to speak, but I could barely breathe.

"Hi, I'm... sorry... to be... knocking... on your door... like that... but... my name... is Nikole... Turner... Is Byron home?" He just stared at me as if I had just come to the door and said, "Excuse me, I know you're married, but can I please suck your dick until I explode?"

"Byron!" he yelled. My friend came running down the stairs and met us at the door. "What the hell kind of foolery are you into? Don't be bringing that nonsense in my house," his father said and walked away.

Byron stepped outside and shut the door behind him.

"I'm sorry 'bout that, yo."

"It's fine." I had caught my breath by then. "I can only imagine how I looked banging on the door like that and speaking all... discombobulated." He just shook his head. "But... uh... are you going to Hampton at all today?"

"Yeah. Why?"

"I just got fired, and I need a way back."

"What? How did that happen?" I told him what just happened, and his mouth was dropped the whole time. "Fo' real, yo?"

"Yes!"

"A'ight. Well, let me get my keys." I sat down on the porch and waited for Byron to come back outside. "A'ight. Let's go."

We got in his Isuzu truck and drove to Hampton. I directed him to Jen's apartment, and he dropped me off.

"Thank you," I said.

"No problem. Just hit me up if you need me."

"A'ight," I said and ran into the apartment.

Paris

"I told you not to move in with that grown woman."

"I'm grown, too, Ma."

"You're twenty-four! She's in her late thirties!" My mother shook her head while she placed the pie crust on top of the pie. "I told you *before* you left, '*Do not move in with that woman.*' And what did she do, Travis?"

"Move in with her," my father said as he ate his breakfast. Between his Chinese accent and him talking with a mouthful of food, it was hard to understand him.

"Moved *right in* with that heifer."

"Ma!"

"What? Didn't she cheat on you? Kick you out into the cold? Burn your clothes? Do I have to go on?" she asked. I just looked out the doorway and down the hall. My mother was a typical black woman— cross her once, fuck you. "Mmm... hmm." She placed the pie in the oven and took away my father's empty plate.

"What in the world is going on in your brain?" my father asked. "You not gay."

"What?" I looked at him.

"Since when you start dating girls?"

"Yeah," my mom said as she crossed her arms and leaned up against the sink.

"I don't have to take this," I said and stood to leave.

"Sit down, Paris Chao!" both of my parents yelled.

"You're in our house now," my mom said. "That means you live by our rules."

"I'm grown, Ma!"

"How? What bills do you pay? You don't even take care of yourself. We take care of you." I rolled my eyes. "Mm hmm. And you can stop all that, too."

My daddy shook his head. "I don't know where we went wrong with you, Paris."

I looked him in his eyes. "You didn't."

He looked down, "Yes, we did." He got up and left the room.

My heart broke right then. I couldn't breathe. The room began to spin, and I couldn't understand her, but my mom was saying something.

Clap!

I snapped out of it and saw my mom's hands in front of my face.

"Snap out of it! Did you hear me?" I just stared at her. "I said, you're not going to stay here rent free. So I suggest you go find yourself a job today, instead of staying locked up in that room like you been doing. And another thing." I looked at her. "You best be in church on Sunday." She started to leave, then turned around and said, "*Every* Sunday," and then walked out.

Jordin

"Hey, baby! You hungry?" my fiancé asked as I walked in the apartment.

I put my keys down and wrapped my arms around his waist.

"Mmm… that smells good. What is it?" I looked around his shoulder and into the pan.

"Blackened salmon, grilled shrimp, and vegetables. And I'm going to put it over rice."

"Oh, that sounds so good." I headed for the bedroom to undress. "Babe, why didn't you go to culinary school?"

"'Cause I didn't want to pay money to learn something I already know."

I pulled my sweater off and shook my head. My fiancé was one of the best cooks I knew, but, instead of pursuing it, he would rather be a cameraman. I was completely naked when I hollered, "Jesse!"

"Yeah!"

"Where's my robe?"

"Is it on the back of the bathroom door?"

I looked. "No, that's fine. I'll just put on my pajamas." I had only got my shirt on when he brought a plate for me into the room. "Mmm… " I kissed him. "Thanks, babe." And sat on the bed. He stood and watched me. I knew what he was waiting for. Every time he cooked, he wanted to see if I liked it from the first bite. But, since I knew he was waiting, I sat the plate down and began to clean my nails.

"Babe!"

"Huh?"

"What are you doing? Eat the food."

"It's too hot, babe." I looked up, and he gave me the most evil look of all. I laughed and picked up the plate, "Okay, okay." I took a bite. "Oh, my God! This is *so* good."

"Okay. Cool," he said and went back to the kitchen.

As I ate, I began to think about Jesse and me. He had been honest with me since the day we met. I knew he filmed porn. But he didn't know that I stripped at Consequences. We met two years ago when I was working at Harris Teeter, down the street in Newport News. That grocery store was twenty-four hours, and I worked overnight, but the pay was horrible. So I quit and became a stripper without telling Jesse. So, whenever I went to work at the club, he thought I was making a long drive to Harris Teeter in Richmond because "they needed help with customer service." I felt like shit every time I thought about it.

"I brought you something to drink." I looked up, and Jesse was holding a wine glass.

"Oh, thanks, babe." I took it from him, and he went around to his side of the bed and lay down next to me. I looked down at him and smiled. "I'm *so* happy you proposed."

"I'm so happy you said yes," he said and picked up my hand and kissed it. "Do you have to work tonight?"

Once Upon A Secret

"Yeah."

"I wish you would quit and let me take care of you. You shouldn't have to spend your whole check on bills." When I was working at Harris Teeter, I made $350 a week. So, when I started stripping, I made sure Jesse only saw $350 a week.

"Babe."

"You're going to be my wife. And my wife won't be stressed out just to make sure the bills are paid."

"But—"

"But nothing." He sat up and kissed me. "I love you."

"I love you, too," I whispered.

He cupped my face with his hands and kissed me softly. He kept kissing me as he ran his hands down my shoulders to my arms and to my breasts. He cupped my breasts from the bottom and massaged them. My breathing became more pronounced. Jesse allowed his fingers to glide along my pink nipples. As he moved his fingers back and forth, my nipples rubbed against the sides of his fingers. In no time at all, my nipples were hard and erect.

Jesse continued to fondle my breasts and stiffened nipples, and my breathing became more erratic. His right hand, then moved lower and made contact with my pussy. He had me sitting straight up and holding him tightly. Jesse's fingers made much more direct contact with my clitoris. The more he rubbed my clit, the closer I pulled him to me. He kept rubbing my pussy faster and faster. I started losing control of my breathing pattern and started humping his hand. After a few minutes of that, my body began to convulse. I climaxed as I held on to Jesse and bit on his shoulder.

ZION

When I finished shaking, I laid him down on the bed, took off my shirt, and undressed him from the waist down. I crawled between his legs and immediately put his penis in my mouth. I licked the tip and then started sucking it in and out of my mouth like a lollipop. I continued to suck his dick, sucking harder and drawing it in deeper and deeper until the head hit the back of my throat and I gagged.

"Oh, yeah," Jesse groaned.

For some reason, he liked it when I gagged. I looked up at him, and he placed his left hand on the back of my head. I tried to wrap my tongue around his shaft and slurped up to his head. I licked the tip and put the tip of my tongue in and out of his hole. He moaned a little more before having an orgasm himself. He nudged me to move, and he stood up on the floor, and I lay down on my back. He lightly grabbed my ankles and told me to move closer to the edge. As I moved, his hands moved up my legs, and he gently spread them apart. Jesse went down to the floor on his knees, with my pussy in front of him. He softly stroked my inner thighs and I relaxed some more. His hands moved closer to my pussy, and he started to rub his thumb along my clit.

"*Please* fuck me," I begged, but he continued rubbing the inner portion of my pussy lips. I moaned, and he put a finger inside my pussy, feeling the tight grip of my pussy muscles.

"Mmm… you're still so tight, baby," he said.

He put in another finger and moved them in and out of my pussy, driving me close to cumming. Jesse inserted three fingers and used the thumb of his other hand to rub my clit. My body started bucking up and down on the bed. And then I had another orgasm. I lay on the bed as Jesse walked over to the dresser and reached in the top drawer.

"What are you doing?" I asked.

He came back to the bed with a seven-inch vibrator and slowly inserted it into my vagina. With the vibrator still turned off, he inched the shaft further into my pussy with each stroke. I started breathing at a rapid pace again. Around about the time he was inserting six inches into my steaming hot vagina, he flipped on the switch. I started to scream from all the pleasure coming over me. Jesse had as much of the vibrator in me as he could while still being able to hold it. Frustrated at not being able to pleasure me the way he wanted, he went back to the drawer and came back with a nine-inch vibrator. He turned on the bigger vibrator while taking out the smaller one. He buried the new vibrator into my pussy and kept thrusting. It didn't take long before I was approaching my third orgasm. I screamed so loud I thought, *Surely, the neighbors are gonna call the police!*

I laid there motionless, and Jesse slowly removed the vibrator and then began to lick my clit. My body jolted at the touch of his tongue, and he lapped harder for a few more seconds and then stopped. I had my eyes closed, but I could feel him staring at me.

"I'll save that for when you get off."

"I want some dick when I get off."

He bent down and sucked on my clit. "Whatever you say, baby."

I moaned and then fell asleep.

ZION

Tori

I was working the bar when an Indian man walked up and ordered a glass of wine. I served him and started to walk away when Emily walked up and sat next to him.

"Hey, baby. You got any money for me?" She rubbed her body against his and put her right leg in his lap.

"Um... I just got here. I haven't even seen you dance yet."

"Really?" she said angrily and then walked away. I bent down to get some clean glasses when I heard Mark, our cook, say nervously, "Emilyy... "

I looked up, and Emily was coming from the kitchen, carrying the cleaning bucket that we put the dirty towels in. She took the Indian man's wine and took a sip.

"*Hey*, bitch!" he exclaimed.

That was when she threw the wine in his face, slammed the glass down, took out a dirty towel, and plopped it on his head.

"What the *fuck*?" Emily laughed. "Look at the towel head!"

"What the fuck is wrong with you?" he yelled as he threw the dripping towel down.

"Aww! Is the towel head baby going to cry?" Emily teased.

"Emily!" Jerry yelled from his office doorway.

Emily looked at him. "What? Fine me!" she said and walked into the dressing room.

Here at Consequences, we couldn't fire any of the strippers because, technically, they didn't work for us.

They were independent contractors. So we worked on a fining system. Fifty dollars for things like showing up late or not showing up at all, and half a night's tips if you assaulted a customer, like Emily did all the time.

"Sir, are you okay?" I asked.

"Does it *look* like I'm okay?" he asked angrily.

"No, but it doesn't look like a problem alcohol can't fix."

"What?"

I winked at him, and as a late reaction, he laughed.

"I'll take a glass of wine and a shot of New Amsterdam, if you have it."

"Coming right up! And I'll get you a fresh towel, too."

I was doing my makeup when Emily walked in.

"Heyy, Nikkiii!"

"Hey, Emily."

"So where's Jen tonight?"

"She has something to do in the morning, so she couldn't come."

"Aww!" She made a pouty face. I looked at her, and she laughed, "I'm just kidding!" She hit me on my shoulder. "But I was wondering, what would I have to do to get in one of your *adult* videos?"

"I actually got fired today."

ZION

"Fired?" She looked more pissed than I was. "What did you do?"

"Long story."

"Oh, come on." She slid her chair closer to me. "Tell me. After all, what are friends for?" I cut my eyes at her as she flashed a wide grin.

"Okay… "

Then, I proceeded to tell her everything that had happened that day. And the whole time, her eyes lit up with excitement. But when I got to the part where Jermaine cursed me out, her expressions changed to hopelessness.

"So… no porno?"

"No porno. But I'm not worried about it that much." I went back to doing my makeup. "I don't know what my parents would have done if they would have found out. And my friend Byron didn't really approve of me doing it… well, he doesn't approve of this either."

"Byron?"

"Yeah."

"Your friend or boyfriend?"

"Definitely friend," I said as I laughed.

"Aaand why not boyfriend?"

"Because… I don't see him that way."

"What way?" she asked as she laughed.

"I can't imagine kissing him or touching him sexually or even—"

"Having sex with him?"

"Or even that."

"Hmm… so, what do you think your parents would have said to you doing porn?"

Once Upon A Secret

"Whatever Medea said when she found out Jason had left her for that princess."

"What?"

"Oh, I'm sorry. I'm a theater major."

"Oh… sooo… "

"They would have been pissed and cussed and yelled and said all types of things."

"Well, I guess that's how parents are supposed to be, right?"

"Yeah."

"I wish I knew my parents."

"What happened to them?"

"I don't know. I was adopted at five. I have three step-sisters and two nieces. But we never talk. I don't know what I did to make them not like me or not want anything to do with me, but… "

"Oh, I'm so sorry to hear that."

Right then, Jordin burst in.

"Where have *you* been?" Emily asked.

"Minding my fucking business. What about you?" Jordin said.

"Hmm." Emily leaned over to me. "Jordin's the type where she doesn't like to talk about her sex life, but you can always tell how good it is by how offensive she is."

"Shut the fuck up, Emily!"

"Giiiirl, I got to get me a man like yours!" Emily said as she stood and headed to the door. "A man who can fuck me *good*." Jordin threw a shoe at Emily as she ran through the door.

"Dumbass," she mumbled. "When do you go on?" she asked me.

ZION

"My first time is with you tonight."

"Good," she said as she slipped on her shoes. "Don't get in my way," and she walked out to mingle with the men.

I put on my Wonder Woman costume and mask and followed behind her. Halloween was just a few days away, and the club was decorated with fake spider webs, spiders, snakes, witches, pumpkins… everything you could think of for Halloween. I sat at the bar by myself and just looked around.

"You're not going to make any money like that." I looked up and saw that Tori was wiping a glass in front of me.

"Well, I figure, the men I want are the men who are willing to chase *me*, not the men I have to chase."

"Two things. This is a strip club. You're a stripper. You're not here to find Mr. Right or Mr. Right Now. You're here to make money. Number two, you don't want a man who will chase you. In here, these men are sad saps, who feel like the only women in the world who love them are in this place. If they chase after you, they'll think they got up on their own, and they'll never stop, even when you're done with them. What you have to do is approach them, so they think you dominate the 'relationship.' That way, when you say it's over, they believe it." I nodded. That was more psychology than I had ever learned in Lions' class. "Here." She put a shot of something dark in front of me. "Take that. Wait a few seconds, and then go get you some money." I picked up the glass and looked at Tori. She crossed her arms and mouthed, "*Do it*!"

Once Upon A Secret

I knocked back the contents of the glass, and my eyes started to twitch. When I opened them, Tori slammed down a bottle in front of me. It was Jim Bean Devil's Cut 90 proof. But she was right. I felt calmer and more confident in a matter of seconds. I smiled and walked up to a man sitting at a table nearby.

"Can I sit here?" I shouted over the music.

"Oh, sure," he said. I sat.

"So what brings you to a place like this?"

"Well… " I slid my chair as close to him as possible and leaned in. He laughed nervously. "Well, the guys at work keep talking about this place. And one of my co-workers got a flyer in the mail, so I thought I'd give it a try."

I looked around. "Who are you here with?"

"My co-worker who got the flyer. He went to the bathroom."

"Oh, okay."

"Oh, he must have seen me talking to you. Look." He pointed. "That's him in the sports coat, walking toward that table over there."

"Oh, I see him."

"Hey, can you do me a favor?" I turned around, and he was going through his wallet. "He's not happy at home. Here's twenty dollars." He handed me the money. "Can you go share some love with him?"

"Of course, sweetheart!" I said as I took the money. I adjusted my Wonder Woman mask and walked over to the man. He was still standing, so I crept up behind him, wrapped my arms around his waist, and said, "Having fun?"

He laughed as he turned, "I am now."

"Oh, my God!" I gasped. The man was my father!

"What's wrong?" he asked, concerned. I quickly put my head down.

"I lost my contact. I'll have to go to the back and get another one."

"Oh, okay! Well, hurry back," and as I walked off he slapped my ass!

Casey

"Dad!" The man looked at me startled.

"Casey!"

"Dad, what the fuck? I thought you were dead! We buried you!"

"Oh, my God! Can we talk about this outside?" I stormed out the front door and he followed, "Okay, look—"

"No! Wait! I'm talking now! What *the fuck* are you doing here?"

"Well, I got this flyer—"

"Not here! What are you doing alive?"

"Okay. Look, baby girl. It's a lot to explain, and I don't think this is the—"

"You know what? Fuck you! As far as I'm concerned, you're *still* dead!" I headed back into the club.

"No, no, no!" He grabbed my arm. "Okay, I'll make it short." He took a deep breath. "When you were a freshman in high school, I lost my job. So I started borrowing money from *bad people*. And they wanted to hurt Daddy, sweetheart. And one day, they did. They came to my hotel room that time when I went to North Carolina for that convention, and they beat me until I passed out. When I woke up, the building was in flames. I broke out and ran out of there, but I knew it would be better if they thought I was dead. And, unfortunately, that meant you had to think I was dead, too." I snatched my arm from him.

"First of all, *Dad*, I am thirty seven. Do not talk to me as if I'm a child. Second, fuck you!" I said and walked back into the club.

I was sitting at my vanity, biting my fingernails when Casey burst in crying. I watched her as she quickly changed clothes and packed her a bag.

"Casey." I slowly walked toward her. "What happened?" She kept crying and packing. "You okay? Did somebody touch you?" She stood up and looked at me.

"Why are you here?"

"Um… "

Her tone and volume caught me off guard.

"You are in college. You have people who care about you. You still have a chance to go somewhere and be somebody." I just stared at her. "If you want my advice, leave and never come back." Then she ran out.

ZION

I didn't know what happened to Casey or why she was so upset, but I had my own problems to worry about. I called Jen.

"Hello."

"Jen, guess who was here tonight?"

"I don't know. Who?"

"*My dad*!"

"*What*? Are you serious?"

"Yes! Apparently, he got a flyer in the mail, and he and a co-worker came tonight."

"Did he see you?"

"I was wearing my Wonder Woman mask, so he didn't recognize me."

"Oh my God. I know you want to leave, but, you have to stay and finish your shift. You don't want Jerry to regret hiring you."

"Yeah, you're right."

I hung up with her and went back out to mingle with the fellas, and I noticed that my dad and his co-worker were gone. *Oh, my God! Maybe he figured out who I was!* For the rest of the night, that was all I could think about. I had to get a few more shots from Tori to calm my nerves. I was sitting at the bar, babysitting my third shot, when a man sat next to me.

"I'll just take a Moscato if you have it." I looked up to see who was so fancy that they ordered wine at a strip club. And to my surprise it was…

Once Upon A Secret

Jordin

"Jesse!" I hurriedly ran into the new girls' dressing room, nearly knocking over two other girls. "Oh my God, oh my God, oh my God!"

I panicked. What was he doing there? I picked up my cell phone and peeped out. I was calling him, but he was not answering! And then Nikole started talking to him! And they hugged each other! Why was he smiling?

Nikole

"Oh, man! What are you doing here?" I asked Jesse.

"Well, I got a strange call from an anonymous person."

"What?"

"Yeah, they came on the phone and asked, 'Do you know where your fiancée is?' And then they gave me this address and told me to come here. I don't know why I'm even here. She wouldn't be anywhere near a place like this."

"Oh, okay," I said awkwardly.

Then, he eyed me. "But I never thought you would be anywhere near a place like this either."

"Times is hard," I said as I laughed nervously.

"Not that hard, Nikki."

ZION

"I didn't want to be a stripper, but the job just fell in my lap. I needed some way to pay my bills,"

"And I'm pretty sure Jermaine wasn't paying you much either."

"Well, I'm grateful. He was paying me $150 a week plus a full tank of gas every Friday *and* a car to use. That's a good deal."

"I dunno. Maybe it's just me, but, that don't exactly sound like much."

"Hmm… well, what does your fiancée look like?"

"She's Caucasian, long brown hair, kinda tall, gorgeous… but I could be describing anybody in a strip club."

"Well, what's her name, and I'll tell you if I know her or not?"

He stood up. "Jordin!"

Jordin

I had gotten all of my things and was headed to the back door when he hollered out my name across the whole club. I didn't even look his way; I just ran. I burst through the door that led to the service room, burst through the exit door, and made it to my car. I was fiddling with my keys when he grabbed my arm, turned me around, and slammed me up against the car.

"Jordin, what are you doing here?" I threw my head back and instantly started crying.

"Babe, please—"

"Please, what?"

"Please, don't be mad at me."

"What's going on, Jordin?"

"I work here."

"Doing *what*, Jordin?"

I couldn't stop the tears from falling, and they were warm as they slid down my face, "I'm a waitress."

"Don't lie to me, Jordin!" He grabbed my arms and pulled me off of the car. Then he wrapped his arms around my waist. "Look at me. Baby, please look at me."

"I can't."

"Baby, please don't lie to me."

I could hear the hurt in his voice, and I knew he was fighting back tears. But I also knew, if I told him, he would cry and be hurt even more. I took a deep breath. "I strip here."

"When? When you're not at the grocery store?"

"No, I quit the grocery store shortly after I met you."

"Oh my God." He let me go.

"I'm so sorry, but, when it happened, I didn't think we'd be dating this long. And I never thought you would propose."

"Why wouldn't I? I'm in love with you, Jordin! That's what people do when they're in love!"

"I didn't think you would fall in love with me. I never pictured myself as somebody's wife!"

He wiped the tears from his eyes, got real close to me, and grabbed my left hand. "And you never will be," he said as he took the ring off my finger, "at least not to me."

"Jesse, Jesse, please! I'm so sorry! I'll never come back!" I was holding on to him, trying to keep him from walking away.

"Get off of me, Jordin!"

"Noooo!"

"Jordin!" he yelled so loud that it scared me and I let go. He just looked at me and walked toward the front parking lot. And all I could do was watch him walk out of my life.

The next day, Jen and I were sitting at the kitchen table eating breakfast for dinner.

"I don't think he knew it was you."

"But why would he leave?"

"Do you think your dad would just leave if he knew you were stripping?"

"Yeah, you're right about that. But, his co-worker said that he wasn't happy at home. I wonder what's going on."

"Who knows? Married people always finna break up." She looked at the clock. "It's 8:30. Let's get ready for this party."

That night was the Johanson's annual Halloween party, and I couldn't wait to go. The year before, I sat up all night with Lonnie, but this year, I would show up and show out. I had ordered a sexy Chewbacca costume online. It was a five piece set that included a lace-up fur mini skirt with a leather band and leather straps that laced up the left side, a leather cropped top that had a deep neckline showing all of my cleavage, fur leg warmers that covered my black six inch heel leather boots, fur hood with attached sleeves and over the shoulder leather satchel.

Jen wore a baseball costume. The polyester dress was light blue with dark blue pin stripes and sleeves like a baseball jersey. It had white accents and "Grand Slam" written across the chest in red sequins. A small "10" was printed in the corner in red as well as across the back. The dress buttoned up the front allowing you to choose how much to reveal. She had it buttoned up all the way and her breasts were still out at the top and her thighs were out on the sides. If she bent over wrong, then her ass would be out. The dress could also be tied up in the front to reveal the included blue stretch knit shorts underneath. The boy shorts had an elastic waist. A red baseball hat and pair of dark blue knee-high socks with white stripes completed the costume. She added some referee boots with it, and she was set for the night.

When we pulled up to the house, Mrs. Johanson was dressed as a nun.

"Come on in, ladies!" she said, clearly drunk. "There's enough liquor for everyone."

We walked in, and all eyes were on us. I loved the attention. Some men were whispering as we walked past, and I just pretended as if I didn't hear them. But one man yelled out, "*Gawwd* damn!"

ZION

I turned and saw a drunk elf holding a bottle of Crown standing in the middle of the living room. "Girl, I would put so much dick in you… so much."

I laughed and walked into the kitchen.

"Jen?"

I turned and saw one sexy Asian Mad Hatter. The girl was wearing a gold, black, and jade dress with a golden shoulder drape and large jade top hat. She had on knee high white socks and a pair of very high black patent leather pumps.

Jen

"Paris?" I looked at Nikole. "I'll catch up with you in a minute."

"Okay," she said and walked away.

"Hey."

"Hey," she said and gave me a hug. "How have you been?"

"Good. What about you?"

"Well, I moved back in with my parents."

"Oh, I didn't know you had gotten your own place."

"No, I moved in with Fish." I just stared at her.

"Excuse me?"

"Wait. You didn't know?"

"No, I didn't know you moved in with my *ex-girlfriend*?"

"Oh my God."

"Yeah!"

"I told her that I would only date her if she got the okay from you."

"The okay from me? I haven't spoken to her since the day she proposed!"

"Wait. She proposed to you?"

"Yes!" Her lip began to tremble, and her eyes filled with tears.

"She loves you."

"No, she doesn't. Trust me."

"No, she does. I can't do anything right in her eyes. She's constantly comparing me to you. She… she cheats on me."

"Why are you still with her?"

"We're not together anymore. I moved back in with my parents, and no doubt she's probably still *fucking* Carl."

"Wait. Carl?"

"Yeah."

"She still fucks Coach Krisby after what he did to Michael?"

"Yeah." She put her head down and began to cry. I hugged her. Even though she had been dating my ex-girlfriend, Paris and I had been friends for years, and I knew she needed me.

"Look. Stop crying. People are starting to stare." She laughed. "Do you have a job?"

"No."

"Well, I got an extra bedroom; no bed though. But you can stay with me until you can get a job and move out."

"Oh, won't your girlfriend mind?"

"Girlfriend? Girl, no, that's Nikole!"

ZION

"Oh, that's the girl that used to be over your house all the time?"

"Yeah, her."

"Wow! She has *really* grown."

"Hey!" I looked her in the eyes, "Nikole is *really* off limits. One, she's straight. Two, she's really vulnerable, and I don't want her to think she's gay when she's not."

"Come on, Jen. Everybody's a little gay."

"Paris, no!"

"Okay, well introduce me." We found Nikki in the kitchen pouring herself a drink.

"Hey, Nikki." She looked up.

"Hey."

"This is Paris. We've been friends for… forever."

"Yeah, I remember her coming to your house a couple of times." Paris stepped forward.

"Oh, yeah. That's right!" As if she didn't just say that a few seconds ago. "So what have you been up to Nikki?"

"Nothing, just school."

"Oh, yeah? What school do you go to now?"

"Hampton University."

"Oh, do you like it?"

"Not really. I mean, I love the people and my professors and even my experiences. But I hate how much it costs."

"How much is it?"

"Like $30,000 a year. But, for some reason, financial aid won't pay for all of it. And that's what's tripping me out because I got accepted into a school in California, and the tuition was $50,000 a year, and my

Once Upon A Secret

FAFSA paid for everything. But, at Hampton," she said as she shook her head, "I had to take out student loans, and my first year, I had a loan for $19,000 on my dad's credit report."

"Wow!"

"Yeah."

"But, other than that, you like it?"

"Pff! No! The dorms are terrible. There's a hole in the roof of VC, and raccoons and opossums come in and run the halls. One girl showed me a picture on her phone of a man catching one. There's mold on the walls, but, when I said something to the dorm director, she shushed me and told me to call it moisture. We pay extra to stay in upperclassman dorms, but the elevators always break down. You share a bathroom with eight plus girls, and they are *disgusting*! And you're paying $10,000 extra to stay on campus! And the *worst* is the people you have to go through every semester—student accounts and office of the registrar. They have the *worst* attitude, and they send you running all over the school when you need help. Over the summer, they never answer the phone, so I don't know *how* anybody from another state can get anything done because I constantly have to drive over there and cuss people out. I remember, I went over the summer, and the lady had the phone on silent! It's ridiculous!"

"Wow! I wouldn't want to go there either!"

"Hmm, and that's not the half of it."

"Weeell," I cut in. "Let's not ruin our night with all of this negative talk. You shoulda went to Norfolk State."

"Yeah. I shoulda."

"Alright, ladies." We all raised our glasses. "Let's get drunk!"

CHARLOTTE

I was in Jermaine's office sending my one hundredth text to Paris when he put his head in his hands and groaned, "I'm so clueless."

"What's wrong?" I asked.

"I don't know what to do. I can't think of any good ideas. Hell! I feel like I can't think—period."

"Why don't you just swallow your pride and hire Nikki back?"

"What? You must be tripping."

"Why are you so mad at her?" I knew the answer, but I had a point to make.

"Why? Because she watched as people were fucking in my bed! That was one of the first things I told her—no one is allowed in my room! But I go upstairs, and she and Jesse are watching and recording the madness. I would have fired him, too, if you had let me."

"Jesse's the best cameraman we have. Of course, I won't let you fire him. But you fired Nikki because some porn stars were fucking in your room. What the hell did you think was going to happen? Your house is a porn studio! These people fake fuck on camera, trying not to cum too fast. You're basically getting them as hot and horny as possible and then sending them on their way. Except this time, these people fucked before they left. And you're mad because your production assistant didn't stop the 'madness'? You're crazy. Before Nikki, we would sit in this office and try to think of something great to shoot and make money. After Nikki, she thought of things that just came to her. But you fired her, like a dumbass, and now we're sitting here looking at each other like... what the fuck?"

He just shook his head.

"Alright, I didn't want to tell you this."

"What?"

"Jesse filmed the people having sex in your room, and, when you barged in, he edited it, and uploaded it to the site."

"What?" I could see he was furious.

"That was four days ago."

"Charlotte, what the fuck? I didn't give you... "

"We have over one million views and likes on that one video. And we have almost a thousand more people subscribed to the website."

His face went blank. "What?"

"Yeah, so, if, Nikki had stopped the tragedy, then you wouldn't have these new people paying their five dollars a month."

He looked down at his desk.

"Call her," I said. "I'll be in the living room."

I walked out of the office and shut the door behind me. Paris hadn't texted me back. We had gotten into a big fight, but, I knew she couldn't possibly be through with me. And yeah, I cheated, but, it wasn't the first time, so, why was she acting all brand new? I called her phone. She let it ring three times before she ignored the call.

"Hey, this is Paris. Sorry I missed your call, but, if you leave me a brief message, I'll be sure to get back with you. Unless this is Charlotte, and if it is… drop dead, bitch!"

Beep.

"'Drop dead, bitch'? Ha! You're funny. Call me back, so we can get this all straightened out. I miss you, Paris. Love you, baby." I hung up and just stared at the phone, hoping she'd call me right back. After two minutes of staring at the screen, I realized she wasn't going to call back, so I went back into the office.

"So?" I asked Jermaine.

"She's on her way."

Nikole

It was a Wednesday, and I was on my way to Marshall, one of the male dorms on campus. The day before, Jermaine had hired me back, given the car back to me, and asked me to try to get a dorm room for the gay porn scene we were going to shoot. I had a friend who stayed in Marshall, so I was going to ask him if I could use his room. Cameron was waiting outside by the street because females weren't allowed in the rooms on weekdays.

"Hey! How you been?" Cameron asked as he hugged me.

"Good. How about you?"

"Good. I missed you!"

"I know. I've been really busy this semester." One thing my daddy said was "be around people who *celebrate* you, not *tolerate* you." I felt Cameron celebrated me every time he saw me or talked to me. It was like, for those few moments, I made his day.

"Oh, yeah? Well, I can understand that." He put his hands in his pockets. "So, what's up?"

"I need a favor."

"Okay."

"Well, part of the reason I've been so busy is because of my job."

"Yeah, well, that's understandable."

"Yeah, well, my job is… I direct porn."

His eyes got big as he leaned forward. Then he nervously started laughing. "I'm sorry, I'm not judging you. I should've known. Of *all* people, you'd be the one."

I laughed. "Why do you say that?"

"I think you're the perfect type to direct porn. You have the personality for it. You take no bullshit, and people are scared of you, but you're cool to get along with. I can see you directing porn as a job and not as something perverted."

"Well, thank you," I said. I had heard that rumor that people were scared of me and that I was mean and a bully and ghetto, but I didn't pay it any mind. "Well, the favor that I need is to use your room."

"My room?" His eyes got wide again.

ZION

"Yeah, I need to shoot a video in a male dorm room."

"Oh, well, I don't know how you're going to get the girls in there."

"It's actually going to be boys."

Cameron's eyes got so wide that I thought they would fall out of his head. "You want to shoot gay porn, like dude on dude... in *my* room?" he asked. I didn't say anything. "Ummm, Nikki, I love you and all, but I think I'm gonna have to draw the line right there. That's a little—"

"Look. I understand you might feel awkward about this, but we'll strip the sheets off your bed. The mattress is made out of that hard, plastic shit anyway, so we'll put different sheets on and wipe it down when we're done. Give us about three hours, and we'll be gone." His face still said no. "And we'll pay you $150."

His eyes grew again. "Really? One hundred and *fifty*?"

"Yeah."

"Well, alright," he laughed. "When?"

"When can you and your roommate be out of your room?"

"Well, some dude snuck a girl in last night, so we have a mandatory meeting to attend tonight, and then he and I can go to the Harbors and chill. You can just text me when you're done."

"Okay."

"The meeting is in the lobby, though," he said.

"That's fine," I assured him. "We can make that work. Just leave ya window open."

"Alright. The meeting's at seven, so..."

Once Upon A Secret

"We'll be here at seven. I'll leave the money under your mattress."

"Okay," he said nervously.

I kissed him on the cheek. "Thanks, babe."

~~~~

That night, I was in my room getting dressed, and Yasmine was studying on the bed. "What you doing tonight, Nikole Turner?"

"Shooting a porno at Marshall."

"Are you *crazy*?" she screamed.

"What?"

"*What*? What if the president finds out?"

"Fuck him."

"Nikole, think about this. He is an old man. He's been married for a while and probably doesn't like having sex with his wife anymore. He probably watches porn. What if he sees this video?"

"It's gay porn."

"Oh, *laaawd*!" She threw herself back on the bed.

I laughed. "You wanna come?"

She sat up. "Excuse you? One, I don't watch porn, and two, if I did, it wouldn't be *gay* porn!"

"Okay. Suit yourself." I laughed.

She shook her head. "I just don't understand you, Nikole Turner."

~~~~

At 6:50, I left my dorm and made the short walk to Marshall. Jermaine, Diontae, and the three guys were in Jermaine's car parked on the road next to Marshall. I walked up to the driver's side window.

"Okay, so how are we going to do this?" Jermaine asked.

ZION

"There is a mandatory meeting in the lobby at seven, so we'll have to sneak in through the window," I told him.

"Girl, do you know the *last* time I snuck in another man's window?"

I gave him the "boy, please" face.

"Never mind," he said. "Continue."

"The meeting will probably be less than an hour—"

"What?"

"But Cameron is going to take his roommate somewhere else for a few hours," I explained.

"Oh, okay."

"These rooms are small, so no lights. Just us."

Everyone climbed out of the truck and followed me to Cameron's window. Thank God he had left the light on for us. I climbed through first, and everyone else followed. Cameron had taken his sheets off the bed, so I knew which one was his.

"Diontae, can you put sheets on the bed please and try to take down anything in here that says *Cameron's Room*?" I asked.

Jermaine was looking around. "This is where y'all *live* at?" His face was frowned up. "All that money Hampton got, and y'all can't get any livable rooms? I'm glad I went to school in California."

Diontae finished the bed and combed the room over.

"Okay, guys," I said to the three men. "For right now, I need all of you out in the hall until I tell you it's safe to come in." All three shuffled past Jermaine and into the hall. "You too, Jermaine."

"Girl, I'm not even arguing with you on that one!"

Once Upon A Secret

"Okay, Diontae, I need a shot of the first two coming into the room and then the rest of the scene up until the third boy comes in."

I stepped out into the hallway. "Okay, guys. Let me give you your character names. That's how I will address you from now on." I pointed to the blond-haired, blue-eyed one, "You're CJ." I pointed to the tall, skinny, black one, "You're Prince." And I pointed to the caramel-skinned one. "You're Ronney. CJ and Ronney come in first, and, when I cue you, Prince, you come in last. Everybody got it?" I asked.

They all said, "Yes," in unison.

I went back in the room and stood next to Diontae. "Rolling," he said.

"Action!" I yelled. CJ and Ronney walked through the door.

"My roommate went to the football game," CJ said as he shut the door behind him.

"So we have the room to ourselves for a couple of hours?" Ronney asked, as the two of them walked toward the bed.

"Cut," I said.

"Still rolling," Diontae stated.

I went into the hall, "For now, you guys can come in and sit on the roommate's bed."

Jermaine and Prince followed me back in the room, and I stood next to Diontae by the door. "You guys ready?" They nodded. "Action!"

CJ and Ronney finished walking to the bed, and Ronney started to take CJ's coat off. When it was on the floor, CJ did the same for his partner. They both took each other's pants off, and Ronney laid on the

ZION

bed. CJ climbed in front of him and hovered over his dick. Ever so gently, he touched his tongue to the tip of his cock. Then, he got a little more earnest and licked a little more of his dick. He moistened his fingertips and gently slid his slippery fingers across the whole top ridge of his penis. CJ gently pushed the semi-hard cock upright, while he lowered his wide open mouth straight down over Ronney's dick, without even touching it, just exhaling with his mouth completely over it. Ronney smiled, and he was starting to get bigger. CJ's warm, moist mouth completely engulfed Ronney's cock as it grew erect in his mouth. Ronney's penis was a full seven inches, and, when CJ came up for air, he just looked at it in amazement. He gently licked his dick and kept using his fingertips to lightly tease that top ridge, his head, and his balls. At times, he would slowly move his mouth, lips, and tongue down his rock-hard shaft.

Ronney's pre-cum was dripping out, and CJ took pleasure in sucking it all up. He kept his mouth licking and sucking as Ronney was gripping the sheets and gasped for breath. CJ used his fingers on one hand to hold the base of his cock gently upright while he slowly lowered his mouth over its entirety one more time and sucked on it hard and long. At the same time, he took his other hand and played with his balls while his mouth was moving up and down. Ronney was about to cum, and CJ pulled up, so his mouth was clamped down on just the top half of his dick. We could hear his tongue flapping on Ronney's head, and a few seconds later, Ronney hollered as he came in CJ's mouth.

Once Upon A Secret

The two boys took their shirts off, and Ronney got up and laid CJ down. He kissed CJ on the lips, and then he started to kiss and lick his way down his partner's body, stopping to suck his nipples. Then, while playing with CJ's nipples between his thumb and pointer finger, he continued to lick down his stomach and stuck his tongue into CJ's belly button. At that point, he swung around so that his ass was just in front of CJ's face. CJ kissed and massaged it as Ronney kissed his shaft and gently sucked his balls.

Ronney held CJ's shaft in his hand, gently took his dick between his lips, and started to suck and circle his tongue around his shaft. Then, he bobbed up and down, taking in only two inches while he pulled at the shaft. Soon, he took in more of CJ's dick, to the point where I thought he was going to gag, but that didn't happen. CJ got excited and started humping Ronney's face.

"I'm about to cum," CJ said.

Ronney took his mouth off of his dick and began to beat him off. Immediately, CJ came, and it shot up into the air like a fountain. Ronney stopped jacking and started sucking. CJ's body was jerking violently, but Ronney didn't stop sucking till he stopped.

"Cut!" I yelled.

"Still rolling," Diontae said.

"Okay, Prince. I need you outside. We're going to shoot you coming in."

"Okay." He got up and went outside.

"Action!"

Prince rushed in, and, when he saw Ronney on top of CJ, licking up his cum, he said, "What the fuck?" and

ZION

turned to leave, but Ronney hopped off of CJ and grabbed Prince before he could leave. "Get off of me!"

CJ ran over to help Ronney. CJ held Prince's arms behind his back, and Ronney pulled his pants off.

"Get the fuck off me, CJ!" CJ turned Prince around and bent him over. Ronney spat on his dick and slowly began to insert it into Prince's asshole. Prince was yelling out all types of curse words and obscenities. Soon, Ronney was all the way in, and he began to thrust his hips a little faster. CJ was holding Prince's head up, and he shoved his dick in his mouth.

"I don't like biters," CJ said as he face-fucked his roommate.

For the next five minutes, Prince was getting double penetrated, and, soon, Ronney came all in Prince's ass.

"I loosened it up for you," Ronney said, and he and CJ switched places. Prince's knees buckled, and CJ grabbed his hips to keep him up.

"Nah uh… it's my turn now."

CJ put his penis in Prince's ass, and Prince bit his bottom lip.

"You like that?" Ronney asked him. Prince nodded. "Good."

Ronney put his dick in Prince's mouth, and Prince began to suck and jerk him off. Ronney just held on to Prince's head and enjoyed the oral sex. CJ bent over Prince's back and began to jerk him off as he fucked him. Prince held on to Ronney's right hand and began moaning his pleasure onto Ronney's dick. CJ kept thrusting faster and faster, and Prince's moans got louder and louder, until he shot his load out onto the floor. CJ came in his ass, and Ronney came in his mouth. The three were past exhausted, and when CJ and Ronney pulled out of their human sex toy, they led him to the bed, and all three lay next to each other. Prince rubbed on CJ's dick; CJ rubbed on Ronney's, and Ronney rubbed on Prince's, and they all exchanged kisses.

"Cut!" I yelled. "Good job, guys. Get dressed. Diontae, can you help me clean this place up?"

"Yeah."

I looked at Jermaine. "So… what did you think?"

"That was awesome! I was over here 'bout to fuck my damn self!"

I laughed. The guys got dressed and waited in Jermaine's truck. It didn't take us long to clean up the mess and clear the bed. Jermaine gave me the money; I put it under the mattress as promised, and I texted Cameron to let him know that we were done. As soon as Jermaine and the boys pulled off, I got a phone call.

"Hello," I said.

"Hey, baby." It was Lonnie.

"Hey, Lonnie."

"I miss you."

"Okay."

"I do. Can you come over?"

I thought about it for a moment. I didn't have to work that night, and I hadn't seen him in a while. "Yeah. When?" I asked.

"Now."

"A'ight. I'm on my way."

I got in my car and drove to Lonnie's house. I walked around back and through the kitchen door.

ZION

"How did you get here so fast?" Lonnie asked startled. He was standing there in a pair of shorts eating a piece of bread with Cheez Whiz on top.

"What the hell are you eating?"

"I'm hungry."

"Your mamma didn't cook?"

"Yeah, but I don't want that." Then, he gave me the puppy dog face. "Can you make me some burgers, baby?"

"What? No!" I made homemade burgers for Lonnie one year, and ever since, he begged me to make them.

"Why not?"

"Because the meat is frozen. It's going to take forever to thaw out, prep, and cook."

"*Pleeaase*?"

"You obviously don't understand cooking. No." I went in the living room and sat down. I heard him squirt more Cheez Whiz on top of his bread. "Ugh."

When Lonnie finished eating, he laid on the floor to watch TV.

"Baby?"

"What?"

"Lay down here with me." I got down on the floor and laid next to him. "I love you."

"Uh huh."

"I do."

"Okay."

He got on top of me and looked me in my eyes. "Nikole."

"What?"

"I love you."

"Okay."

Once Upon A Secret

He kissed me, and the whole time I was hating him and loving him at the same time. Nobody kissed me like Lonnie did, but I knew that Hampton was full of bitches he had been kissing. He stopped kissing me long enough to undo my belt and slide my pants off. He lay on the floor and pulled me on top of him.

"Wait."

"Uh uh." He pulled his rock-hard dick out and put it at my hole.

"Wait."

Then, he pushed me down on it slowly, and I moaned a little.

"See, it's not that bad," he said as I began to rock back and forth. "It doesn't hurt?"

"Uh uh." I moaned, moving faster and faster.

"Nikole." I looked down at him and stopped moving. "It doesn't hurt?"

When I didn't say anything, Lonnie threw me off of him and cut on the light. He searched his dick for any signs that he had broken my hymen.

"You said you were a virgin."

I didn't say anything.

"Bitch, I'm talking to you." Every muscle on his body tensed up, and the crazy man inside was starting to come out. I reached for my underwear.

"Lonnie, calm down."

"Bitch, don't tell me to calm down!"

"You're going to wake your mother," I said as I slid my underwear on.

"Fuck her!" I stood up to put on my pants, and Lonnie grabbed me. "Who you been fucking?"

"Lonnie, nobody!"

ZION

"You been fucking somebody! And it ain't been me! So, you cheating on me now?"

"Didn't you fuck that bitch in August?"

"That's different!"

"How?"

"Get the fuck out my house!"

"Nigga, you ain't got no house!"

He grabbed my hair and pushed me to the front door. "Get ya ugly ass out!"

"Dumb-ass nigga. Whoever I fucked probably was better than you anyway," I said as I opened the door.

Lonnie punched me in the middle of my back, and I flew through the door and down the porch steps.

"The fuck you say?"

I was trying to stand up when he kicked me back down. He grabbed the back of my head and slammed my face into the ground.

When I could speak, I screamed, "Lonnie, get off of me!"

He turned me around and wrapped his hands around my neck and squeezed. I stared at him with a face that said, *You're not hurting me.* And then, without control my eyes rolled back in my head. He let me go right when I started to black out, and I heard him say, "Get the fuck off my yard," and then I heard the door close.

I took my phone out of my bra and called Byron.

"Hello." There was a lot of noise in the background.

"Byron." I could barely whisper.

"Hello? Nikole?"

"Byron, come get me."

"Where you at?"

Once Upon A Secret

I don't know what I said because I blacked out. When I came to, I was in Jen's house on the couch with a serious headache. I started to sit up, and I heard, "Where you going?"

I looked over to the kitchen and Byron was sitting at the table, watching me.

"What are you doing here?"

"I brought you here."

"You did?"

"Yeah, you called me last night, and I came and got you."

"Oh, my God. Where's the car?"

"Jen drove it over here." He looked at me, concerned. "You were outside with no pants on, yo. What's going on?"

I laid back down and immediately started crying. I don't know why, but I valued Byron's opinion of me, and I was sure it was about to get worse.

"Nikole, what's wrong?"

"You're going to hate me if I tell you."

"Oh, Lord. The last time you said that it was something bad." He sat on the couch by my feet, and I stared at the ceiling.

"When I met Lonnie, I was a virgin. He thought I was still a virgin because he didn't know that I was fucking my teachers for As."

"What?"

My tears were flowing really heavily. "Yeah, and when Lonnie and I started to have sex, he found out I wasn't a virgin, and he beat me."

"C'mon, yo." He shook his head, and my eyes were filling up with tears. I told him how my life was spinning out of control. How I didn't feel comfortable with my teachers anymore, how I saw my dad at the club, and how, overall, my life was a disaster.

"You need to go back to church," he said, "and all this nasty, unholy shit you doing needs to stop."

"Okay."

Charles

"Christian!" I shouted as I walked into my three-story townhome.

"Up here!" my wife shouted from the bedroom. I went upstairs and found her putting up clothes. "Hey."

"Hey! How was your day?"

"Good, and yours?"

"Good," I told her. I went to the dresser and then walked back to her. "Chrissy, we need to—"

"What's wrong, Charles?" she asked with a concerned tone.

"You might want to sit down for this," I told her. She sat. "Before I met you, my name was Marcel Anton Lovette, and I lived in Williamsburg, Virginia, with my daughter, Casey Lovette."

"What?"

"Wait. Let me finish. I got into some trouble, so I faked my death. Then, I restarted my life, leaving my daughter to be taken care of by strangers." I took a deep breath. "A few nights ago, I went to this strip club in Richmond with a co-worker, and I found out that

Casey worked there. She saw me. So, now... I don't know."

"Strip Club?!" She just stared at me. "So let me get this straight. My *husband* is someone else and has a daughter by another woman? Where is the girl's mother?"

"She died in labor."

"How old is the girl?" she asked.

"She should be thirty-seven by now."

"You have a thirty-seven-year-old daughter, and, for twenty years, you didn't tell me about her? When were you going to tell me you were a different person, Charles? Or whatever your name is."

"Honey, maybe you don't understand how this works. When you get rid of an old identity, you don't bring it up again."

She gave me the most evil stare with those big grey eyes. "So why are you telling me this?"

"Because I think Casey and Nikole should meet."

"Oh, hell no! Not my daughter! If she's a part of your past that you didn't bring up for twenty years, then let her stay there."

"Christian! She's my daughter! I love her as much as I love Nikole."

She stood up. "I'm going to let you make the decision on this. And it better be the right one."

She turned on her Italian heels, flipped her golden hair and stormed downstairs.

I took a deep breath and went after her. "I don't know who the hell you think you're talking to, but you better get it together!"

ZION

"Excuse you?" She stopped at the bottom of the stairs in the dining room.

"I'm the head of *this* house, and, if I say I want to bring my doggone daughter here, then that's what we are doing!"

"Who's the head of this house?" she asked.

"Me."

"*Me*? Me who?"

"Me. Ya husband."

"My husband's name is Charles Anthony Tucker, and, about five to ten minutes ago, I found out he doesn't exist. So you ain't the head of *shit*, nigga!" She continued to go down to the first floor.

"Look, Christian. You better get it together 'cause you ain't gonna be talking to me any damn way!" I yelled from where I was standing.

"Don't cuss at me!"

I ran down the stairs. "Don't feel good, do it? But you like to cuss at me when you get all mad and upset. But let me cuss at you, and it's a doggone problem!"

"When have I ever cussed at you, Charles?" She threw down the shirt she was folding.

"When we was upstairs you said, 'Oh, hell naw!'"

"That's not cussing at you. That's a phrase."

"Well, phrase this: both of my daughters will be coming home for dinner. And I suggest you look cute and cook something good and leave ya attitude and phrases somewhere else." I started to walk away.

"So my opinion doesn't matter?"

"Not if your opinion isn't 'Sure. Bring 'em over.'"

"Let me ask you something." I turned around, and she asked, "How in the hell am I supposed to feel?

'Cause you know so much about hiding identities and shit."

"There you go cussing again."

"Tell me this," she raised her voice to speak over me. "What was I supposed to say when the man I married tells me he's not the man I married? How was I supposed to react? 'Cause I think I'm handling that pretty damn well! But, to put the icing on the cake, you want to introduce some grown-ass woman from the strip club to my daughter. Nigga, have you lost your mind?"

"Call me nigga one mo' time, Christian!" I held my finger up.

"And what you gonna do?"

"You just wait."

"You gonna leave and start a new identity?"

"I'ma walk away before I end up hurting you." I walked back up the stairs and headed for my bedroom.

Christian followed behind me. "Hurt who? Not me! I'd love to see you try."

"Keep on pushing me, Chrissy. You just keep right on like you doing. You gonna see a side of me you never seen before."

"Oh, is the other man gonna come out? What was his name? Marquavious?"

"Marcel!" I shouted as I went into the room to look for my keys.

"Oh, Marcel think he gonna put a hurting on me," she said as she went in our bathroom. "Let me get my Vaseline out."

"Go on 'head and get it out then!" I grabbed my keys.

ZION

"Where you going? To go grab some mo' chapters from ya past?" she yelled.

I ignored her and slammed the front door behind me. But she opened the bedroom window and shouted out, "If you find anymore skeletons in your closet, I suggest you leave 'em there! This house is too small fo' all your baggage!"

I slammed the door to the car and sped off to the barber shop. My pastor was also my barber, and I felt that I needed somebody with Jesus to give me some advice. It was a Thursday evening, around six, and when I arrived, I was shocked to see how busy he was.

"Charles!" he shouted as I walked through the door. "¿Qué pasa, baby?"

I exhaled deeply as I stood next to him. "I need somebody to talk to."

He looked me up and down. "Alright. What's wrong?" he asked.

"Well, I can't talk about it with people around."

"A'ight. Look. I got one, two, three more. You can wait or leave and come back in 'bout thirty minutes, and I'm all yours."

"I'll wait." I sat on the cream colored couch that stretched the length of the wall and watched CNN as I waited for my pastor to finish cutting his clients' hair. At 6:45, we went outside to talk.

"Okay, so what's up?"

I explained everything about my past, seeing my daughter, and the conversation I had just had with my wife.

"Oh, wow," he exclaimed.

"Yeah, and I'm pissed."

Once Upon A Secret

"Of course, you are! I would be, too. But I, also, understand why your wife is mad. You didn't think she was going to be calm about all of this, did you? She married you twenty years ago, and you just basically told her that she married somebody that doesn't exist."

"But, Bishop, I'm the same guy; I just changed my name."

"No, you're not the same guy. The real you has a daughter that's a stripper. The fake you has a daughter that's in college and a wife who loves you. The real you is in debt with people who want to hurt you. The fake you has good credit. You see where I'm going with this?" he asked.

"Yeah, but, all the same, both Casey and Nikole are my daughters, and I want them to meet. And I want to be in Casey's life again."

"And you should. And I'm saying that from a father's perspective. But, as a husband and your pastor, this type of decision should be made with your wife. But, as a man, I wouldn't let her talk to me like that, especially if I'm the one paying all the bills and working like I'm working. Did she go out and get a job yet?"

"Uh, naw," I told him.

"I knew she didn't! But, if she got a problem with your daughter, that's her problem. You made a mistake. Now, you want to fix it. Good. I am all about a man handling his business."

"Okay, so, Chrissy definitely doesn't want them to meet. Should I still go ahead with it?"

"Charles, you're a grown man. You don't need me to tell you what to do. I would bring the two together.

ZION

Sure. But that's a decision you need to make on your own."

"Yeah, you're right."

"I know I'm right. Now, make sure you bring your wife to church on Sunday, so I can put plenty of oil on that head."

I laughed. "Thanks, Bishop."

"No problema. A'ight. I'm going inside now; it's cold out here."

"A'ight. I'm going home," I said as he went back inside, and I headed toward my car. I dialed my daughter's cell phone number.

"Hello?" Nikole answered.

"Hey, baby."

"Hey, Dad. What's up?"

"I wanted to know if you could come home for the weekend and maybe go to church with me and your mama."

"Uh, yeah."

"A'ight. cool. Well, I'll see you Friday or Saturday?"

"Actually, I have a lot of work to do, so I'll just come Sunday morning. Church starts at 9:30, right?"

"Yep."

"Okay. I'll be there."

"A'ight, baby. Talk to you later."

"Okay. Bye, Dad."

I hung up the phone and smiled. I was so proud of my daughter. I couldn't wait for her to graduate and actually be successful at everything she wanted to do. She was great at whatever she put her hand towards, but, if she could just pick one thing to get started on, she would be very successful!

Once Upon A Secret

Sunday morning Nikole and her roommate, Yasmine, had ridden with Jen. We all sat together, and I was anticipating a great word from the bishop. The congregation stood and read Luke 15: 13-24 together, the story of the Prodigal Son.

"Before you take your seats, look at your neighbor, eyeball to eyeball, and say these words: 'When are you...'"

"When are you," we all said in unison.

"Going to come..."

"Going to come..."

"To yourself?"

"To yourself?"

"Y'all better take your seat. I feel something pushing me already. Tell somebody on the other side, 'cause that person might didn't hear you. Look at the other person next to you and say: 'Aint it 'bout time...'"

"Aint it 'bout time..."

"For you to come..."

"For you to come..."

"To yourself?"

"To yourself?" We all clapped.

"I know y'all heard the story. I know you heard it plenty of times. I know you've heard it preached. I done preached it plenty of times. I went through the text over and over again, Toot." Bishop liked to address members of the congregation while he was preaching. "But, this time, I ain't never seen it like this. I've been preaching now for twenty-two years, longer than that really. And it seems like, every time I preach this word, I see something else there. And here, first of

ZION

all, if you study the text in its totality, Augustine, you see that the boy had no right to ask for nothing. Boon, he was arrogant. You don't know nobody like that, do you?" he said sarcastically. "Full of pride, full of himself; he's not the oldest; he's the baby. He's the youngest, and this joker walked up in the house, Clair, and asked his father for his inheritance *before* he was even due. That's one point. Are y'all okay?"

"Yeah!" someone in the congregation shouted.

"The next point is, why try to hurry your blessing?"

"Alright."

"When most of the time, if you hada waited for your blessing, you would have been mature enough to handle it, when you got it? Anybody up in here? But you was *so* in a hurry to get *something* and to have *something* so that you could walk around and parade how bad you was. But God allowed you; watch what you pray for. Look at somebody and say, 'Watch what you pray for.'"

"Watch what you pray for."

"'Cause you just might get it. So what happened to the boy? He was so bad. He was so arrogant, so he walked up to his father and he said, "Father! Give me what's bestowed to me. Give me what's mine." He said, 'Okay, son.' Let me tell you what he did. He divided his inheritance, and he gave the older brother his, and he gave the younger brother his, and the younger brother decided to leave, and the older brother stayed home. But I didn't understand it before, Judy, when I was young in the ministry. I didn't understand, if the older brother had such a problem, why didn't he leave? But, according to Jewish custom, the oldest always stayed home and took care of the parents. Y'all ain't gonna help me preach!"

"Go 'head, bishop!" one lady shouted.

"Go 'head!" another one shouted.

"So because of the older one's responsibility, he wouldn't leave first; he would leave last."

"C'mon, bishop!"

"I got to help y'all in here. When you understand this text, it messes with me so much. The boy left home, he took everything that his father had for him, he was rich, he had all of his inheritance, and he went to a faraway country. In other words, he travelled all the way to the far side of the globe and got as far away from home as possible. You don't know nobody like that, do you? That tried to get as far away from folk that love them as possible?"

"C'mon!"

"Every time you turn around, they tryna get further away. The more people try to keep you closer to them, you don't like that, you want to be further away. He tried to go somewhere where nobody knew his name, where nobody was his pedigree, where nobody knew where he was coming from. All they knew was he gotta lotta money, and he got it going on. Y'all don't wanna talk to me. And so the Bible says that he went to a place, and he spent all that he had on riotous living. In other words, he was partying every night." The congregation laughed. "He was doing what he was wanting to do. He was in the Big Apple, Royal Blue, and every other club you want to talk about." The bishop named the clubs that had been popular when we were younger. "The boy was jamming. He had a Rolls

ZION

outside; he had a Bentley; he had a Jag; he had it going on. He had everything! You don't know nobody like that, do you?"

"Oh, yes!"

"That had it going on and had success and had everybody tooting his horn and talking 'bout how bad he was? But, in the midst of everything, he lost. The Bible says, a famine came in the land, and he spent all he had on riotous living, and guess what? When he had nothing else to give, he had nobody else."

"Come on!"

"Y'all ain't gonna help me. You ever understand that everybody blowing up your phone and texting you all night long is only doing that for as long as you have something for them. But the moment you stop putting out, folks stop calling you. They don't know where you live no mo'; they ain't calling to see how you doing. Whoaaa, but, when you had it going on, they was calling your phone late at night. 'Girl, what you doing? What you up to tonight?' But, when you're broke, lost your job, got home with yo mamma and them. Y'all ain't gonna help me preach in here. Watch this. And the text says, and nobody gave him… " He paused for us to finish his sentence.

"Nothing," a few members chimed.

"I don't think y'all want to read it. I had y'all speaking awhile ago."

"Anything!"

"Nothing!"

"Seems like somebody would have said, 'Look here, man. I remember when you looked out for me when I was going through. I think I might look out for you. I think I might return the favor.' Isn't it ironic. Do you mind if I take a seat?" he asked a visitor and sat next to her in the pew. "Isn't it ironic that the person you do the most for is the very person that does the least for you when you need them? And the one you done the least for, is the one that ends up coming through for you."

He got up and ran to the back of the church while everyone clapped and cheered him on. He ran back to the center of the church. "Isn't it *ironic* that the one you broke your neck for and stuck up for the most is the one that hurt you?"

"Yeaaah!"

"I don't know why God do us like that. And guess what? The person that we say we ain't gonna do it for again. Well, God puts them right back in our pathway and makes us do it *all over* again!"

"C'mon now, pastor!"

"Why in the world does God do us like that? He knocked on folks' doors. He went to folks that he had been looking out for, and, every time he asked folks, the text says—I didn't write this. I am not exaggerating right now; I am not putting my own stuff in. Did y'all read the text? He said, '*Nobody...* gave him... *anything.* That's tough. I've been reading this text for a long time. Seems like—"

"*Somebody.*"

"Somebody, could have gave him—"

"*Something.*"

"Something. I'm talking to about five of y'all in here, that ain't nobody gave you nothing. Oh, it's about five of y'all. Ain't nobody gave you jack, and, if they said

ZION

they did, you would lay them out right now and say, "Don't you *tell* that lie! You saw me when I was hurting the most!" I'm talking to some folk in here right now. Some folk, then, rode past your house to make sure that you *did* lose it!"

"C'mon!"

"That's right!"

"Made a special trip! Don't even live nowhere near your neighborhood. Rode ten miles out of the way and caught up in the curb to see if you was still there!"

"Yes, they did!"

"Yeah!"

"And got mad when they saw you packing your boxes to move to a better place!"

"Whooo!"

"I'ma help you get free today! Got upset! Went a little crazy! 'I don't believe that she got a man helping her!' Ain't it something when you ain't got no man? I'm talking to about three or four women in here that ain't got nar' a man, ain't nobody help you with the mortgage, light bill, water bill; every time you can pay it, all you can say is 'Thank you Jesus for allowing me to have what I have!'"

"Yes!" All of the single women shouted.

"Alright!"

"You go, bishop! C'mon!"

"Whoo, you preaching!"

"Take ya time. Take ya time."

"And so, and so, and so, it seems to me, Clareatha, that somebody should have gave him something."

"Yeaaah."

Once Upon A Secret

"While he had everything, you know how it is. You got to step over folks in your house. Everybody slept over your house. But, when you ain't got nothing, you got an echo. The text says... watch this. It says that he went and done something that some folk in here need to do; he went and got a job."

Only one or two people said, "Amen."

"Let me come over here 'cause y'all looking at me real messed up." Pastor went into the pulpit and stood by the drummer. "If anybody come over here, Kerry, you get them, okay? The Bible says, he hired himself out; catch this revelation. He left a rich place with all of his inheritance, but he lost all that he had, and now he understood how other folks felt. He lost everything, so he could get from up there —" Bishop stretched his hand up high above his head "—to down there." He stooped down and pointed to the ground. "So now he understood how everybody else felt. Before, he had never worked a day in his life. His daddy was rich. Y'all ain't talking to me. The boy had everything; the boy had *everything*. Look at somebody and say: 'He had everything.'"

"He had everything," we all said.

"He lost everything. He had everything. Ain't it something when you had it and you lost it? But now that he lost it, he hires himself out. His job is to take care of the swine. If it hadda been us, we could roll wit' it. We African-Americans... Mexican-Americans We used to being in the pig pen. C'mon now. You from New Light, Crestwood. I still remember Mr. Brooks had a pig pen on Dunn Street. C'mon now. Don't get brand new. When I was going to Ms.

ZION

Novella's store, it was a pig pen back there. We smelled pigs all night long. Don't get brand new. Don't get deep in here like y'all from the city or somewhere. What bothers me with this here, Chris, is that he's a Jew… in a pig pen. Jews don't even touch a pig."

"Yeah," Georgia Mae said.

"You wanna finish preaching this, Georgia?" She burst out laughing and laid down in the pew. "'Cause you know already, there's a place where God will put you, where you said when you was up and had everything, that I would—"

"Never!" everybody, including the bishop, said.

"Oh, but there's coming a day. Who am I talking to up in here? Where you ending up doing the very thing that you said—"

"You would never do," the congregation said.

"Desperate times call for desperate measures. Don't ever say what you ain't gonna do, especially when you hungry, you ain't had nothing to eat, you ain't had a good bath; baby, when you're desperate, you don't know what you gonna do. My daddy told me, 'You ain't got no business going 'round there telling them white folks all of your business and getting food stamps.'" I said, 'I'ma tell you right now. I'ma get these free lunch tickets.'" He said, "Ain't no son of mine gon' get no free lunch tickets. You take this money and go buy you a lunch.'"

"I took his money… but, I also got my—"

"Free lunch tickets," the congregation said.

"This boy messed around, and he's in a position that he would have never put himself in. He's in the hog pen, eating what the swine eat. He was pushing the

Once Upon A Secret

pigs out of the way so that he could get the best parts. And the text never implies, Chris, how many days he stayed in the pig pen. But I just want to say, one day is too many when you come from a mansion and wind up in a pig pen. And the Bible says, while he was scraping for food, while he was looking to get filled… " Bishop reached behind the podium and pulled out a mirror and looked in it. "The Bible says, he came to himself. He looked at himself. You say, 'Bishop, the man ain't have no mirror.' Ain't it ironic that God can show you; you don't need no mirror. But, baby, when you get in a bad situation, you can turn around and look at yourself and tell yourself, 'I don't have to be like this. I can change my life. I can change who I am. I can change what I am.' Who am I talking to here?"

I looked over and saw Nikole's roommate nudge her.

"Touch three people and say, 'He's talking to me.'"

I looked over again, and Yasmine was poking Nikole in the leg and making a face at her as if to say, "This message was just for you."

"I got to change my life. I got to learn who I am. Lord, have mercy! And the boy got up and shook himself. He said, 'I ain't got to live like this. How many servants are in my father's house?' In other words," he explained, "if I'm gonna work for anybody, let me work for my daddy. And he started on the journey all the way back home. But y'all ain't missed the best part of the text. The father never went looking for him. He never left home. He never put out a search party. He knew that, one day, his boy would come to himself!"

ZION

Jen

Church was awesome that Sunday, and I couldn't help but feel that my dad was talking directly to Nikole and me. But more so Nikole. I remember I used to call Nikole a Huxtable because she was African-American with both of her parents. She never had to go without, and whatever she wanted or needed, she got. So she reminded me a lot of the prodigal son because she went from having everything she wanted to directing porn and becoming a stripper, so she could pay some bills, have a car to drive, and money to go whatever she wanted. But I knew that she was in her hog pen experience at that time, and Dad said that the prodigal son had to come to *himself*, so I knew that it wasn't up to me to tell Nikole. She needed to change.

Sunday night, Nikole stayed in her room with Yasmine, and Paris was still crashing at my place. I had to go to work, so I left her there to chill, and I went on to Consequences. I walked into the dressing room and began to undress and get changed.

While I was looking for a costume to wear, Emily stood close to me and whispered, so nobody else could hear, "That was crazy what happened the other night, huh?"

"What other night? What are you talking about?"

"You didn't hear? Casey's daddy came back from the dead, and Jordin's fiancé broke off the engagement."

"What?" I said. "What are you talking about?" I didn't like to gossip with Emily because I knew she was bad news, but that was news I needed to hear.

Once Upon A Secret

"Okay, so listen, I'm not one to gossip, so you didn't hear this from me."

"Yeah, yeah, whatever," I said, trying to rush her.

She moved in closer. "Okay, so you know Casey's dad died when she was in high school, right?"

"Yeah, that's what I heard." I actually had heard it from Emily my first night working there.

"Okay, well, apparently, he got in bad with some people and faked his death to get away."

"What?"

"Yeah."

"And what did she do?"

"She just cussed him out. I'm pretty sure she was shocked. But, just when we were all winding down from *that* fiasco, Jordin's fiancé spots her from *across the club* as she's trying to leave."

"Leave?"

"Yeah. Apparently, he didn't know she was a stripper! So she was trying to sneak out the back door before he could see her."

"Wow!"

"Mmm hmm, but he saw that ass."

"That is crazy." I was wondering how Nikole didn't notice any of that. But she probably was too flustered about seeing her dad anyway.

"Yeah, I thought we would get a *little* drama when I invited Charles and Jesse to come, but not *that* much!"

"Mmm," I said as I flipped through the costumes. Then, it hit me. "Wait! What?"

"Oh, girl, yes. I went into Jerry's desk drawer and got Nikole's home phone number and called Mr. Turner to let him know that, if he came to the club, it would be a night he would *never* forget. I had a feeling Jordin's fiancée was a good man and wouldn't be caught dead in a strip club, so I had my friend, Kevin, call him and ask if he knew where his fiancée was that night?"

"What the fuck is wrong with you?"

"What? I wanted my night to be a little more exciting. How was I supposed to know that Jordin would end up single and Casey's dead father would walk through the door?"

She walked away, and I ran up behind her. "Do you know that you basically ruined people's lives? What if Nikole's dad had recognized her? Do you know what her parents would have done?"

"No. In fact, that's what I was trying to find out." She walked away again.

This time, I grabbed her by her hair and pulled her head back; she screamed. All the girls in the dressing room looked over at us. I chopped Emily in the throat, stood her upright, and kicked her in her back.

"You bitch!" she yelled when she got her balance.

"You're the bitch!"

She ran toward me, and I bent down to scoop her, but she stood firm, grabbed me by my waist, and kneed me in the stomach. I doubled over and was on my knees when she brought her foot down in the middle of my back. I was pinned to the floor.

"You don't know me, Jen! I whoops ass!"

I rolled over really fast, grabbed both of her feet and pulled really hard. She fell, and before I could do another move, she kicked me in my face. I wiped the blood from my mouth and stood up. "Oh, hell naw!"

Once Upon A Secret

And before I could do anything, Jerry grabbed my arm and pulled me away from her.

"Jen! What the hell are you doing?"

"Whooping this bitch's ass!"

"Not likely," Emily said.

I tried to run around Jerry to get to her, but he held me back.

"Jen, you're fired!" Jerry yelled.

"What? You can't fire me! One, I'm an independent contractor, and two, I did nothing wrong. She—"

"Is fired, too," Jerry said, cutting me off.

"The fuck?" Emily yelled.

"Emily, you have been giving me *and* my customers problems from day one!"

"But what about me?" I yelled. "I ain't done shit!"

"I've been the manager here for over five years and never have I seen a fight break out this bad." He looked at me. "Who started it?" I just crossed my arms. "That's what I thought. I want both of you out. Now!" Jerry headed for the door. "If you're not out in five minutes, I'll have security drag you out!"

Emily and I looked at each other. "Now I don't have a job because of you," she said.

"Right back at ya," I said, and started to gather my things.

What was I going to do without a job? I had just moved out, and the money I had saved would be used up fast if I didn't come up with a plan.

ZION

Casey

It was 6:00 p.m., and my alarm was going off. I slapped it off, but there was still noise in my apartment. Someone was knocking on my door.

"Can I help you?" I asked as I answered the door.

There was a tall, slender white man standing there in a gray three-piece suit, a fedora, a pair of the shiniest Giorgio Brutini shoes I'd ever seen, and Ray Ban glasses. He was too fresh to be a cop, so I assumed he had the wrong address.

"Hello. Are you Ms. Casey Lovette?" he asked.

"Look. If this has anything to do with my father, you tell him—"

"Ma'am, this is about Mrs. Twine."

I just stared at him. "What?" I stepped out into the hallway and looked at her door.

"May I come in?" the man asked.

I looked at him. "Um, sure." I let the man in and led him to the living room. "Um, would you like some water or something?"

"No, thank you, but maybe you should sit down." I sat. "Mrs. Twine died yesterday at two in the afternoon," he told me.

"What?"

"Yes. She had a massive heart attack in her apartment."

"I know she lives alone. Who found her?"

"The superintendant came up an hour later to work on her heat, and he found her."

Once Upon A Secret

"Oh, my God! Well, I know she has one daughter, but I don't know who she is or where she lives," I said, wondering why he was visiting me.

"Yes, I have contacted her."

"And who are you again?"

"Oh, I'm sorry. My name is Antwon Jackson." He handed me a card. "I was Mrs. Twine's lawyer."

"Oh… well, why are you here?"

"Because Mrs. Twine has left you something in her will. To receive it, you must attend the funeral and reading this Friday at ten a.m."

"Of course, I'll attend the funeral, but did she tell you why she left *me* anything? We barely knew each other. She just came over and prayed for me and cooked for me."

"All of that will be reviewed at the reading of the will."

"Okay," I said.

The man stood. "I'll be going now."

I walked him out and sat down on my bed. I couldn't believe Mrs. Twine had died. She was the only person in this world that genuinely cared for me. I wondered what her daughter was feeling. Probably the same thing I felt when I had *thought* that my dad had died: grief, despair, loneliness. I thought for a few moments more, and then I got ready to go to work.

When I got in the dressing room at Consequences, everyone was eating.

"What's going on in here?" I asked one of the girls.

"That new girl, Nikole, cooked dinner for us and, *girl…* "

ZION

She didn't even bother to finish her sentence as she shoved some food in her face. I sat my bag down, and it was like, immediately, my stomach started growling. I hadn't eaten because Mrs. Twine didn't bring over anything. Just the thought of Mrs. Twine brought tears to my eyes.

"Hey, Casey." I looked up, and Nikole was standing behind me. "I made this for you."

I looked down, and she was holding a small cake no bigger than a man's hand. The frosting was a white cream cheese with pecans sprinkled on top. I took it from her. "It's my way of saying 'sorry' about the last time I was here. I didn't mean to get you that upset."

"Okay. No, Nikole. I was upset about something else and took it out on you. I should be the one apologizing," I told her.

"Well… " She handed me a fork. "I hope you enjoy."

She walked away, and I sat down at my vanity and pulled a forkful away from the cake. It was two layers: red velvet and chocolate. I took a bite, and immediately I nearly passed out from the goodness. It was as if the two flavors were in my mouth, giving each other orgasms on top of my kinky taste buds.

I went over to Nikole. "You made this?" I asked her.

"Yeah," she said with a smile.

"Nikole, you are what? Twenty-two?"

"Twenty."

"There is no way a twenty-year-old should be able to make cakes this good!" I continued to stuff my face.

"Well, don't get full off of cake. I made chicken lasagna, garlic bread, braised short ribs, garlic roasted red potatoes, asparagus and almonds, and cornbread."

Once Upon A Secret

I just looked at her like she was a crazy person. "What? Why did you cook all of that? I would have went insane trying to prepare all of that food."

"Oh, I love to cook. And I was thinking about what you said about being better than this. I went to church on Sunday, and he was basically saying the same thing. So, as soon as I get caught up on my bills and have some money saved, I'm going to try to open my own restaurant."

I smiled. "That's good, Nikole. I don't know if this means anything to you or not, but I'm proud of you. And, if that food tastes as good as it sounds, your restaurant will be a huge success."

"Actually, that means a lot to me," she said and smiled from ear to ear.

I was sitting at the table outside of Professor Lions' office, waiting for the girl that was seeing him to finish up, so I could go in there and have a talk with him about my grades. That was when Byron called.

"Hello," I said when I answered the phone.

"Hey. Where are you?"

"Hampton, waiting to meet with one of my teachers."

"For what?" he said angrily.

"Calm down. This is a different teacher, and it's to talk about grades."

"Is it a guy?"

ZION

"Yeah."

"Then, I don't trust him. What building are you in?"

"MLK, second floor in the psychology office."

"A'ight."

"Byron, what did you call me for?"

"I wanted to see if you wanted to go out for lunch. I'm hungry."

"Okay, yeah. Cool. I should be ready in thirty minutes or less. I'll call you when I'm done."

"Okay."

We hung up, and I saw the girl leave Professor Lions' office. I knocked on his door, and, when he saw me, his face lit up.

"Nikole!"

"Hey! How you doing?"

"Good! Please have a seat." I sat in the chair next to his desk. "So what brings you by today?"

"Well, it's about the letter assignment we had."

"Okay."

"You gave me a B, and I was sure it was an A paper."

"It was. There was just some grammar that needed to be corrected."

"Um, grammar brought my paper down a whole letter grade?"

"Well, I can show you if you'd like."

"Yeah, sure." I sat back in the chair and crossed my legs. My skirt had a deep split in it, and my thighs were exposed. Professor Lions bit his lip while he searched for the assignment on his computer.

"Okay. Here it is." I stood up and bent over behind him so that my breasts were lightly touching his shoulder. He stuttered as he showed my mistakes to me. With each one, I exhaled deeply, causing my breasts to fall on his shoulders. I didn't want to act like a slut, but Lions was the only professor I had that I actually fantasized about.

"Well, I guess that's that then." I picked up my purse, and my keys fell.

"Oh, I'll get them." Professor Lions got up and bent over to pick up the keys, and I quickly stood behind him and grabbed his waist. He stood straight up. "We shouldn't be doing this."

"I don't see why not," I said as I took my keys from his hand and sat them down with my purse. I put his hands up my shirt, so he could feel my breasts. "You can't tell me that you've never wanted this."

He didn't say anything, and I rubbed my hands along the shape of his penis in his pants. I no longer needed to guide him as he moved his hands along my hard nipples and groaned his satisfaction.

"Wait a minute."

He stopped, slammed the door, and then rushed back to me, grabbed me, and kissed me really deeply and long. My teeth bit at his bottom lip, and, whenever he stuck his tongue in my mouth, I sucked on it and stuck my tongue back into his. Professor Lions picked me up and laid me down on the extra desk in his office. I lifted my skirt, and he unzipped his pants. And before either of us could think twice, he was deep inside of me touching all of my walls and trying to reach my G-spot. I spread my legs as far as I could and fucked him back. He grabbed my ass and pulled me in close to him. I grabbed the back of his head and started to moan louder and louder.

ZION

"Nikki, shh."

I was quiet for about thirty seconds, but I was living a long dreamt fantasy, and I couldn't stay quiet. I closed my eyes and leaned my head back and moaned more and more.

The next thing I knew, Lions was out of me so fast that I didn't know what was going on. I opened my eyes to see Byron on top of him, pounding him in the face.

"Byron, wait!" I hopped off the desk and tried to pull my friend off my professor.

Byron stood up and looked at me. "Are you okay?"

"Yes! What are you doing here?"

"What am I doing here? What are you doing, Nikki?"

"Byron, it's not what you think. I'm passing Lions' class."

If looks could kill, I would have been chopped up and put into a tree shredder at that moment.

"So, whatchu saying, yo? You *wanted* to fuck him? Just because?"

I looked him in his eyes. "Yes."

At that moment, I saw his eyes fill with tears, and he walked away.

"Byron, wait!" I grabbed his arm, and he pulled away.

"Don't touch me! Don't call me, text me, tweet me, Facebook me. Don't try to communicate with me at all!"

Then, he was gone.

I looked down at Lions. "I am so sorry."

"I think you should go," he said quietly.

Once Upon A Secret

I gathered my things and ran to my car feeling the pain you feel when someone you love walks out of your life. My heart was supremely broken, and I didn't know what to do. Byron was my best friend and the only one I could call on day or night, and he had just walked out of my life. But I had opened the door for him. Right then, in my Prodigal Son experience, I realized I was completely surrounded by nothing but pigs, and I was metaphorically desiring to eat what the pigs ate.

Charles

It was a Wednesday, and I was coming home from work. My wife was cooking in the kitchen, and I went in to meet her.

"Hey." I bent down to give her a kiss.

"Hey," she said and dodged my lips.

"Really?"

"How was your day, Maurice?"

"Marcel. And I'm still Charles to you."

"Right."

"What are you cooking?"

"I'm fixing me some chicken alfredo."

"Whatchu mean *you*? You not cooking for the both of us?"

"I don't know what you like to eat."

"What? I'm still the same guy!" She just shrugged her shoulders. "Okay, look. I called the girls today."

ZION

She turned abruptly and gave me a death stare. "And what did you say?"

"They're coming home for dinner tomorrow."

"I know they're not!"

"Well, you better learn before they get here!"

"I told you. I don't want my *daughter* to meet that girl! And you go behind my back and do it anyway."

"First of all, that *girl* is my child. Second of all, I didn't go behind your back. I'm grown. I'll do what I want."

"Oh, you grown, huh?"

"Yeah."

"Well, now you grown and single." She walked away and stormed upstairs.

I went to my car, grabbed an envelope, and ran up the steps to our room. The door was locked, so I kicked it in.

"The door was locked for a reason!"

"You said I'm single. Here!" I took the papers out of the envelope and handed her a pen. "Make me single, and sign these papers."

"Oh, fuck you, Julius—"

"Marcel!"

"Whatever! I'm not stupid! We're going to court to settle this. Now, get out!"

"You must have forgotten that I paid for all of this shit! I ain't going nowhere. But you better start looking for a place to move into *real* soon." I headed for the door.

"So, you already went to a lawyer? You never expected this to work after you told me your big secret, did you?"

Once Upon A Secret

I turned, and she was sitting on the bed with her arms crossed. "Any woman, who wants nothing to do with my child, means *nothing* to me."

The next night, I was at Applebee's eagerly waiting for my daughters to show up. I really wanted to have the conversation over a home-cooked meal, but I didn't want to do it at my house with all of that negative energy. I didn't know if Casey was going to show. I called the club she worked at and left a message with the bartender that answered the phone. But the chances were she wasn't going to show either because she didn't get the message or she didn't want anything to do with me. Either way, I was hoping she would show. Nikole walked in the door.

"Nikki," I hollered out to her. She waved and came to the table.

"Hey, Daddy." She gave me a hug.

"Hey." She sat down, and I couldn't help but notice the despair on her face. "What's going on?"

"Nothing." She picked up her menu and then sat it back down.

"You already know what you want?"

"I'm actually not hungry."

"You already ate?"

"No." She looked out the window. "So where is this person you want me to meet?"

"She should be on her way?" She looked at me.

"She?"

"Uh, yeah. I guess it's good that she's not here yet, so I can talk to you first." Her face looked so nervous that it made me uneasy to say what I had to say. "Well, before I met your mother, I was somebody else."

ZION

"What do you mean 'somebody else'?"

"My name was Marcel Anton Lovette, and I lived in Williamsburg." Her eyes grew wide. "I had a daughter named Casey, and, when she was a freshman in high school, I faked my death."

"Is this a joke?" she laughed and some color began to come back to her face.

"No. I moved to Virginia Beach, and, later that year, I met your mother. And the following year, you were born."

"I'm sorry. What?"

"Okay, Nikole, my name is Marcel Anton Lovette from Williamsburg, Virginia, and the person I called you here to meet is my daughter Casey Lovette." She took a deep breath and exhaled slowly.

"Okay."

I was shocked at her response. "You're okay with that?"

"You did what you thought was right, right?"

"Yeah."

"Okay, and now you're trying to do what's right by both of your kids. That's cool. I'm with that," I smiled.

"Boy, I tell ya. I did a good job raising you."

"Yeah, well… "

She hesitated for a moment, and, before I could say anything, Casey came storming over to the table.

"Make this quick. I drove a long way to get here, and I just want this to be over and done with."

I stood. "Casey, this is—"

"*Nikole?*"

Nikole looked up. "Casey?"

"Wait! You two know each other?" I asked.

Once Upon A Secret

"Yeah, we work together," Casey said.

"Work together where?"

"At my day job in Hampton," Casey said. "Nikole and I are waitresses at the County Grill." Casey sat down next to Nikole. "Is this who you wanted me to meet?"

"Yeah, but, y'all already know each other."

Nikole just stared at Casey in amazement.

"Wait. This is your *daughter*?" Nikole asked.

"Yeah," I responded.

"Shocker, isn't it?" Casey said nonchalantly.

"But you have red hair and my hair's blonde."

"My mother's hair is red. Your father's hair is brownish blonde."

"I'm your father, too," I interjected. She just picked up her menu.

"We don't even look alike," Nikole said, still bewildered.

"Well, both of you take after your mothers. I must have recessive genes. Casey is tall and slim with distinct curves like her mother. And you're petite with golden hair and skin and grey eyes like your mother. Nikole, you're black and Italian, and Casey is black and Lithuanian, so that has a lot to do with bone structure and appearance as well."

"Well, who taught her how to cook?" Casey asked.

"What?"

"Nikole can cook like it ain't nobody's business. Last I remember, you almost burned our apartment down when you tried to make homemade soup that one time."

ZION

I laughed remembering that night. "Must have been from her mother."

"And Food Network," Nikole chimed in, "but, where is Mom? Wouldn't she like to meet your other daughter?"

"Yeah, and I would love to meet the lady who found you to be a catch," Casey stated.

"Well, uh, she's at home. She didn't approve of the two of you meeting."

Both of my daughters crossed their arms and frowned their faces.

"Why not?" Nikole asked.

"She felt that Casey should stay in my past, and I didn't feel that way. So, uh… " I rubbed my head. "We've decided to get a divorce."

"Wait! What?"

"I'm sorry, but, Casey is important to me and—"

"Oh, please!" Casey started. "If I was so important, you would have found me a long time ago. The only reason why I'm here now is because you just so happened to come into the club where I work."

"Casey, you don't understand what kind of trouble I was in."

"And that's fine, but, don't use me as an excuse for why you're getting a divorce. Some other stuff was going on in that house. I was just the cherry on top of the cake. And why am I here anyway? In a few years, you won't even remember who I am."

"Casey, please don't say that. I'm actually trying here." I could see tears fill her eyes.

"I *buried* you, Dad. I buried you! I had no family. I had to stay with foster parents who didn't give a fuck about me. Do you know how badly I wanted to go to college?" Nikole put her head down. "But I couldn't go because my foster parents hadn't filed their taxes in years and refused to fill out a FAFSA 'cause they thought they would get caught. I started stripping at seventeen, when I graduated high school, so I could get my own place. I kept stripping, so I could go to school, but I never went. And because I never got a degree, I can't get a good enough job to leave the club. I understand that you're *trying,* but I heard somebody once say that 'trying is nothing but failing with honors.'" She got up from the table. "It is hard to raise somebody from the dead, especially after they've been dead for twenty years." And with that she walked out of the restaurant.

"You guys ready to order?" the waitress asked.

"Naw, I think we're just going to go."

Nikole and I got up and left the restaurant.

MICHAEL

It was 10:00 p.m., and Scarlet was knocked out cold in the bedroom. I was in my office feeling guilty as hell, but I was addicted. Oh, Jesus. On my computer screen were two gay guys fucking in a dorm room. I squirted a lil bit of lotion in my hand and just ent ahead and lubed up my dick. This boy was suckin' some other boys thang and it was getting my booty moist. I spread my legs and played with my balls a lil bit. Now when that boy gripped them sheets, I said *thwap, thwap, thwap*! Then, they did 69; my favorite position. I aint never *seen* my arm go so fast! My toes began to curl, and I started to arch my back. Then, in came *another* boy! I stood up and bent over my desk, and, as one boy fucked the other one's asshole, I put a small vibrator in mine. I'm a freak, I know. My knees were buckling and sweat was dripping all over my po' lil keyboard. When that boy came, so did I. Don't ask me which one it was. It didn't matter. He squirted, then I squirted all over the floor and under my desk. I grabbed my penis and kept pulling at it until I couldn't cum anymore.

I cleaned up the mess and hurriedly typed in another website to get the two gay dudes off my screen. Lord, I couldn't let nobody see that gay mess! The first thing that popped in my head was Craigslist. Why, Jesus? I was sitting at the computer almost in tears, thinking about what I had just done. I was a married man, and I had a baby on the way; a baby! And there I was, still addicted to porn. I never wanted to say it out loud, but I was still gay. Late at night, I craved for a nice, hard one to be rammed into my ass until I begged him to stop. I was so frustrated, and masturbating wasn't doing it anymore. I was still horny. I looked at the screen. *Personals? No, I couldn't… but it wouldn't hurt to look… would it?*

I clicked on the link that said *Strictly Platonic*. "My Sexy Panties For Sale-W4M- 21", "Geek/Nerds I want to chat with someone I can learn from and vice versa - W4W - 28", "Heartbroken 32 blk man - M4W - 32"; those were some titles to the ads people were posting. I

Once Upon A Secret

clicked the back button and clicked on the *Men Seeking Men* link. "Ready to Suck Cock Now", "Vers needs some long pipe - M4M - 19", and "Your Feet in my Face - 28" were some of the titles of ads posted. I clicked on *Ready to Suck Cock Now*. The ad read: *Suck your cock while you sit back and enjoy. No recip. necessary. Love to swallow your sweet load while you pump it in my mouth and throat. READY NOW, no BS or games. Hit me up if interested, discreet home and neighborhood. Black, White, Latino, hairy, uncut all +++++*. I swallowed hard and clicked on the anonymous e-mail at the top left. I thought for a moment, *What would Scarlet think if she found out? What would my father think?* I started typing, "To whom it may concern." I erased that. "Hey, looking for a onetime thing. Your place, really discreet. Are you interested?"

I looked it over and then pressed send. I was wishing I could get the e-mail back when I got a reply.

"Can you come now?"

Now? I looked at the clock at the bottom right-hand corner of the screen. 11:10 p.m.

"What's your address?"

A tear came to my eyes. What was I doing? I love Scarlet. I love Scarlet. I love Scarlet. I said over and over again.

"Seventy-five Manteo St., Portsmouth, VA."

My tears fell as I replied: "OMW."

I grabbed my keys and left out the door.

ZION

Nikole

I'm pretty sure I was sending the twenty-fifth apologetic text message to Byron's phone. And I wasn't anticipating a reply, but I *was* hoping for one. I couldn't remember the last time I ate. Yasmine was so worried about me that sometimes, I found her just staring at me. She would even sneak food out of the café and beg me to eat it. In the midst of being ignored by my best friend, I wasn't even acknowledging the fact that my parents were getting divorced. I don't know the last time I went to class. I hardly left the room. The only time I did was when Yasmine begged me to take a shower because I was stinking up the room.

My phone began to ring. It was Byron.

"Hello."

"Yo."

"Hey."

"Hey." There was an awkward silence.

"I'm glad you called."

He exhaled deeply. "I don't know why I care about you, but I do. But I don't wanna protect somebody who don't want protecting."

"Okay."

"You know, if you were any other girl, I wouldn't even be talking to you right now?"

"Yeah, I know," I said with a smile.

"Please, Nikole. Please promise me you'll stop doing all of this craziness."

"I promise, Byron. I'll never strip or fuck again!" Yasmine lifted her head up.

"We'll see. We never did go out to lunch."

"Naw, we didn't."

"So you wanna go out now?"

"Now? Like right now?"

"Now what?" Yasmine asked, trying to figure out what was going on.

"Well, I'm at the crib, so in thirty to forty-five minutes?"

"Uh, yeah!" I said a little too excited. I was hoping he couldn't hear it in my voice, but he did, and he laughed.

"A'ight. I'm on my way."

"Okay." I hung up the phone with a wide smile on my face.

"What?" Yasmine asked.

"He's on his way to take me out to lunch."

I jumped up out of the bed and ran to the shower. In about thirty minutes, I had on a cute sweater dress. My hair and makeup were done, and I was in my jewelry box looking for some cute accessories.

"I'm glad he finally called you. You were looking rough before. You look like a new woman now."

I laughed, and my phone rang. It was Byron.

"Hello."

"I'm downstairs."

"Okay." I looked at Yasmine. "I'll see you later," I said with a smile.

"Mm hmm."

I met Byron in the lobby, and the girls that were just sitting around started gawking at us.

ZION

"Why are they looking at us?" Byron whispered.

"You tend to draw attention." I said. Byron was sexy, but I don't think he thought so. That didn't matter because every girl thought he was, and they threw themselves at him every chance they got.

"Let's go," he said, and I followed him out the door. When we were in the truck, I asked, "So, where are we going?"

"Where do you wanna go?"

"I don't care."

"That's what I thought. You wanna go to Olive Garden?"

"Olive Garden? Oh, you fancy, huh?" He made a face, and I laughed. "Yeah, let's go to the Olive Garden." I looked at what he was wearing—a black sweater with a purple shirt underneath and a black and purple tie, black pants and black shoes. "Besides, we look too good for McDonald's."

He laughed. When we got to Olive Garden, he opened the door for me, and I smiled as I walked into the restaurant.

"How many?" the hostess asked.

"Two," I said.

"Okay. Right this way." She led us to a table in a corner and handed us our menus. "Your server will be Reba, and she will be with you shortly."

"Okay." I looked at the drink menu and started to lick my lips at the different types of alcohol listed.

"Whatchu gonna get?" Byron asked.

"Um, I dunno. I was actually looking at these drinks, trying to figure out which one I wanted."

He eyeballed me. "Alcohol?"

I lowered my menu. "Yes."

"You don't need alcohol."

"Why?"

"Because you don't. What benefit is it giving you?"

"It tastes good."

He frowned at me.

"Okay. I won't drink." I picked my menu back up. "I'll get lemonade instead." The waitress came to the table.

"Hey, guys. How are you doing today?"

"Good," I replied.

"Great. Can I start you two off with some drinks?"

"Water," Byron answered.

"Strawberry lemonade," I said.

"Okay, and are you two ready to order?"

"Um, we need a little more time," Byron answered.

"Okay, that's fine. I'll be back with your drinks," and she headed back to the kitchen. There was a terrible, awkward silence while we looked at our menus, so I decided to break it.

"So."

He looked up at me. "What?"

"Why did you call me?"

"Because I'm your friend and I care about you and what you do." I looked down. "How many people told you that stripping wasn't a good idea?"

"Two. You and Yasmine."

"And if I wasn't your friend, it would have been only one."

"Right."

"Can you imagine going through life with only *one* real friend?"

I thought about that. "No."

"Neither can I." He sat back in his chair and picked up his menu.

"You know, I was expecting to never hear from you again."

"Hmm." He grunted without lifting his eyes.

"But I'm glad I did." We ordered our food and spent the rest of dinner talking about pleasant things like goals and ambitions.

"So, I took the ASVAB."

"Really?"

"Yeah."

"So."

"So I'm going in the navy."

"Oh, my gosh! Why are we not drinking to that? That is amazing. I am so proud of you, Precious!"

He smiled a wide smile. "Thank you."

"So when do you start basic training?"

"I don't know. They'll let me know."

I could not stop smiling. I was so proud of my friend. He said he was going to do something, and he did it. Now, all I had to do was decide on what to do and do it.

Scarlet

"Scarlet, are you ready to go?" Brittany was calling me from the living room of my apartment.

Once Upon A Secret

"Hold on. I have to transfer some money into my account," I answered as I waddled into Michael's office. I was starting to waddle at four months, and I was hating it and loving it at the same time. I hated walking like a fat penguin, but I had started to accept the life that was growing inside of me, and I loved it nonetheless. I sat at the chair and moved the mouse. His e-mail popped up. There was an e-mail from Clarisa, the lady who monitored his clothing line's sales. I clicked on it.

MIKEY,

UNFORTUNATELY, YOUR CLOTHING LINE ISN'T DOING SO WELL IN THE DEPARTMENT STORES WE'VE CHOSEN, SO I THINK IT WOULD BE BEST IF WE SEND THE LINE INTO STORES SUCH AS WAL-MART AND K-MART. I CAN UNDERSTAND HOW THIS CAN BE FRUSTRATING WITH THE NEW EXTENSION TO YOUR FAMILY AND ALL, BUT I THINK IT'S BEST THAT WE TRY TO FIND A WAY FOR YOU TO KEEP MAKING MONEY.

PLEASE CALL ME WITH ANY QUESTIONS.

I was infuriated. We were married, and that was the sort of thing that married people talk about with *each other*. I quickly went to NavyFederal.com and checked his account. We still had more than enough money to pay our bills. I transferred $100 into my account and logged off.

"What's wrong, sweetie?" Brittany asked when I stormed into the living room.

ZION

"Nothing. You ready to go?"

"Sure." She grabbed her coat and purse, and we were out the door. We had a great mother/daughter day and went out to lunch and perused around a few stores. At around 7 p.m., she dropped me off at home, and I went into the apartment.

"Hey, babe," Michael said as he sorted through the mail. I instantly recalled the e-mail and became pissed all over again.

"Don't you *hey, babe* me!" I slammed my purse onto the couch.

"What's wrong?"

"*What's wrong*? I checked your e-mail today, Michael."

"Oh, no!" Tears came to his eyes, and I crossed my arms.

"So explain it to me."

"Okay, Scarlet. Just sit down."

I began to pace. "No, I'll stand. Because I want to know how you could hide something *this big* from me. I'm your *wife*, Michael!"

"I know, and I'm sorry."

"Oh, you think you're sorry now, but you just wait."

"Scarlet, please don't leave me!" I guess that should have made me curious, but I was so upset that I just fed into it.

"I think I might consider that. I am carrying a child, *your* child, and you go and keep a secret *this big* from *me*. Me. Of all people who have loved you unconditionally since the day we met in that library at school."

"I know, and I am so sorry."

Once Upon A Secret

"So how long has this been going on?"

And that was when he blurted it out, "Only a couple of days, I swear. I thought those feelings had passed the first night we made love, but they haven't. I've just been suppressing them deep inside, and, Thursday night, I found myself replying to an ad on Craigslist. And I kept saying, 'What would Scarlet say if she found out?' But it was as if I couldn't stop myself. The ad said that all he wanted to do was suck dick, and that's all I went over there for, but... that wasn't enough. And... I had sex... with a man... and I don't even know his name."

I plopped onto the couch, and Michael dropped to his knees, face full of tears, and begged, "Please, please, please, Scarlet. Please forgive me. I love you, and I can't live without you." He put his hands on my knees, and I looked him in his sad, pathetic eyes. "Please say *something*!"

"I was talking about your clothing line. What are you talking about?" He just looked up at me.

"Um."

"Um? Michael, you *fucked* another man?" Before he could respond, I punched him in his left eye. "What the fuck is wrong with you?" I stood. "Am I not good enough for you? Do I need to have a dick for you to love me?"

"No, baby, you're perfect—"

"Perfect? *Perfect*! 'Perfect,' says my gay husband. 'Perfect,' says the man who had a dick rammed up his ass for the past few days! 'Perfect,' says my baby's father! *Perfect*? I don't think so. You can keep your ass here, by yourself with your gay lover. I'm going to my parents' house."

"Please." He grabbed my ankle, and I kicked him off.

"Leave me alone, Michael!"

I turned and tried to walk toward the bedroom, but he grabbed my ankle again. That time, he pulled too hard, and I fell flat on my stomach. I looked at him.

"What did you do?"

We both looked down, and the floor was rapidly covering in blood.

"*What did you do?*" I screamed.

The ambulance was called, and they rushed me to the hospital, and, in two hours, we discovered our baby girl didn't make it.

"Scarlet." Michael was by the bed, crying, and I just stared up into the ceiling, "Baby… "

"Don't call me that."

"Scarlet."

"Leave."

"But, please, just let me explain." And that was when the tears began to flow in hot waterfalls down the sides of my face and puddle in my ears. "Oh, baby, please don't cry. I'm so sorry." He bent over me and tried to hold me. "I'm so, so sorry."

"*Get… off… me!*" I yelled as loud as I could. He moved back. "Michael, please leave."

I closed my eyes, and the last sounds I heard were my hospital room door closing. That night, I cried and cried. I had gone from not wanting a baby to dreaming about raising her. I knew she was a girl. I knew it in my heart, and she was. She would have been the prettiest baby ever. My thick hair and pretty eyes, and

Once Upon A Secret

her daddy's nose and beautiful skin. I had dreamed of the day I would see her and hold her and teach her to read and count and spell her name. But in an instant, my selfish, gay husband ruined it all. My *gay* husband.

Casey

Saturday morning, I was trying to find the nerve to go to Mrs. Twine's funeral. I knew she had left me something, but that didn't give me any motivation to go. I think I was so nervous because the last person I buried had risen from the dead. I looked at myself in the mirror. I had taken a shower, put on makeup and jewelry, but no clothes. I looked even closer. It was just the previous month; I wouldn't look at myself in the mirror because I was ashamed of myself, ashamed of what my father might think. But was I still ashamed? I did the best I could to take care of *me*. I shouldn't be ashamed. And my father's opinion shouldn't matter. He had left, proudly if you ask me. Never even rode through town to see if I was okay. If he had, then he would have seen my shitty life and tried to fix it. No, he had another little girl that he was *so* very proud of. Nikole.

Why did I cover for her that night at dinner? Why did I care if her father found out that she worked at the strip club? Maybe it was his fault. Maybe, if he would have raised her right, she wouldn't be shakin' her ass for dollars. I shook my head. I knew I was wrong.

ZION

Aside from leaving me stranded, my daddy was the best father any girl could ask for.

Suddenly, there was a knock at the door. I grabbed my robe, covered myself, and, without checking my peephole, opened the door.

"Hey," my dad said, standing there in a suit.

"What the hell are you doing here?"

"Casey, please. Can I come in?"

I opened the door for him to come inside. He looked around at all of the clutter. "This is a nice place you have."

"Thanks." I shut the door and led the way to the couch. "Have a seat."

"Okay." He sat.

"So, how did you find out where I lived?"

"I followed you home from the club last night."

"Right. I'm sure that consumed a lot of gas."

"You're worth it."

"Am I?"

"What do you mean?"

"Nothing."

He looked me up and down. "Were you going somewhere?"

"Yes... no... I don't know."

"What's wrong?"

I took a deep breath. "My neighbor, Mrs. Twine, was the only person in the world who gave two shits about me. She would come over every night before I left for work and pray for me. And every two or three days, she would cook for me to make sure I stayed healthy." A tear rolled down my face. "She died earlier this week, and her funeral is today."

Once Upon A Secret

"I'm so sorry to hear that."

"Yeah, well, I don't know if I'm going to go or not because… " It got too hard to talk at that moment.

"Aww, Casey." Dad stood up and hugged me. "I can see why funerals would be hard for you to go to, but it sounds like this lady meant a lot to you."

"Yeah, I didn't even realize how much."

"Well, I think you should go to pay your respects. Well, I'm pretty sure my opinion doesn't matter to you." He let go of me and took a few steps back. "But, uh, the reason why I came over here today is because you left so fast from the restaurant that I never got to tell you that I'm proud of you." I couldn't stop crying. "I know you probably don't want to hear this right now, but you mean a lot to me, and I did what I had to do to keep you safe. If those guys were going to kill me, what do you think they would have done to you? Well, whether you care or not, I just want to say that I'm not mad that you're a stripper. I understand that you had to do what you had to do to survive, and I commend you for that. But, uh, I talked to my boss, and he said he would hire you as a secretary."

I looked up at him.

"I live in Virginia Beach, but I work in Norfolk. I know that's a long drive from Williamsburg to Norfolk, so I actually found some places that you might be able to afford." He reached in his pocket and pulled out about four apartment ads from *Apartment Guide* magazine and handed them to me. I took them. "And I know this is asking a lot, but I would be the happiest man on earth if you took the job and moved to Norfolk and possibly started school. And, if I turn out to be a waste of your time or if you ever feel like I am neglecting you, you can come back to Williamsburg and continue stripping in Richmond."

I looked at him and the eagerness and intent he had on his face and I smiled. "School does sound good." We hugged again. "I think I will go to Mrs. Twines' funeral. And, if you're not doing anything else, could you go with me?"

"Of course!" he replied. I ran in my room and threw on my dress and heels. I don't think I'd ever been more excited to go anywhere in my life.

The funeral was a graveside service, and, when we got to the casket, I was shocked to see only three people there; her daughter, her lawyer, and her pastor.

"Who is he?" she barked when she saw my father.

"My father."

"This funeral is invitation only."

"And I invited him. What's the big deal?"

The lady shook her head. "Come on, pastor. Let's start." The pastor opened in prayer, preached a five-minute message, and then opened the floor for anyone to say any words.

"Well—"

"Mmm mmm." Mrs. Twine's daughter cut me off. "We don't have time for all of that. I got a plane to catch. Go ahead, pastor."

We all looked at each other in disbelief at her attitude toward her mother.

"Come on, pastor!"

The pastor concluded the service, and the casket was lowered into the ground. The daughter gave Mr. Jackson a look, and he opened a leather pop-out folder.

"Okay, I will read Mrs. Regina Twine's last will and testament. To my daughter, Donia, I leave you one million dollars and my home in Fernwood Farms. Also, everything inside the house belongs to you and everything inside my apartment."

My mouth dropped. I didn't even know Mrs. Twine had one million dollars to throw around. Nor did I know she had multiple homes.

"And to Casey, the daughter I never had."

"What?" Donia shouted.

"I leave you everything that is left in my bank accounts, all of my stocks, my Atlanta home, and The Niño, my very lucrative restaurant in Atlanta. Over the years, I have hired people to run it, and I have had no need to work in the restaurant. But, if you want to, you are more than welcome. Now there is no excuse for you to stay where you are."

I smiled at my dad.

"I can't believe this!" Donia ranted. "I'm her daughter, and all I get is a measly million dollars? Thanks, Mom." And, with that, she grabbed her purse and headed to her Lincoln Town Car and waiting driver.

"Well, Ms. Lovette, I'm sure you will take care of what you have."

"Yes, sir. I will."

ZION

Jen

"Hey, Nikole, can you come here for a minute?" Paris was out job hunting, so I thought that that was a good time to ask Nikole something.

"What's up?" she asked as she sat next to me on the couch.

"Do you know how much your boss pays his porn directors?"

"Oh, I don't know. Why?"

"Because you know I got fired from Consequences, and I need a new source of income."

"So now you want to do porn?"

"Yeah."

"Oh, my God. Jen, you have so much potential. Use your getting fired as inspiration. Maybe you should write a book. You have so many great stories that are real-life, personal experiences."

"Uh, that sounds like something you would do. Not me. Can you just talk to him and ask him if he could use me sometime soon. I don't want my bank account to get too low."

"Alright," she sighed heavily. "I have to see him today, so I'll call him, and we can ride together."

"Okay, cool. But, uh, you're talking about me having potential. Didn't you tell Byron you were going to stop doing this stuff?"

She glared at me. "I broke up with Lonnie, and I quit the club. But Jermaine just rehired me. I can't just quit now. I have to wait for the right moment."

Once Upon A Secret

"Right," I said sarcastically. She pulled out her cell phone and called her boss.

"Hello. Hey, Jermaine. I was wondering if you needed a female for today. My friend is interested. Yeah… I know… Well, she'll do that on Monday, but, if you like her, maybe you can work with her more. She lost her job at the strip club and is looking for work… okay… alright. Thanks. Bye."

"So?"

"He said he usually wouldn't do this, because you need to get tested first, but, he had someone call out at the last minute today and could use you."

"Oh, great."

"Yeah, so go ahead and get ready and let's go."

"A'ight." I ran in my room and found a pair of black tights and a gray and red NBA sweatshirt. I put on my red and black Patrick Ewings, pulled my hair back into a ponytail, put on my big hoop earrings and was ready to go.

Nikole and I pulled up to a house that was literally up the street from our parents' houses. We went inside, and I immediately recognized Jermaine.

"Well, hello," he said.

"Hey." We hugged, and he whispered in my ear.

"Nice to see you with your clothes on."

"Same to you," I whispered back, and we laughed.

The last time I saw Jermaine, he was wearing nothing but a pair of boxers, standing in my foyer. And I was nude, standing in the downstairs hallway.

"Okay, well, we're going to do a scene upstairs with Carl. He's new as well. But," he looked at Nikole, "I'm not directing this one."

ZION

"That's fine. Can I meet him?" I asked.

"Actually, it's a *her*," Jermaine said.

"Oh, I can't imagine a female porn director."

"Yeah, she should be here any minute."

At that very moment, the front door flew open, and I heard a woman behind me say, "Sorry, I'm late. I've been doing a lot of running around today."

I turned around, and my mouth dropped. "Fish?"

"Jen?"

"Yeah, I kinda thought this would be awkward," Jermaine said.

"Wait," Nikole started, confused. "How do you two know each other?"

"We used to date," I replied. "She's Cat Woman."

"Oh."

"What are you doing here?" Charlotte asked.

"I'm going to do a movie today."

"Oh, which one?"

"Apparently yours."

"Oh, okay. Well, I'll meet you upstairs," and, with that, she went down the hall, and I heard a door shut.

"Wow," Nikole replied.

"Yep," Jermaine stated.

"So," I chimed in, "is there a costume or makeup person or something?"

"Yeah, just go straight upstairs."

I went upstairs, and that was when I met Erin and Ashley. Ashley dressed me in a sheer yellow teddy, and Erin just applied some foundation and eyeliner. Carl walked in wearing a pair of boxers.

"Is this it?" he asked.

"Yup," Ashley said. I had to admit that he was pretty handsome with a low cut and waves. He looked at me and smiled, and I saw every tooth was lined up perfectly, and each one was pearly white.

"How you doing?"

"Good."

"You ready for this?"

I inhaled deeply, "As ready as I'll ever be."

"Cool." He winked at me and walked out.

"Isn't he gorgeous?" Ashley asked us.

"Damn straight," I said.

"You're gonna enjoy fucking him," Erin replied, and we all laughed.

Nikole came in the room. "You ready?"

"Yeah."

"Okay, well, come in the other room, and I'll get you started."

I got up and followed her across the hall.

"Okay, so basically, Carl is going to be lying in his bed, and he's going to start masturbating. You are going to be coming to his room because you had a nightmare and you want to sleep with him. You're going to stand at the foot of the bed and watch him, and he's not going to notice you. When he does, you take over the jerking off, finish that, lay on the bed, order him to take your clothes off, and then you can feel your way through the rest."

"Gotcha."

"Okay, you stay in the hall, and Charlotte will be right up." I stood up against the wall and patiently waited. The last time I had seen Fish, she was proposing to me. That was in January. Now, here we

ZION

were about to work together on a film. I was angry and nervous at the same time. But I was also feeling those same feelings I had when we were together. I had fallen in love with Fish, and she had trampled on my heart. I thought I would never see her again, but here we were.

Fish came up the stairs and looked at me.

"You'll stay here until your cue. This will be about a minute into Carl jerking off."

"Okay." She started to walk into the room. As she did, I said, "I like your hair." She had about twenty-four inch long Indian Remy hair in. When we were dating, she rocked a 'fro. Now, she was wearing a weave.

"Thanks," she said and smiled. I heard some muttering going on in the room and then, "Action!" I peeped into the room and saw Carl lying in the bed, tossing and turning. He looked at the doorway. I guess to see if "anybody was there," and then he laid back in the bed, pulled off his boxers, and began to play with his penis. He put a few pumps of lotion into his hand and began to jerk slowly at first and then sped up his rhythm. I walked in the room and watched him. Then, I stood at the foot of the bed and watched him bite his lip and grab his bedsheets. He opened his eyes and saw me. He jumped up.

"Uh, uh, it's not what it… I mean—"

I crawled into the bed next to him. "It's okay. Let me finish that for you." I closed my hands on his shaft and began to stroke it slowly up and down.

In only a few moments, he hollered out, "I'm going to cum." And he came all over my hands. I licked the cum off and lay on the bed.

"Undress me."

"What?"

"You heard me. Do it."

The teddy clasped in the front, and he undid it, and I sat up. He pulled the spaghetti straps off my shoulders and threw the teddy onto the floor. I laid back down and lifted my hips and pulled off my thong.

"Lay down." He did, and I climbed off the bed. "Now close your eyes." He followed my instructions. I reached under the bed and pulled out some handcuffs. I handcuffed both of his ankles to the footboard and both of his wrists to the headboard. "I'm not going to hurt you. Well, maybe just a little."

I stood over him with one foot on each side of his torso and my butt pointed toward his face. I bent over with my ass in the air and kissed the head of his cock. It throbbed a little as I bent down and began to suck it with my pussy in his face but still too far away for his tongue to reach. It didn't take long for him to cum in my mouth, and I opened wide for the camera to see before taking a large swallow.

I turned around and smiled at my victim. I bent over and put a nipple right up against his lips. Without hesitation, he stuck his tongue out and flicked it back and forth, making my nipple hard. I moaned out a little, and I let him suck a little more. After a few more seconds, I brought my legs up by his head and hovered my pussy right over his mouth. I looked into his eyes,

ZION

"Your turn," I said and lowered myself onto his mouth. At first, he licked my labia and got my lips nice and wet. Then, he used his tongue to burrow into my slit and licked my clit. I moaned loudly as I remembered the first time Charlotte had eaten me out. I cut my eyes at her, and she was looking at me. I had known before I even walked in the room that I had to give her a show. I arched my back and moaned louder. I was riding his face and screaming until I came, and it was dripping in his mouth. When I was able to move, I sat back on his stomach and licked my pussy juices off of his face.

"Mmm," I moaned. I slid my body backward until I could feel his penis at my opening. I looked at him. "Are you ready?"

He nodded, and I sat on his fully erect penis. We both moaned in excitement. I lifted my hips off of his pelvis and then drove them down again. I felt him fucking me back, and when our bodies met, he went in deeper and deeper. I quickened my pace, and my pussy was squeezing his cock all over. We fucked hard, and I didn't bother to hide my screams. We were covered in sweat, and I was feeling so good that my eyes were rolling back in my head. I was riding him even harder, and he exploded inside of me. I screamed as I came at the same time.

When my shaking had stopped, I looked down at him.

"Did it hurt?"

He shook his head, and I smiled.

"Good." And I left out of the room, leaving him there.

"Cut!" Fish yelled. "Alright. That was good you two. Go ahead and get changed." Ashley brought me a rag, and I washed in the bathroom before putting my clothes back on. Once I was fully dressed, Carl approached me.

"Hey."

"Hey."

"You were really good in there," he said, obviously trying to make conversation.

"Well, you weren't too shabby yourself."

"Well, I don't know if I'm breaking a code or anything, but would you like to go out sometime?"

"Uh," I had no intentions of going out with this man, but I said, "Sure." I gave him my phone, and he put his number in. "Call me whenever you're ready."

"Okay." We both walked downstairs, and Nikole met us with envelopes.

"Here is your pay, and we'll call you the next time we want to use you. But it's always good to call us and let us know that you're available. You know, remind us that you exist. And you're both free to go."

Carl left, and I sat on the steps while Nikole finished up her meeting with Fish and Jermaine. When the office door opened, I stood up. Fish walked toward me.

"So, Jen, how terrible would it be if we did some catching up?"

"What do you mean?" I said as I adjusted my sweatshirt.

"I mean, let's hang out, and I'll take you home."

I thought about it for a moment and then said, "Okay."

She smiled from ear to ear. "Let's go."

ZION

I looked at Nikole. "I guess I'll see you later."

Charlotte took me to her house, claiming that she had to change clothes. I sat in the living room as I waited and remembered all of the things that had just happened the previous year...

"Hey, Jen. Can you come here for a minute?" I went up to Charlotte's room, and she was completely naked, holding two dresses. "Which one should I wear?"

"Uh, neither."

She smiled, assuming I was flirting with her.

"I'm dressed like a bum; I don't think you should be dressed like *Project Runway*."

"Oh," she said, and her smile diminished.

"You look good."

She looked up at me. "Thank you." She laid the dresses on the bed. "Jen, I never got to apologize for what I did to you and how I treated you."

"You're good."

"No, I'm not." She stepped close to me, still naked. "I didn't recognize that you were the one person in the world who loved me more than anybody. I think about you every day and every night. You can't tell me that you don't still think about me."

"No, I don't," I lied.

"Oh, well, okay." She walked toward her closet that was in her bathroom. "I'll find some jeans and T-shirt, and we can go out."

"It's too cold out for a T-shirt," I hollered to her as I sat on the bed. I had missed Fish. I really had. And sitting on the bed and seeing her naked was doing nothing but reminding me of what we used to have and making me horny. She came out of the bathroom, still naked, and headed out of the room.

"I'm going to go check the laundry room for my sweatshirts and sweat pants."

I don't know what I was thinking, but I took off my clothes and laid on the bed. Charlotte came back up, still naked.

"I still can't find—"

She stopped speaking when she saw me. I put two fingers in my mouth and let my tongue coat them with saliva. Then, I put my fingers down on my vagina and moved them up and down, paying special attention to my clit. Charlotte ran to the bed and was on top of me so fast that it almost scared the wind out of me. She held my left hand down with her right one and kissed me while playing with my right breast. Fish took one of my nipples between her lips and sucked it, using her tongue to flick it again and again. I moaned. I remembered how much I loved her tongue as it licked all over both of my nipples. I was fingering myself as deep as I could with my two fingers. Fish let go of my left hand, and I grabbed her breast and put it in my mouth. She moaned. I pulled my fingers from my pussy and put them in her mouth. She licked them, sucking all of my juices off my skin. Then, she put her fingers deep inside me and fingered me as she sucked on my nipples. My abs tightened, and I jerked up as my whole body shook. I came all over my ex's fingers. She pulled her hand out, and I licked my cum off it.

My eyes were closed, but when I opened them, I looked Charlotte dead in hers and flipped her onto her back. I spread her legs, and almost immediately, my tongue was deep inside her pussy. She whimpered with each motion of my tongue inside of her. I pulled my tongue out of her hole and swirled and flicked on her hard clit while I had my index finger inside of her. I looked up, and her back was arched, and she was moaning louder. As I sucked on her clit, I inserted another finger and moved faster. And it wasn't long before she sat straight up in ecstasy, pulled my hair and screamed as loud as she could.

I had never had Fish cum this much in my mouth. She was pulling my head into her pussy, and I kept lapping like a dog.

She yelled out, "Fuck!" And then fell back on the bed. I stopped licking her and looked into her face. Her eyes were closed, and she was still shaking a little. I kissed her on her lips and laid next to her. I couldn't believe I had done that. I thought I was over her, but obviously I wasn't.

Nikole

It was a Sunday night, and I had gone to the club to formally tell Jerry that I could no longer work for him.

"I understand," he said. "A strip club is not for everybody."

"Thank you so much for understanding and thanks for the opportunity. I can't say I didn't learn anything while I was here." He gave me a hug, and I started to leave when I saw Casey come from the dressing room.

She wasn't in costume, though, just a pair of jeans and a coat. I smiled at her and headed for the door.

"Hey, Nikki!"

I turned around. "Yeah."

"Why don't you have a drink with me?"

"Okay." I sat at the bar, and Tori served us one tequila shot each.

"So, you quitting this place?"

"Yeah, I have dreams and goals, and I think I should actually go for them. Thanks to this job, I'm out of debt, so there are no more excuses, right?"

"Right." We toasted our shot glasses and knocked them back. "So what *are* your dreams and goals?"

"Well, after college, I plan to move to Atlanta and go on as many auditions as possible and try to make it. Plan B is to work in a salon and one day own a salon. But I do have a dream of owning a restaurant; I just… don't know where that fits in my plans." Casey gave me this awkward look, as if I were the answer to her prayers. "What about you?"

"Well, mine are not as extravagant as yours, but I want to move to Norfolk, go to Tidewater Community College and, from there… be somebody. And actually develop a relationship with my father."

I smiled. "You know, he's actually a great guy."

She looked down into her empty shot glass. "Yeah, I know."

"You wanna know what my greatest fear is?"

"What?"

"That I won't be successful. That I'll be the kid that tried but never… made it. I have dreams, but I don't wanna waste my time chasing a dream that might not ever come true."

"How will you know unless you try?"

I looked away. "Yeah, that's what I tell myself every day."

"Can I ask you something?"

"Yeah," I looked at her.

"If you got a million dollars today, right now, what would you do first?"

I laughed. "Thank God! But I think I'd start that restaurant."

"Why not invest it into your acting career?"

"Well, acting is my passion, but it's unstable. My biggest fear is that I won't be successful. With a million dollars, I'd own a successful restaurant. You know, have something to leave for my kids."

She smiled at me. "You know, you're a smart kid."

"Yeah, that's what they tell me."

"There's something I want to give you, but you can't see it now."

"What?"

She reached into her purse and pulled out some papers. "As of yesterday, I own this restaurant in Atlanta. But I don't know how to run a restaurant, and I don't want to." I looked at her, wide-eyed. "But I believe you can do it if you want to." She smiled at me. "When are you scheduled to graduate?"

"Twenty-fourteen."

"Well, May 2014, you will own your own restaurant as my graduation present to you."

"Are you serious?"

"Yeah. I don't know anything about cooking. But you, you can cook like a slave who's scared she's gonna get whooped if the food ain't good!"

I laughed. "Why are you doing this for me?"

She shrugged her shoulders. "What are sisters for?"

I smiled and hugged her as hard as I could. "Thank you so much!"

CHARLOTTE

I had invited Paris back over to my house for an apology dinner. After a few days of leaving voicemails and sending text messages, she finally replied and said yes. I cooked some zesty Italian chicken, white rice, and fixed a tossed salad—something simple. The candles on the table and all around my bedroom were lit, and I had on a black leather dress with my leather pumps. I looked out of the window and saw Paris pulling up, so I hurriedly poured two glasses of wine and fixed two plates. When I had finished, she still wasn't inside. Looking out of the window, I saw that she was still sitting in the car. *What is she doing?*

ZION

Paris

I saw Charlotte trying to discreetly look out of her *sheer* curtains. I hadn't gotten out of the car because I was still asking myself, *Is this right?* I was confident that things would be good between Charlotte and me for a few months, but then she would go back to drinking and cheating with Carl Krisby. I put my hands on my keys to start the engine, but then I thought, *What could one dinner hurt?*

I still had my key, so I let myself in. It smelled good in the house. I didn't even know Charlotte could cook. I walked through the foyer, past the steps, through the living room, and into the kitchen. The lights were down low, and the candles were lit. Charlotte walked over to me with two wine glasses; she gave me one.

"Hey, baby. I miss you."

"Hey," I said as she pecked me on the lips. We both sat at the table and I looked at the food. "So who did you get to cook?"

She laughed. "*I* cooked."

I just looked at her. "You *never* cooked the whole time we were together."

"Well, I can. I just don't like to."

"Oh." I took a bite of the chicken, and it was surprisingly good. We ate in silence for a while and then she blurted out, "So how have you been?"

"Good."

"You enjoy living with your parents?" she asked sarcastically.

I laughed. "Actually, I moved in with Jen."

CHARLOTTE

I dropped my fork and started choking on my rice.

"Drink some wine!" Paris yelled. I knocked it back and cleared my throat.

"My ex, Jen?"

"Yeah, I saw her at the Johanson's party, and I told her about us, and she offered for me to stay in her apartment with her until I could find a job."

"Oh… so are you fucking her?"

"What?"

"I mean, we had that thing last year, and now you're living with her."

"Because you kicked me out!"

"You were staying with your parents! You had somewhere to live."

"So what are you implying? That I'm a whore?" And before I could answer, she said, "Well, you're a liar."

"What?"

"She didn't know about us."

"What are you talking about?"

"I told you, when we first got together, I would only move in if you told Jen about us. You said you did. Jen said you didn't." I didn't speak. "Are you going to say anything?"

"No. You caught me. But you would have done the same thing."

ZION

"No, I wouldn't."

"You wouldn't? You're dating somebody, and you really want to take it to the next level, but they say you have to get *permission* from your ex, someone you've let go of. You wouldn't have lied?"

"No, because she was *your* ex. She was *my* friend. And friends will be there, even when your girlfriend burns all of your clothes on the front lawn."

"Okay, can we move forward please? I brought you here tonight to apologize and ask you for a clean slate. I want this to work."

"Work toward what, Charlotte? I'm tired of going through the motions with you. What are we working toward? A year? Two years of dating?"

"No, marriage." I pulled a ring box from my lap and opened it. I got out of my chair and stood next to her. "Jen is my ex-girlfriend, but when I think of you, I think of my *wife*. My life was miserable when you were gone. I missed coming home and having the door opened before I could get my key put in. Or how you would push the hair away from my face when we kissed. Sometimes, in life, we make mistakes in who we decide to spend the rest of our lives with. Sometimes, we think we know better than God who our soul mates are. But, in all actuality, he picks the perfect people out for us, and we turn them away. Well, I'm sorry for turning you away." I took her hand. "Paris Chao, will you marry me?"

Once Upon A Secret

Paris

I stared at her in disbelief and took the ring out of the box. It was gorgeous. It had three diamonds on the silver band, the center one was the biggest. I looked at the inside of the band, and it said, *Love Always, Charlotte*. The Charlotte looked kind of funny, but I paid it no mind. I put the ring on my finger and smiled.

"Yes."

She looked at me, shocked. "You will?"

"Yes! Yes!" I stood up and kissed her. I think we both were the happiest women on earth that day. She got on her knees.

"Paris, I am so sorry for making you feel like you weren't loved and… ." I cut her off by lifting my skirt, and since I was conveniently not wearing any panties, I straddled her face, pulling my pussy lips apart.

CHARLOTTE

I stuck my tongue out, eager to taste Paris again. She lowered her pussy just onto the tip of my tongue. As I began to tongue the damp pussy in front of me, Paris held the back of my head hard against her mound. I looked up and could tell by the looks on Paris's face that she was enjoying the attention she was receiving. I continued to flap my tongue on her clit and threw myself into the task with added enthusiasm. Gradually,

ZION

I began to get three slick fingers working in and out of her pussy hole. And soon she had a massive orgasm. My face was covered in Paris' juices.

My lover helped me up and escorted me upstairs to my room. We both removed our clothes, and I went into my "party drawer" and pulled out my strap-on. I put it on and gave Paris the look. She got on her knees in front of me and began to lick and kiss the dildo. When the fake dick was covered in saliva, I pulled Paris up and pushed her onto the bed. I lined the dildo up with Paris's soaking slit, running it up and down a few times before plunging it in deep in one fluid motion. Paris's body rose off the bed with the rough intrusion. She had about eight inches of fake cock inside her as she relaxed back down onto the bed. As I began to pump in and out of her, Paris relaxed and moaned with pleasure.

While I was fucking her, I kissed and played with her breasts. Her nipples were nice and erect as I kissed and sucked them into my mouth. Paris tasted so sweet and so nice. I twirled my tongue around the nipples, switching between breasts. I looked up at my fiancée, and she was panting so much with the pounding she was getting. I grabbed her hair and heard her gasp in pleasure, and her hips began to rise off the bed to meet my thrusts. That was when she started yelling out curse words, and I increased my pace. It was obvious Paris was about to cum, and I picked her panties up off the floor and put them in her mouth as a gag. And when she came, it was amazing. As she came, her hips bucked up so fast and violently that she nearly knocked me off the bed.

Once Upon A Secret

Instead of pulling out, I left the dildo inside of my lover and kissed and held her. As Paris's breathing came back to normal, I withdrew my strap-on and laid on the bed. Paris helped me out of my toy and began to finger me. She kept adding more and more fingers, and I got worried. Then, she withdrew and took a tube out of the drawer in the nightstand. She spread the gel over my pussy and her fingers.

Again, she opened me up and got my pussy ready for the strap on, Paris pushed the dildo into me, and I exhaled deeply. She stroked slowly for a while and then pulled almost all of the way out and then forced the whole thing inside of me. I screamed out in pain, and she shoved her panties in my mouth. She kept slowly fucking me, and, as she picked up the pace, I found my pleasure increasing as my hips rose to meet her thrusts.

Paris

I was getting tired, so I took the strap-on off, but I used my hand to keep stroking Charlotte with the dildo. I paused only for a moment to lube up my other hand. I took the dildo out of Charlotte and lubed up her pussy. I put in three fingers at first and then four. And as I moved in and out, she was being stretched wider and wider. And then, I put my thumb in. I could feel my fiancée's pussy muscles tightening around my fist.

ZION

She grabbed my wrist and pulled me into her as she thrust her hips upward.

Soon, I had my whole fist in her and half of my forearm. I kept fisting her, punching her G-spot as she was approaching the biggest orgasm of her life. She came so hard, and her pussy was so tight that I couldn't move my fist if I wanted to. When Charlotte calmed down, I slowly removed my arm from her hole. She just looked at me.

"You've never done that before," she said.

"There's a lot I haven't done, but when we get married, I'll do them all." I kissed her and that night we fell asleep holding each other.

I was in Jermaine's office, meeting with him and Charlotte about our plans for that day. The website was a hit, and Jermaine was begging me to think of something new. We all had been there for an hour, and nobody had come up with anything.

"I got it!" I yelled. "Aliens!"

"What?" Jermaine said.

"Who watches porn the most?"

Jermaine and Charlotte looked at each other. "Men?"

"No. People without a sex life. And who doesn't have sex lives?"

"Nerds?"

"Yes! And what do nerds like?"

"Aliens!"

"Yes. How about an alien with tentacles who uses the tentacles to fuck a curious little human girl."

"I think that might work," Jermaine said. "Charlotte, you call Ashley and Erin and give them the rundown. Nikole, call Steve and see if he has any ideas. And I'll call some actors." We all got on our phones and started calling. Steve told me some really good ideas on how to decorate the backyard, so it looked like aliens had just landed.

Erin told Charlotte that she could do the makeup, but didn't know how to make the man look like he *really* had tentacles. And Ashley was excited about buying new costumes.

"Okay. Nobody's answering the phone," Jermaine said, "but I'm going to call my sister, Elicia. She studied costume and makeup at her school, and hopefully, she's in Virginia this month. She moves around a lot. Nikole, I found two guys, but can you keep calling the females to see if anybody can be here by six?"

"Okay."

Jermaine stepped out to make his phone call, and I continued calling the actors where he'd left off. Surprisingly, a majority of the numbers we had on file were disconnected, and the ones that weren't, nobody answered. I left voicemail after voicemail and sent text after text until I got to the end of the list.

"Nobody answered," I told Charlotte.

"Well, what about Jen?"

ZION

"No." I shook my head. "I asked her before I came here, and she said she had an interview in the morning, so she wouldn't be able to come."

Jermaine came back into the room. "So what's going on?"

"Nobody answered the phone."

"*Nobody?*"

I shook my head. He plopped down into the chair and bit his bottom lip as he thought for a moment. And then he looked at me.

"Why don't you do it?"

I looked at him. "Why don't *who* do it?"

"Nikole Turner, I have never needed you like I need you now."

"Why don't we just do it another day?"

"Because we are on a roll, and I don't want to lose my customers."

"Don't they pay per day?"

"*Exactly*! And lately we've been giving them something new every day and something *awesome,* at *least* once a week. I don't want them to log in and see the same old stuff and then not be motivated to log in for a few days. That's going to slow up our cash flow. So, please, I'm begging you." I put my head down. "I'll pay you your pay *plus* the actors' pay."

I sighed heavily. "I'll do it."

"Oh, thank God."

"But I won't be back after this."

"What?"

"I have a great guy in my life. And, even though he's just a friend, I'm pretty sure he's one of the only people on this earth who care about me. And I *promised* him I would stop stripping and filming porn." Charlotte and Jermaine's eyes grew wide. They didn't know I was stripping. "I didn't know how to tell you, but… that's it."

Jermaine took a deep breath. "I understand."

By 3:00, Erin, Ashley, Elicia and our two male actors had arrived and went upstairs to get made up and into costume. The men were wearing brown burlap pants and had their top halves, feet and calves painted a deep brown. I was curious, so I asked Elicia how she was going to make the guys into aliens.

"Well, first, I'm going to tape the guys' fingers together, and Erin and I are going to paint the whole hand the same color as the rest of the body. Look at this." She pulled out two big Ziploc bags filled with something. She opened the bag and pulled out some small diamond-shaped pieces. "This is some felt that I've cut to be the scales on the aliens. I chose felt because it's going to be dark outside, and, if I put something shiny on them, when the lights hit, it's going to reflect into the camera. Now, check these out." She picked up two long tentacles on two straps. "This is going to go on their backs. They'll wear it like a back pack, and the tentacles will hang off."

"But won't the straps show?"

"No, because I'm going to have them wearing these olive green leather vests."

"Oh, wow."

"Yeah," she looked at me. "You okay?"

"Yeah. Why?"

"You look nervous. You ever did this before?"

"No."

ZION

"Then, why are you doing it?"

"To help out your brother."

She shook her head. "If you didn't do it, he probably would be mad, right?" I nodded. "But, if you did do it, what happens to your future?" I just looked at her. "I mean… what do you see yourself doing? Who do you see yourself being?"

"Well, my plan A is to be an actress, plan B is to do hair and eventually open up my own chain of salons, and Plan C is to own my own restaurant."

"Okay, listen to your plans. If you become a successful actress, picture the headline on *The Enquirer*, 'Nikki T Sex Tape Found' or 'Guess Who Did Porn to Pay for College?'" She stared at me, "Do you see what I'm saying? You have to do what's best for *you*, not Jermaine." Just then, Ashley came in the room.

"Hey, Nikki! I found you a cute costume. Come try it on."

I looked at Elicia and then Ashley and back at Elicia. "I'm sorry," I mumbled and followed Ashley out the door.

Jen

I wanted to go with Nikole that night. God knows I needed the money. But, the next day, I had an interview with this modeling school for a teaching position. I kept thinking about the bishop's message that Sunday:

"You can't help 'em if you keep right on going after 'em. But, if you stop going after 'em and let 'em come to themselves! Uh uh, don't you go after 'em. I know he strung out right now, but let 'em keep getting high. Let 'em keep right on drinking. Let 'em keep on smoking. Let 'em keep on partyin'. Job said, I pray for my children because I don't know the mischief that they might be doing. Your job is to *pray… for… them*!"

And, after waking up next to Fish the other day, I knew somebody had been praying for me. I had "come to myself" and realized that I was better than my situation. I knew I was beautiful, but that didn't mean that any man in the world had the *right* to see my naked body. I was both mortified and angry with myself. So that was why, on that particular day, I opted to stay home.

At around 4:00, Paris came running through the door with a huge grin on her face.

"Well, who jumped in *your* panties?" I asked.

"Charlotte!"

"*Charlotte?*" I was shocked. I thought Paris and Fish were through.

"Yeah, she proposed!" She stuck her hand in my face, and, when I saw that ring, my bottom jaw hit my chest. "Now, I hope this doesn't come between us, Jen. I love you like a sister. And I know she proposed to you at one time, but I love her. *I really love her!*"

I stood up and looked at Paris. "Give me the ring."

"What?" She took a step back.

ZION

"I just want to see something."

She reluctantly handed me the ring, and I quickly went to the engraving; *Love Always, Charlotte.* The *Charlotte* looked a little funny, and I knew why.

"Okay, Paris, this is going to be hard to explain, but bear with me. Part of the reason why I didn't say yes to Fish was because I noticed that on the ring she gave me, it said, *Love Always, Kadeem.* Kadeem was her ex fiancée." Paris looked lost. "Kadeem proposed to Fish. She turned him down. Then, years later, she proposed to me with *the same ring,* and I turned her down. Now, she's proposing to you with the *same ring.*"

Paris took a step back. "I don't believe this."

"Yeah, I know. It's—"

"You would actually make up a story *that* ridiculous, just so I won't marry your ex-girlfriend."

"Paris, it's way more to it than that!"

"Charlotte *loves* me! Plus, she has enough money to buy *ten* fucking rings if she wanted to! Why would she keep reusing a ring some *man* gave her years ago?"

"Because that's how much she values us. We aren't worth a diamond ring that she would actually take the time to pick out. We are only good enough for what's left over."

"Oh, please, Jen! You are something else! Give me my ring back."

"Knowing Fish, she proposed to you the *exact* same way she proposed to me. Did she get down on one knee?"

"No." I didn't bother telling her that she had for me.

"Okay, when Charlotte proposed to me, she said some bullshit like, 'When you had hurt yourself, I didn't say, I hope Jen is alright, or I hope my girlfriend is okay. I said, what happened to my *wife*?'" Paris's eyes grew wide. "She went on to say that she couldn't live without me and some spiel about thinking we know better than God when it comes to finding our soul mates." Paris's eyes were tearing up. "Did she say that to you?" She nodded. "Paris, you can't marry her. She doesn't love you. She just wants somebody to be in that big house with her."

"I'm so stupid." She managed to say through sobs. I hugged her.

"No, you're not. You're in love." She cried on my shoulder and I looked at the ring, pissed.

Fuck you, Charlotte.

Scarlet

It was 5:00, and I was packing the last of my things to put in storage. After the incident, I told Michael that I wanted a divorce and I was moving out. I found a nice place closer to my job, but I couldn't move in till after Thanksgiving. So I put my things in storage and decided to move back in with Brittany and Jack until I was able to get the keys to my new place.

Michael had stayed in a hotel until I was completely moved out. I couldn't believe how quickly my life had changed in a day. I went from being a wife and expectant mother to single and without child. But I was mad at myself. Just the previous December, Michael was gay. But, in January, I had convinced him that he wasn't, and I had married a gay man. I should've known those gay feelings would come back again. I did this to myself, and I was finding myself getting a divorce and moving out.

Oh, if my mother could see me now, she would shake her head and say, "Scarlet, what in the hell is wrong with you?"

Nikole

It was 6:00, and the sun had already gone down. In the backyard, there were fog machines and lights, and both cameramen had to be on duty. I was upstairs in one of the bedrooms sitting on the bed. Nobody was in the house as I began to pray.

"Lord, I know that over the past month I haven't lived right, and I know you must be *so* disappointed in me. I apologize from the depths of my heart, and I rededicate my life to you. I need you now, more than ever, to come into my life and take charge. Satan, I rebuke you now. You no longer have authority over me or anything that I do. Jesus, I invite you into my heart, and I am forever yours. Amen." I opened my eyes, and Jesse was standing in the doorway.

"You didn't ask for forgiveness, you know?" He came and sat next to me on the bed.

"I don't think I'm worthy of forgiveness. I just want him to love me again."

"Nikole, he never stopped loving you. He's just been waiting for you to come back to him. But one thing God believes in is forgiveness."

I looked up at him. "Did you forgive Jordin?"

He sighed heavily. "No, but I will because she didn't cheat on me. She just got herself into a situation that she didn't see a way out of. And I don't approve of what she was doing, but I looked back at all of those times when I didn't know how the bills would get paid and Jordin's check would be conveniently big enough for us to handle it. If she wasn't doing what she was doing, I don't know what would have happened to us." He looked into my eyes. "I love her *so* much, and I hate living without her."

"You ready?" We both looked up, and Charlotte was standing there. Jesse squeezed my hand and then picked up his camera. I nodded and got under the covers. "Okay."

"Camera rolling," Jesse mumbled.

"Action!" Charlotte said into a walkie-talkie, and lights flickered outside my window. I hopped out of bed and ran over to see what it was. I put my shoes on and ran out of the room. "Cut!" Jesse and Charlotte went down to the bottom of the stairs, and I stood at the top.

"Still rolling."

"Action!" I ran down to the bottom of the stairs and headed to the back door. Once outside, there was a bright light shining in my face, and there was a heavy fog coming from the same place the light was coming

ZION

from. I put my arm up to protect my eyes, and, suddenly, the silhouette of a man came walking toward me. I turned to run, but there was another alien right there. I stood looking from one to the other until both of them grabbed me. I screamed, and they threw me down onto the lawn chair. I pulled my legs in close to me, and one of them grabbed my feet and pulled them out. I was trying to free my legs when the other one, all of a sudden, caressed my face.

That was when I calmed down. The alien that was holding my feet pointed a tentacle at my vagina, and I pulled my thong off. He let go of my feet and started to rub on my pussy lips. He separated them and started to put his tentacle in my hole. I jumped, and, when I turned my head, there was a penis in my face. I looked into the alien's eyes and then opened my mouth. He inserted his penis, held my head, and face fucked me while his alien friend was nearly fisting my vagina.

I had gagged about five times and had a tear rolling down my face when the two decided to change positions. I was encouraged to get on the ground in the doggy style position, and, before I knew it, my pussy was full of alien cock. I bit down on my bottom lip and moaned until I started to slurp on some alien dick. I was being doubly penetrated—one penis in both ends. The one in front of me was grunting and moaning, and his head was rolling from left to right. The one behind me was gripping my hips and thrusting hard into me.

And that was when he made a noise. It was all too familiar. I remember, the first time I heard it was from Professor Elmo. That sound meant that he was about to… and he did. He came all inside me, and I don't think I ever felt as bad as I did at that moment. And just as I was about to cry, I had another load being shot down my throat. I couldn't believe it. I was, at that moment, the definition of a cum dumpster.

But that wasn't it. The alien I was sucking laid down in the grass and pulled me onto him. I sat on his penis and leaned forward. Then the other one put his penis at my asshole and slowly began to insert it. I screamed out, and the one below me covered my mouth. I was held tightly at the hips as he kept slowly pushing in. I was taken over by so much pain that I was pulling the grass up by the roots. But the alien kept going slow until it wasn't as uncomfortable. When I stopped trying to scream and pull up the grass, the one below me started to stroke as well. He let go of my mouth and wrapped his tentacles around my back. They both were thrusting. The penis in my ass, taking long, deep strokes. Pulling out almost all the way, then back in. The one in my pussy, however, was giving short, hard thrusts. And with each impact, the pain lessened until it was entirely replaced with an odd hunger for more.

When the alien in my pussy came, I came as well. It was the first time I had ever done so. It was the most amazing thing. I had no idea that it was even possible for a person to feel so good. The alien in my ass came, and once all three of us were spent, I was picked up and placed back on the lawn chair, and they both went away.

"Cut!" Charlotte yelled. "Okay, you guys go get cleaned up." I slowly stood up from the chair, and everybody who walked past me smiled and mumbled,

"Good job," as they went back into the house. Elicia came up to me and smiled.

"You might make it as an actress. You really convinced everyone you were enjoying that." And then she went inside to help the guys out of their makeup and costume.

"You okay?" Jesse asked me.

"I think so. First and last time."

I went upstairs and hopped in the shower. I must have been in there for a long time because Erin and Ashley came to the door twice to see if I was okay. I cut the water off, and, as I was drying off, I whispered, "Lord, please forgive me for what I have just done." I picked up my phone and called Byron.

"Hello."

"Hey. What are you doing?"

"Nothing. What's up?"

"Nothing. I'm hungry, and I'm in Virginia Beach. So I was wondering if you wanted to get something to eat."

"Where?"

"Kelly's?"

"A'ight."

"Okay. I'm on my way."

"A'ight."

I hung up and got dressed. When I came out of the bathroom, the men had gone, and Erin, Ashley, and Elicia were cleaning up.

"Jermaine wants to see you in his office," Ashley said. I went down to the office where Charlotte and Jermaine were waiting for me.

"Here you go," Charlotte said as she handed me the envelope. I took it.

"Well, Nikki," Jermaine started, "I really enjoyed working with you these past few weeks, and I'm sad to see you go. But I understand why you have to. And I hate to do this, but I'm going to need the car keys."

"Oh, yeah." I took the key off the ring and handed it to him.

"Do you need a ride back to campus?"

"No, I'm good."

"Okay. Good luck in everything you do."

"Thank you and same to you."

"Bye, Nikki," Charlotte said with a sad look on her face. I left the office and called Byron back.

"Hey! Can you come get me?"

"Where are you?"

"In your neighborhood. I had to give the car back."

"A'ight." I gave him directions, and he picked me up. He was dressed to impress, and I was in jeans and a sweatshirt.

"Oh, wow," I said as we headed to Kelly's.

"What?"

"You look nice, and I look like a bum."

He laughed. "Naw, you look nice, too."

I smiled. "Well, I do try," I said playfully. When we sat at our table at Kelly's, I looked over the menu. "Have you ever eaten here before?" I asked.

"Yeah." He looked up at me. "You want me to order for you?"

"Oooh, yeah! That would be fun." I closed my menu and sat it down.

ZION

"You guys ready to order?" our waitress asked as she approached the table.

"Yes, ma'am," Byron said. "I'll have a water, and she'll have a sweet tea. We'll have the marinated steak bites as our appetizer. I'll have the sirloin beef tips, and she'll have the chipotle chicken fettucine."

The waitress repeated the order to him, and Byron confirmed it. "I'll be right back with your drinks."

"So what's been going on?" my friend asked me.

"Well, I quit all of those jobs you hated."

"For real?"

"Yup."

"Good. What's going on with you and school?"

I shook my head. "I can't remember the *last* time I went to class."

"That's not good."

"No, it's not. But I just wasn't comfortable anymore."

The waitress came back and gave us our drinks.

"Well, now what are you going to do?"

"I'm going to drop my entrepreneurship minor 'cause I've learned a lot, and I *really* just want to get out of the department. And I'm going to focus on theatre, and I should be graduating next semester."

"And then what?"

"Well, a family member just gave me a very lucrative restaurant in Atlanta. I inherit it after I graduate."

"So you're going to move to Atlanta?"

"Yeah. I'm actually pretty excited."

Our appetizers were delivered.

"Well, I just found out that I leave for basic training next year in June."

Once Upon A Secret

"Oh, that's great!" I said as I grabbed some food.

"Yeah, but I've been doing a lot of thinking, and I don't want to leave you."

I smiled, "Aww! That's sweet, Precious, but, you don't have to worry about me anymore. I stopped being a whore, and I quit my naughty jobs, so I'm good."

"No, I don't want to leave you behind. I want you to go with me."

"But... I don't want to join the navy."

"No... maybe I'm doing this wrong. I want you to be my girl, and, when I go away, I want to know that there's somebody back here waiting for me."

I stopped moving right as I was about to shove in a mouthful of food. "You don't have to be *my man*. I assure you I'm not going to date or have sex again."

"Nikole," he said sternly. "I love you." He stared at me. And not knowing what else to do, I shoved the food in my mouth. "I didn't have a chance to buy a ring, but I promise I'll buy you one when I get back." I couldn't speak. Because my mouth was so full, I could barely chew. "You're going to Atlanta, right?" I nodded. "There are two naval bases in Georgia. NAS Atlanta, just outside of Marietta, is about thirty minutes away from Atlanta. And King's Bay Submarine Base is... well, that's kind of far. Like five hours far. But the point that I'm trying to make is I'm not asking you to change anything about you or your goals. I just want you to say yes." He took my hand from across the table. "Nikole Turner, will you marry me?"

I still had food in my mouth, so I held up a finger to ask for a minute to get myself together. As I slowly chewed, I began to think. I loved Byron, but not like that. I mean, I couldn't even imagine myself kissing him, much less *having sex* with him. I thought, Maybe he's just scared about leaving. But he was only going to *basic training*. I remembered all of the stories he'd told me about the girls he slept with and how crazy they were because of how he had played with their hearts. But he was *proposing* to me. I just had this feeling that it was going to work. He was different, and, as I finally stopped chewing, I said,

"Yes."

He waved a Tiger Woods fist and said, "Yes!"

The waitress sat our plates in front of us. "Here you go."

"She said, yes!"

The waitress looked at me. "Oh, congrats!" Her eyes darted to my naked ring finger and then at Byron. "So, how long have you two been dating?"

"Uhh… " We both grumbled.

"We never dated," Byron said.

"We were just friends two minutes ago," I chimed in.

"Ooh," the waitress sang. "Well, you guys want me to take a picture?"

"Yeah!" I pulled out my phone, put it on the camera, and gave it to her.

"You two make a cute couple. Say *marriage*!"

Once Upon A Secret

Charles

I was helping my wife pack up Nikole's things while she was out getting packing supplies. I found a picture of my daughter, Casey, and I smiled. Our relationship was actually working, and, even though she had inherited all of that money, she was the most humble person to be around. Eventually, my wife came to her senses and accepted Casey into our lives. I picked up a photo frame and smiled at the picture inside. It was a picture of Nikole and Byron on the night he proposed six months ago. The story was kind of funny. They both were on opposite sides of the booth, and, when the waitress got the phone, the two leaned across the table with their faces next to each other, and, when she said, "Say *marriage*," Byron grabbed Nikole's face and kissed her. I wrapped the picture up and sat it in the box.

Byron was scheduled to go to boot camp next month, June, which was good because he was able to see Nikki graduate, and when she was to go to Atlanta, she would have three months by herself to get adjusted to the area and oversee the restaurant. I smiled as I looked at Casey and Nikole together in Nikki's graduation picture. I was proud of both of my daughters.

Christian walked into the room.

"What are you doing, old man?" she asked as she wrapped her arms around me.

"Nothing." I kissed her.

"Mmm, I see that. You're supposed to be packing this stuff up." She let go of me and picked up the big picture from over the bed. It was a picture Nikole had blown up of herself, Casey, and me on the swings. "So when are we going to the dealership?"

"I don't know." My wife and I had decided that we were going to surprise Nikole with a new car before she moved to Atlanta. "Maybe, it would be better if we all ride in the U-Haul together and we go look for a car when we get there."

"Yeah, that's a good idea." My wife hugged me. "You are a great father and husband. And I love you more now than I ever have." She gave me a big kiss, and we continued to pack.

I had been spending a few nights at Jen's house, helping her go back and forth, helping Paris move into her own place right up the street in Chandler's Warf.

"That's all of it." Paris finally said after a long day of going up and down the street.

"Whew! Okay. It's time for me to go," I said. "Byron's taking me out tonight. We're trying to spend as much time together as we can before he leaves next week."

"Aww, you guys are so cute," Jen said.

"Alright. I'll see you guys later."

"You want me to drive you back to my apartment?"

"Naw, you good. I'll walk."

"You sure?"

Once Upon A Secret

"Yeah, I'm good."

She looked at her watch. "It's ten o'clock."

I laughed. "I'm good. I ain't scared. Please! I wish a nigga would!"

We all laughed. I hugged both of them and left the apartment. It was the last week of May, and the air felt good, but I was power walking to the apartment because I didn't want to keep Byron waiting. He had let me borrow his truck while I helped Paris move, and I knew he was waiting on me. I was passing the liquor store and was almost to the apartment when I passed a group of guys.

"Hey! Excuse me!" I heard a guy yell. I turned around. "I'm sorry. I don't want to scare you or anything, but you look really familiar."

I stepped toward him. "I'm sorry. I don't recognize you."

"Did you go to Phoebus High?"

"No, I'm from Virginia Beach."

"Oh, well, I can't think of anything else. I'm sorry."

"You're fine." I turned and headed back to the apartment.

"I know who she is!" Another guy yelled. I turned. "You that alien chick."

"What?" The first guy asked.

"Remember that video we saw online? With that bitch that got fucked by them aliens?" All five guys looked at me, and I immediately got scared.

"Oh, yeah!"

"Ay, yo! Let me talk to you for a minute."

"Come here, shawty."

ZION

I took off running and tried to get my cell phone out of my pocket. When I finally did, I tripped, and the phone fell into a puddle. I got on my knees to get up, and I was immediately pushed down by a man laying on top of me.

"Where you going, sexy?"

"Get off of me!" I grunted as I tried to move under his weight.

"Hey! Leave her alone." I looked up, and it was the guy who first approached me.

"Naw, nigga. This all me right here," the man on top of me said. I rocked from side to side, but I was getting nowhere.

"I said, 'Leave her alone.'"

"Man!" The man got off of me, and I jumped up. All five guys surrounded me, all eyeing me like homeless men eyeing a steak dinner.

"Touch me, and I'll kill you," I said.

They all laughed, and a guy grabbed my arm. In turn, I grabbed his, yanked it, and head-butted him in the nose. He fell. Another one came up behind me and grabbed me, and I elbowed him in the ribs. He let go, and I gave him a right and left jab to the face. The last three looked at each other, smiled, and ran toward me.

Byron

I was at home waiting for her, and all I kept thinking was, *Where the hell is she?* I knew she was helping a friend move, but it was eleven o'clock, and she hadn't even called. I remember calling and texting and never getting a reply. That was when I began to get worried. I called Jen.

"Hey! Is Nikole still with you?"

She hesitated. "No, she left a long time ago."

"Oh, I'll call her dad then. She's not answering her phone."

"Okay. I'll call you back if I hear anything." I hung up and called Mr. Turner.

"Hello."

"Hey, Mr. Turner, have you heard from Nikole?"

"Not since this morning. She said she was going to Jen's to help Paris move."

"Yeah, and Jen just said she left a while ago. I'm starting to get worried." My phone beeped. "Hold on right quick." I clicked over; it was Jen. "Hello."

"Hey, I just pulled up to my apartment, and your truck is still here."

"*What*?"

"I was at Paris's house, and Nikole said she was ready to go and didn't need me to drop her off, so she walked back."

"Oh, my God! I'm calling the police." She gave me her address, and I called the cops. I can't even begin to explain the pain I felt from hearing "she walked back" to hearing, "Mr. Parker, we found her body." My body went numb, and I had no emotion. My face went blank, and I just sat there as they explained that she had been tortured and that she was almost unrecognizable.

"Did you catch the guys that did it?" I asked.

ZION

"We caught one. He said he won't tell on his friends, but he confessed to doing it."

"Did he say why?"

"He said he wanted to see if she was really as good as she looked in the pornos."

"What?"

"Mr. Parker, your fiancée was a porn star. Didn't you know?"

I just lowered my head. And now it's my last Saturday in Virginia, and I am sitting at a graveside funeral. Earlier this week, my best friend and fiancée was beaten and raped to death while she was out walking in Hampton. I feel angry and sad and terrible all at once. I thought she had changed. I thought she had become a better person. But she hadn't. And I hate to say this, but she had to face the consequences.

Once Upon A Memory

Here's A Sneak Peak Of:

Once Upon A Memory

A MODERN UN-FAIRY TALE

Paris

"You must think I'm stupid, bitch." I said.
"What are you talking about?" Charlotte asked before taking a sip of wine.
"This ring."
"Yea."
"You don't think I know?"
"I don't know what—"

ZION

"*Love Always, Kadeem*, bitch!" She froze as she looked at me, "Oh, don't give me that look. You're caught, Charlotte!"

"Paris, I wanted to give you a ring and I didn't have time to shop around so, I gave that ring to a guy I know and–"

"You proposed to Jen with the same ring."

"No I didn't. I never—"

"Hello, Fish." Charlotte turned around to see Jen standing in her foyer.

"What are you doing here?"

"I told her to come." I said as Jen came toward me. "Hey, baby." I gave her a nice, sloppy kiss right there so Charlotte could see exactly what she missed out on.

"What *the fuck* is going on?"

"We came for an apology."

"For *what*?"

"One," Jen started, "for dating me only because I look like your crush in college—"

"I already did that."

"Two," Jen raised her voice, "for proposing to me with the same ring your ex fiancé gave you."

"Three," I chimed in, "for stringing me along for almost a year. Making me believe that you loved me when you were still in love with Jen."

"So she says," Jen mumbled.

"Four, for having *sex* with Jen behind my back and last but not least, proposing to me with the same ring you proposed to Jen with."

"You have to be out of your cotton pickin' minds! Fuck you! Both of you." Charlotte stood up, "Now get out of my house before it gets ugly in here."

Once Upon A Memory

"Oh, it's been ugly in here." Jen said.

"Iight, stand there." Charlotte started heading towards the kitchen drawer where she kept her 45 and immediately, Jen and I ran towards her. Before she could put her hand on the drawer, Jen grabbed her, by all twenty six inches of Indian Remy hair and pulled her back. I slapped her as hard as I could and she screamed and kicked me in my abdomen. Jen let her hair go and Charlotte turned around and gave her a right jab to the face. I hurriedly reached in the drawer and pulled out Charlotte's gun.

"Hey, bitch!" I yelled. Charlotte turned around and I slapped her across the face with the butt. She collapsed to the ground and Jen and I just stared at her.

"Let's move her upstairs."

Zion is a recent graduate of Hampton University, majoring in Theater Arts. In 2011 a professor told her she should write a story and a recent break up gave Zion a lot to say. Pen met paper and a story was birthed. In the process of writing her first manuscript, the student discovered she was with child. This motivated her even more to finish her story and get it published. Once the manuscript was complete and the search for a publisher began, the young author was rushed to the hospital. Seven days later she gave birth to a daughter she named Zion. Two hours later, Zion passed away. This loss changed the author forever, but in the midst of it, she decided whenever she was achieving greatness she would go by the name of Zion.

More titles

from the 21st Street

Publishing group...

21st Street

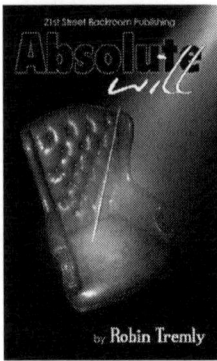

Absolute Will by Robin Tremly

Faith knew what she wanted. Her career, her own life, and the occasional play partner. She had planned out her existence and was quite capable of fulfilling it on her own, no man needed. She was self-reliant and strong. At least, she considered herself to be. However, a few martinis and a chance encounter with a woman that she expected would be a casual fling, ended up turning Faith's world upside down and her beliefs in strength and independence turned inside out. Take a journey with Faith as she learns true courage in offering absolute submission to another; another who accepts nothing but absolute obedience to his will.

**For credit/debit card purchases, please go to:
www.21StreetUrbanEditing.com
Free shipping with all on-line orders!**

Once Upon A Fling by Zion

Experience the pulse racing, erotic true-to-life-tale of characters you can connect to. Their tangled web of secrets and desires come to life on these pages. Witness them jump relationship obstacles as they explore sexuality, hoping for happiness and contentment while catering to their hunger for intimacy.

Experience the gruesome pain of deception. Witness innocence being ripped off of the backs of the unsuspecting. Can love still exist in the heart of a young girl, taken from her mother? Does compassion elude a boy lost in a hurricane of mixed feelings?

Is love in the air? Does it exist? Or are the streets of Hampton Roads flooded with the lust, deception and regret from five very confused lovers?

To place an order using check or money order,
please send your list of titles
and $14.99 + $2.99 per book to:
21ST Street Publishing Group
P.O. Box 171, Lake Bluff, Illinois 60044

21st Street

21st Street: Straight Outta Zompton by Bryant Jones

From the mean streets of Chicago, Bryant Jones gives us our first look at his contribution to the hood trilogies. Meet Sassy, the flavorful white girl who roamed far from suburbia and stole the heart of Zion's most feared and respected drug lord known on the streets as Bang.

The dope house shared by Bang, his brother and two nephews, use to be a hangout for Sassy and her cousins. When she moves in with them it seems that all hell breaks loose. Hated and envied by almost everyone for being Bang's woman and a white girl, takes Sassy on a rollercoaster ride that has her facing twenty-five years in prison. Bang's nephews, Black and Jack, use to hate Sassy. Just like the rest, have now become her best friends and they will do anything and everything to protect each other.

Find out what happens when Bang suspects Sassy and Jack are becoming a little too close for comfort, Jack feels like Bang takes Sassy for granted, and Sassy isn't sure if her feelings have gone further than they should for the nephew on the come up. This story will have you begging for part two long after you read the last page.

**For credit/debit card purchases, please go to:
www.21StreetUrbanEditing.com
Free shipping with all on-line orders!**

Ten Toes Down by Avron Loveface & Jocelyn Estes

Living in New York, Rush learned that someone was out to kill him. He moved down south to Arkansas, where no one knew him but his Uncle Tony. Finding himself behind bars, getting sex from a female guard was a piece of cake until he got her pregnant. After time served, Rush was a free man and found himself working at a Cracker Barrel with his jail cell mate, B-Lo. Rush knew he had a daughter to take care of, and his hourly job wasn't paying enough. Robbing drug dealers was the fastest way to come up, but not just any drug dealers, the ones with duffle bags full of money and drugs. Their first attempt was successful.

B-Lo came up with a play to rob Big O, a big time drug dealer. It would be hard for Rush and B-Lo to run up on Big O since he had a whole army of killers on standby, ready to lose their lives for him. Rush knew the only way to get Big O's money was though Karla. What started as a set up, turned into Karla catching feelings and moving in with Big O. Rush was furious about his girl sleeping with Big O so he raped Karla and hit her in the head with the butt of his gun. From that point on, it was war.

To place an order using check or money order,
please send your list of titles
and $14.99 + $2.99 per book to:
21ST Street Publishing Group
P.O. Box 171, Lake Bluff, Illinois 60044

Evenings of Score by Doni Matlock

At a young age, Ream was scarred by a long time best friend, which left a permanent bruise when it came to females. Then at fifteen, she was with her cousin at a party, where she was drugged and raped. She tries to put that behind her as well. After her mother was murdered, she was lonely and unknowingly opened up to the wrong man thinking that he was a gentleman. When she finds out different, her wrath becomes merciless on the person responsible for a domestic crime and Ream is out for vengeance.

Mar thinks she can change her boyfriend's abusive ways. After a tragedy, her Aunt Fancy helps her realize her worth and she is ready to break it off with him, but then again, there may not be a need to.

Relly finds herself in lust with DJ, and lets jealousy get at the people closest to her because of a family secret. She doesn't think about any of her actions, and could care less about anybody but herself. Then when DJ hooks up with her cousin, she decides enough is enough and wants to expose them for who they really are. Only Relly didn't expect her envy to backfire.

Sir got out of jail and received an almighty hit from his cheating ways and his *Evening of Score* has him doing a disappearing act. Will they get their lives together before karma completes its circle?

For credit/debit card purchases, please go to:
www.21StreetUrbanEditing.com
Free shipping with all on-line orders!

A Young Lost Soul's Journey by Doni Hill-Matlock

They say a hard head makes for a soft ass and these two, *Lost Souls,* are going to have to learn the hard way.

Jeramiah's teenage years consisted of him getting his feet wet with street behavior that his father tried to warn him about. Eventually, he had an epiphany when he woke up in a hospital bed. It was then that he finally understood a reoccurring dream. He realized the error of his ways and stood firm on making swift changes in his life.

Jacky Smith, aka, Jacqueline Miller and her, don't care-about-anything attitude, had her heading to a life that her mother and aunt tried to keep her away from. Money and lust made her melt right into the scheming hands of a man that put her life at stake. After many unsuccessful attempts of trying to escape him, she gave up all hope.

Jeramiah helped Jacky evade her deranged pimp as her many identities became horribly misconstrued. Sadly, the innocent lives of their loved ones were taken, and they found themselves involved in more situations than they ever thought possible.

Will Jacky and Jeramiah make it through this journey together?

To place an order using check or money order,
please send your list of titles
and $14.99 + $2.99 per book to:
21ST Street Publishing Group
P.O. Box 171, Lake Bluff, Illinois 60044

21st Street

Dirtiest Revenge by Cha'Bella Don

Kendra LaSalle, aka "Spice", is a stripper from Los Angeles, California who decides to exchange the pole for a chance at love with Trenton "Trent" Moore. But being with a boss doesn't come easy, and Momma always said what glitters isn't always gold. Lies, deceit, and trust issues are becoming Kendra's worse nightmare. With deception in her view and Wiz nearby, Kendra is ready to move on until the unthinkable happens. Dreams, hopes, and love aren't enough anymore! Will she go to depth's end to seek the, *Dirtiest Revenge*?

**For credit/debit card purchases, please go to:
www.21StreetUrbanEditing.com
Free shipping with all on-line orders!**

Bound by Blood, Loyal by Choice:
The Loe-Lie Chronicles by Milas Williams

Ethan and Donovan Blake are two of San Antonio's most notorious street gang members on a fast track to the top. Unlike most crime duos, these two have reigned successfully and inseparably for years with loyalty never being a question or issue. They are true blood brothers. Because of their strong bond and even stronger armed tactics for "getting it done", they have become untouchable. Ethan is the oldest and quick-tempered. Donovan is the humble yet silent striker. Together they make the perfect recipe for creating unsolved crimes.

When fate has it that Ethan goes off to prison, Donovan is left in the streets alone to grow. The brothers are separated by the hands that they are dealt. Both brothers experience life-altering changes that will bring them to decide to reign together. Now on the verge of an uprising, the once-betrayed Old Man Lei must find a successor to his empire built on loyalty. After encountering the young Ethan in prison, Lei finds respect and honor in the young warrior. Will Ethan have the heart to handle what may be in store for him? Is Lei making the right decision? If not, will it cost both of them their legacies or more, their lives as they know It?

To place an order using check or money order,
please send your list of titles
and $14.99 + $2.99 per book to:
21ST Street Publishing Group
P.O. Box 171, Lake Bluff, Illinois 60044

21st Street

Alani's Bigger Hustle by Kai Storm

Growing up in the '80's when crack was just becoming an epidemic was not easy for Alani but she used it to her advantage and learned quickly. She got her teachings from Tracy, a pedophile that targeted her as an easy conquest. While becoming Tracy's sex toy, Alani observed and noted every trick and lesson needed to become a major player in the game. With these lessons and her three best friends; she did what it took to reach the top.

Everything was going so well that she decided to bring in a childhood friend that she hadn't seen in years but never stopped thinking about, Angelique. But what Alani didn't know is that this move would change the game forever. Angelique was not the same person that Alani knew as a child. After living a life filled with prostitution just to survive, Angelique was jealous and full of hate and when got a taste of Alani's fortune. Angelique wanted to do everything she could to destroy Alani and would stop at nothing.

Sex, drugs, money and murder. When in crime, never blindly trust anyone!

**For credit/debit card purchases, please go to:
www.21StreetUrbanEditing.com
Free shipping with all on-line orders!**

Alani's Hustle Gets Bigger by Kai Storm

Sex, drugs, money and murder. When in crime, never blindly trust anyone. Alani learned this lesson the hard way. In the end, she lost everything, her home, her friends and most of all, her man. To survive she had to run back to Panama, go into hiding and live a quiet life... but was this the end?

With patience, a plan and the right backing, she was ready to go back for her throne and nothing was stopping her. Did you love the ride that was *Alani's Bigger Hustle*? You will love *Alani's Hustle Gets Bigger*. *Bigger* things are in the air!

To place an order using check or money order,
please send your list of titles
and $14.99 + $2.99 per book to:
21ST Street Publishing Group
P.O. Box 171, Lake Bluff, Illinois 60044

Alani's Hustle: La Familia by Kai Storm

Alani has her man back, she's reunited with Sophonia and Cali, and most importantly, she has climbed comfortably back on her throne. Some people are missing though, like her family. The original people that had helped her start all of this—those who were there for her from the beginning—deserved to live in the kingdom just like she did.

What will she do to get them back? Find out in the final part of the trilogy of La Familia Alani. It's time to get the family together!

**For credit/debit card purchases, please go to:
www.21StreetUrbanEditing.com
Free shipping with all on-line orders!**

You Just Don't Know by Kai Storm

Randy loved his life because he did what he wanted, when and how he pleased. Fantasy and reality were equal playgrounds and he played every day. Only now there would be a price to pay to play. But what would it cost?

Tania was not one to be played with. She had rules and when she met Randy, she made it clear that her rules could never be broken; ever. However, Randy lived life breaking rules all the time and never got in trouble; and that was part of the fun... until now.

Tania was on to him, she knew his game and planned to end it with... Pain, Pleasure, and Punishment!

To place an order using check or money order,
please send your list of titles
and $14.99 + $2.99 per book to:
21ST Street Publishing Group
P.O. Box 171, Lake Bluff, Illinois 60044

***Where Is My Daddy* by Kai Storm**

Agodess, a child conceived in love, started out her life without the main entity that she thought she would always have-- her father.

Her loving mother raised her. Her sister helped her with her ABC's, played with her, and kept her in good spirits. But in her mind, she always had thoughts of her father. Key moments in the early stages of her life have her analyzing her beginnings as she tries to find the answer to the question...

Where Is My Daddy?

**For credit/debit card purchases, please go to:
www.21StreetUrbanEditing.com
Free shipping with all on-line orders!**

Fast Lane by Shakeera Frazer

Trish Grand has it all. Looks, money, cars, clothes and all the men she wants; her life is perfect. But all that is about to change- only she doesn't know it yet. Why? Because someone wants everything she has. The leading lady of the re-released novel The Fast Lane has reinvented herself into the infamous Trish Grand. She has come a long way from Patricia "Patty" Grand, the poor girl in the Astoria Projects in Queens. She has done things in her past that she would never want anyone to know but that is far behind her and that's where she intends for it to stay, until her world suddenly gets knocked upside down by someone she considered her friend. She will do anything to protect the image she has built but where can she turn? Who can she trust?

Meet Crystal Dawson, a beautiful, young, successful lawyer has the world at her feet. She plans on moving up in the firm when she suddenly gets pregnant. Crystal's pregnancy brings out skeletons that she thought she buried deep in her closet. Secrets that no one will understand. She will do anything to keep her secrets hidden but what will it cost her? Her career? Her friends? Her family?

To place an order using check or money order,
please send your list of titles
and $14.99 + $2.99 per book to:
21ST Street Publishing Group
P.O. Box 171, Lake Bluff, Illinois 60044

21st Street

Meet the Jordans by Jen Booth

This summer will make or break the women of the Jordan family. Betrayal, revenge and greed is rampant and each must decide where their loyalties lie. Long buried secrets resurface and irreparable damage is done. Lo, the girlfriend of notorious Atlanta business man Ace, is adjusting to being Ace's wife, dealing with his former relationships and all that his "occupation" brings.

Taking a stand against her older cousin Tracy has also cost her the respect and support of those closest to her. Gabby's relationship with Ace's right hand man, Vinnie and role as Lo's confidant brings her to the forefront of turbulence in Ace's organization. Still scarred from an abusive childhood, she navigates through life looking out for the one individual she trusts; herself.

Tina is dealing with a divorce from her cheating NFL husband and the lifestyle she once knew. Hustler by blood, she is prepared to do whatever necessary to provide for her daughter. Tracy, the unofficial captain of the Jordan women and Ace's partner of more than a decade, is coming to a crossroads in her life. With her children going off to college and the emergence of a new love interest, she battles with wanting to get out of the game completely versus her addiction to the excitement. Can she break all ties with Ace and start over with the life and love she deserves?

**For credit/debit card purchases, please go to:
www.21StreetUrbanEditing.com
Free shipping with all on-line orders!**

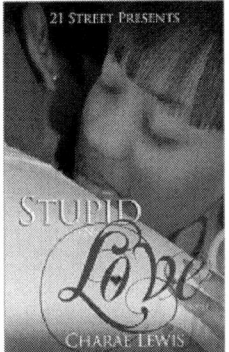

Stupid -n- Love by Charae Lewis

It is said one man all by himself is nothing, but two people who belong together make a world. What happens when you thought you had love but it was all a mistake? Kennedy James had to find out the hard way when it came to her first love Kyrell. Her love for him ran through her veins. But soon her life takes a turn for the worst and her strength is tested. Her love is on the line when tragedy comes knocking her way. Kennedy's world is turn upside down and it seems there is no light at the end of the tunnel.

Will love conquer all or will she face reality and relieve the burden off of her shoulders.

Then, there's the sexy and charming Kam "Cash" Mitchell. He comes and revives Kennedy from all the pain she has endured from her past. She never felt love like this and believes it is too good to be true. Her happiness is rudely interrupted by a familiar figure that refuses to let go.

Secrets are revealed and love is tested is this whirlwind drama. Will she follow her heart or will she die trying?

To place an order using check or money order,
please send your list of titles
and $14.99 + $2.99 per book to:
21ST Street Publishing Group
P.O. Box 171, Lake Bluff, Illinois 60044

21st Street

Self-Publishing Guide to Urban Fiction by Niccole Simmons

**For credit/debit card purchases, please go to:
www.21StreetUrbanEditing.com
Free shipping with all on-line orders!**

The Don Divas by Keisha Howard

Meet five of Virginia's most well-known exotic dancers... *The Don Divas*. Luscious, the big sister type, Chocolate, the feisty chic that doesn't hold her tongue for anyone, Juicy, the diva, Golden Brown, the not so well put together one and Bay-Bay, the atheist. These ladies will do whatever it takes to make ends meet, even if it means setting up gangsters or hustling what their mamas gave them for a quick buck. Ride along with these ladies on their journey of deceit, heartaches and pain, ups and downs and all the grimy things that they will do to get their money by any means necessary.

You will find that every dancer has a story and a reason for what they do for a living and maybe understand the hustle a little more. These ladies have been through it all but have persevered every obstacle that stood in their way!

To place an order using check or money order,
please send your list of titles
and $14.99 + $2.99 per book to:
21ST Street Publishing Group
P.O. Box 171, Lake Bluff, Illinois 60044

21st Street

Money by Jack Onasis

Meet 'Money' and his new girl-friend Shayna. What starts off as a drug dealers dream come true, turns in to a living nightmare because of unforeseen betrayal and deception.

What happens when the Mexican Cartel finally begin to deal their cocaine to the black drug dealers they've always refrained from working with? Was the divide between races put in place long ago by their ancestors for a reason, or can they all eat and get paid together?

Can Money trust the new love of his life, Shayna or a better question is, can a man in his position trust anyone?

Love, violence, betrayal, crooked federal agents, and racial tension are all part of what will quickly make this raw, 21st Street book, one of your new favorites.

**For credit/debit card purchases, please go to:
www.21StreetUrbanEditing.com
Free shipping with all on-line orders!**

Men Do What Women Allow by Sam Sylk

We all have heard the sayings...

"There are no good men out here... "

"All men are dogs... "

"All men cheat... "

"He's a womanizer... "

Some of this could be true. However, could it be that you're to blame for some of his behavior? Could it be that you could have controlled or manipulated the situation and then let your emotions get the best of you?

In this book we will take a raw, un-cut journey on how and why men do what they do. Also, what women can do differently in the relationship to prevent heart-break. I want to help prevent you being broken up and up late at night crying on the phone with your girl. I don't want any more of you stalking your baby daddy or acting un-lady like. I want to enlighten you on the thought process of many men and help you have a healthy successful relationship.

After reading this book you will have a better understanding and see where you went wrong in choices of men and how to correct them. I want to help you move forward and understand that, *Men Do What Women Allow.*

To place an order using check or money order,
please send your list of titles
and $14.99 + $2.99 per book to:
21ST Street Publishing Group
P.O. Box 171, Lake Bluff, Illinois 60044

21st Street

Gettin' It by Dion Hayes

Iesha is a young girl who has seen it all and endured way too much at a very young age. Her close childhood friend, Brooks, has been by her side through all of her life altering challenges. Iesha is a very street smart girl, who is willing to do anything necessary to survive with her man lovingly and unconditionally by her side.

Rob was a well-known hustler who always felt he should be at the top and would't accept anything less. Rob's best friend, Cool, grew up with him in the same neighborhood and stood by Rob's side no matter what he was up against. They went from chasing girls - to chasing dreams. Now that they are older and times have changed, the empire they built together is now in jeopardy. Around every corner someone is threatening to push them out. Rob now wants to step away from the drug business and put his girlfriend through school, but he soon finds himself dodging the police and eluding death.

Will Gettin' It be their demise or will they make it out alive? All of the sex, love, money murder, greed and betrayal *21ST Street* brings in their books is available again in our latest release, Gettin' It.

**For credit/debit card purchases, please go to:
www.21StreetUrbanEditing.com
Free shipping with all on-line orders!**

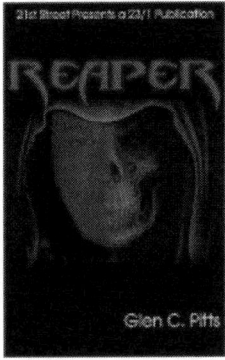

Reaper by Glen C. Pitts

In the early 80's, gang activity was at a peak. Ronald was living the lifestyle to the utmost. The back room of his mother's house was off limits to the rest of his biological family. The room was a place for members of his other family, his organization. It is where they would discuss business, store their guns, bag up their drugs, smoke weed and talk about women.

Ronald's younger brother, Cornelius was born a wild child. He was fearless and had a dark heart. Ronald knew the only person Cornelius would ever love or respect was their mother and anyone else could get it. His violent actions indicated this to anyone he'd came across, ever since he was old enough to walk and talk. Cornelius admired the comradery that his older brother Ronald and his associates shared. He was fascinated by all of the sex, drugs and money and wanted in. By eight years old, Cornelius was begging Ronald to allow him to join his gang, but his brother always refused. Ronald knew if Cornelius had a taste of this life, there would be no turning back for him.

To place an order using check or money order,
please send your list of titles
and $14.99 + $2.99 per book to:
21ST Street Publishing Group
P.O. Box 171, Lake Bluff, Illinois 60044

21st Street

Loyalty is Everything by Jon Jersey Auletta

Loyalty is Everything, by a man whom the Don Diva Magazine dubbed as America's Youngest Gangsters is a fast paced, urban novel that will take you back to the way the original urban fiction authors wrote.

**For credit/debit card purchases, please go to:
www.21StreetUrbanEditing.com
Free shipping with all on-line orders!**

Made in the USA
Columbia, SC
20 June 2017